Saved by You

by

Kimberly Daniels

Finding You, Book 2

Saved by You

Cover Art by *Kristian Norris*

The Wild Rose Press, Inc.
PO Box 708
Adams Basin, NY 14410-0708
Visit us at www.thewildrosepress.com

Publishing History
First Mainstream General Edition, 2019
Print ISBN 978-1-5092-2672-6
Digital ISBN 978-1-5092-2673-3

Finding You, Book 2
Published in the United States of America

Footsteps approach. I feel a light touch, and then hands gently finding their way around my waist. Camryn lays her head on my shoulder and squeezes. Gavin stands up next to me on the other side of the bench and links his arms around my neck.

"Daddy, are you mad at me?" he asks.

I lift my head, pull Gavin onto my lap, and tilt his chin toward my face. "You listen now. I could *never* be mad at you for talking about the baby. You will be the best big brother anyone could ask for. So, you talk about the baby all you want." I lift my thumb. "Thumbs up to the best big brother in the world."

He touches his thumb to mine. "Thumbs up to the best daddy in the world."

As the pain melts away, Camryn squeezes my waist and kisses my shoulder. "Are you ready to go, best-daddy-in-the-world?"

I gently kiss her lips and assure her, "With you, I'm ready for anything." The meaning of my words run deeper than the family dinner awaiting us at home.

She stands up from the bench and turns toward me. "Let's start small then." She reaches her hand out. "One step toward home?"

The distant roar of the waves slamming the shore, and the strength in Camryn's simple words, fortify my resolve. I reach out to my wife, my lifeline, and grasp her hand, knowing she is the only one who possesses the power to save me.

Dedication

To my husband, Dave.
A true love story never has a final chapter.

Chapter One

Present

Thump-a, thump-a, thump-a...

I know there will never be a more perfect sound. My gaze is glued to the tiny, white speck bouncing around the fuzzy background. The technician lists the details of the ultrasound, but the only thing I hear is the sound of life filtering through the room—our baby's heartbeat. Tightening my grip on Camryn's hand I glance over to her, my heart melting at the tearful joy in her eyes.

I lean down to kiss the top of her head. "I've never seen anything more beautiful."

Our baby bounces to the rhythm of Camryn's breathing, and I can't look away, for fear I might lose sight and break the connection. The spot on of the screen is so tiny, yet it holds such immense meaning.

Camryn nuzzles her head into the crook of my neck, her warm breath against my skin. "Our baby...perfect in so many ways."

I run my hand through her long, silky hair, dragging my nails beneath her loose gown, and gently down her arm. Goosebumps instantly rise beneath my fingertips and I smile. With Camryn in my arms, the life growing within her, and our son clutched to my elbow, I never want to leave this moment.

Feeling a tug on my shirt, I peek down to see Gavin staring at the screen with confusion. In a most serious tone, he asks, "Daddy, is there a baby on TV? Because I don't see one."

A smile tugs at the corner of my lips, and Camryn giggles at the innocence of our son. Pointing to the small, white outline on the screen, I explain. "Gav, this is the baby. See it? Right here…He or she is just really small right now and needs more time to grow in Mommy's belly."

His mouth drops open. "*Wow*. That's my brother or sister? I just thought Mommy ate a jellybean."

Camryn and I smile at his response. I let go of her hand and crouch down to hoist Gav in my arms. He continues to stare in awe at the ultrasound. Giving him a kiss on the nose, I declare, "Well, buddy, you just performed the first task of being a big brother."

His grin stretches from ear to ear. "What did I do?"

"You just gave the baby its very first nickname…Bean."

With Gavin's brotherly pride and Camryn's contentment, this moment will forever be imprinted in my memory. It's the day I'm given a second chance at a family; the day where I can finally, just maybe, put my past grief to rest.

As the doctor verifies a late August due date and discusses specifics with Camryn, my mind drifts to everything we've endured over the last nine months. But as I watch my wife find comfort at a place that once tortured her dreams, I find strength in those struggles. The revisit to our connected pasts has been agonizing, but merging our futures is worth the fight.

I lead Gavin into the hallway, letting Camryn

change out of her hospital gown, when I lock eyes with a part of my past that won't surrender. Her short, blonde hair bounces with each stiff step toward me. I peek over to check on Gavin, relieved to find him occupied playing with the buttons on a water fountain.

Turning back around, hell-on-heels herself is quickly approaching. There is no doubt about it, we are on a collision course. She extends her arm out, in an attempt to give me a half-hug. Marking my boundaries, I take a slight step back, her hand grazing my chest.

"Did you get the go ahead to surf again?" Tara asks empathetically. She points to the door behind me, labeled *Physical Therapy*.

I ignore her question and snap. "What the hell are you doing here? Are you following me?"

"Ummm…no, Cole. You're standing in a hallway of a medical building, you know, one with lots of offices?" She nods to the door I just walked out of. "I have an appointment."

Well, *that* was embarrassing. "Shit. I'm sorry. Didn't mean to snap like that," I mumble.

Tara reaches out again, but this time her eagle-like talons land on their mark, gripping my bicep. "No worries. I'm quite used to your snippiness." She leans in close. "In fact, it was always a bit of a turn-on for me."

Flinching at her candidness, I jerk back. Searching for Gavin over her shoulder, I find him still trying to outsmart the automatic water fountain. Before I can shut down her advances, I feel a body hovering next to me. Swiveling my head to the side, I am met by Camryn's glare, burning a hole through Tara's hand on my arm. Attempting to squash any anger, I plant a kiss

3

on her lips.

I pull away and flash her my dimpled grin. "You ready to go, wifey?"

Ignoring Tara's noticeable huff, Camryn's eyes soften. "All set, hubby." Then, she turns to face the proverbial thorn in our side. "*Goodbye*, Tara."

She pushes passed us, talking under her breath. "Not even close."

It's unbelievable. Despite Todd's surrender, Tara refuses to follow his lead. She holds on to the memories of us and, in her twisted mind, believes we were more than two fucked-up kids who tried to find comfort in each other for so many years. She thinks what we had was real, but it was just a way to cope with the shit in our lives, masking the realities that we would have to eventually face head on.

Gavin, his shirt soaked from his battle with the fountain, runs over to us and leaps up and down. "Mommy, Mommy. Can we go buy some jellybeans on the way home? I think the baby will like them."

Our heads snap up at Gavin's announcement, hoping Tara is out of earshot. But the sound of her trembling whine proves otherwise.

"Is it true? Well…is it?" Her voice raises with anxiety as she inches toward me. "Are you having a baby? With *her*?"

I close the distance between us to avoid the impending scene about to take place. Her cold disposition morphs into a look of pain and suffering. Tears pool in her eyes, her bottom lip quivers. She stands frozen; unable to come closer but unwilling to walk away.

"It's very early on. We're keeping it quiet for

now," I calmly whisper.

A high-pitched sob escapes her, and she clutches her stomach, as if mourning the emptiness of it. With tears streaming down her cheeks, she averts her attention to Camryn, her icy glare on her waist.

Tara cries out, "What the hell is wrong with you?" Her head snaps back to face me. "Do you want to replace her? How could you do this?" Whimpers muffle her words. "How could you do this to our baby...*our* Rose?"

Although I know what she said is irrational, rage quickly replaces any sympathy I just felt for her. Grabbing her wrists, I jerk her closer. Making sure to lower my voice, I say, "Don't ever think, for one second, I'm not fucking shattered from losing Rose. She'll *always* be my baby girl."

Grief pools in her eyes.

I release my grip. Tara is always able to strike a chord and bring me back down to reality. With her around, it's impossible for the past to stay buried. Turning around, I storm down the hallway. Even with Tara behind me, I'm still able to hear her, crying out apologies. I fling open the glass doors leading outside, and sink down into a wrought iron bench next to the entrance.

The pain Tara brings to the surface is unbearable, making me realize I still hold on to a good deal of anger and grief. Camryn and I had thrown that damn wooden box into the depths of the inlet last summer, but obviously, I never let go.

Bent over, with my elbows pressed into my knees, I lace my fingers behind my head. *Would this sorrow ever go away?*

Visions of Rose, my sweet baby girl, flash through my mind. Her tiny hand involuntarily grasping my index finger. The flutter of her eyelids as they struggled to open. The curl of her legs that never had enough time to stretch out and feel the earth below them. And the machines. Those fucking machines controlling her life.

I squeeze hands over my ears, and hum, rocking back and forth. No matter what I do, I can't drown out the memory of those machines and their incessant beeping. And then…that one note. The deafening sound of death.

Footsteps approach. I feel a light touch, and then hands gently finding their way around my waist. Camryn lays her head on my shoulder and squeezes. Gavin stands up next to me on the other side of the bench and links his arms around my neck.

"Daddy, are you mad at me?" he asks.

I lift my head, pull Gavin onto my lap, and tilt his chin toward my face. "You listen now. I could *never* be mad at you for talking about the baby. You will be the best big brother anyone could ask for. So, you talk about the baby all you want." I lift my thumb. "Thumbs up to the best big brother in the world."

He touches his thumb to mine. "Thumbs up to the best daddy in the world."

As the pain melts away, Camryn squeezes my waist and kisses my shoulder. "Are you ready to go, best-daddy-in-the-world?"

I gently kiss her lips and assure her, "With you, I'm ready for anything." The meaning of my words run deeper than the family dinner awaiting us at home.

She stands up from the bench and turns toward me. "Let's start small then." She reaches her hand out. "One step toward home?"

The distant roar of the waves slamming the shore, and the strength in Camryn's simple words, fortify my resolve. I reach out to my wife, my lifeline, and grasp her hand, knowing she is the only one who possesses the power to save me.

Chapter Two

Present

The early, Saturday morning sun filters through the small spaces in the blinds, warming my face. I reach over next to me, but find nothing but crumpled blankets. Squinting, waiting for my eyes to adjust, I look at the wrinkled sheets that still hold her outline. One of her pillows is scrunched up at the bottom of the bed. She can never sleep without it wedged between her legs. However, last night, the pillow had no chance...not when I provided her comfort all night long.

After a long night filled with a late family dinner and some extra-curricular activities with my wife, I coax myself out of our king-sized bed. Stumbling into the bathroom, I splash some water on my face.

Gavin spent the night at Heidi and Dusty's house, and I'm meeting them in an hour at the beach. There's nothing like winter surfing to awaken every bone in your body. Even the full-body wetsuits, made for this type of surfing, don't protect fully from the initial blast of cold that hits your body. There really is nothing better than surfing in the middle of February. The beaches are desolate, and the water is darker, which creates this feeling of the waves thickening around you. It's pure therapy for the soul.

I squeeze my eyes closed to prevent any water from seeping in, and blindly reach for the monogrammed *S* towel hanging on the rack next to the sink. Camryn insisted on these towels after thumbing through a *Pottery Barn* catalog. I went along with it, as I'd quickly learned never to mess with a woman and her linen selections.

Instead of the towel, I grab a familiar breast, her pert nipple nestling between two fingers. With a flirty laugh she dries my face, and I open my eyes to the most beautiful smile I've ever seen. Now *that*'s the best wake-up call I could ask for.

Bringing my other hand up, I massage her chest. Her dark, alluring eyes draw me in, and I wrap my arms around her waist. Her body presses my erection against my stomach and I give a little thrust.

Camryn is *my* gift, one that I'm about to open for the second time this morning. I lean into her mouth and suck on her plump bottom lip, before sliding my tongue in to meet hers. The vibe between us shifts and moans escape from her throat. With our lips still connected, I move closer to her, imagining that talented mouth on other parts of my body.

"What did I do to deserve an encore performance?" I ask, huskily.

Her hand travels down to my arousal, takes hold of my cock firmly, and strokes up and down. At the top of each stroke, her thumb rubs circles on the underside of the head. She knows what that does to me.

A devilish grin spreads across her face. Bringing her mouth to my ear, she flicks the lobe and whispers, "I guess I just can't keep my hands off of my sexpert." She giggles at her nickname. "See the thing is...you're just too good to me. I keep coming back for more."

My breath hitches as her hand does a swirly thing around the sensitive tip. After making a few hard thrusts, I drop to my knees. She leans against the sink counter as I remove the sexy boy shorts she wore to bed. They are my favorite accessory, riding just above the perfect curve of her ass.

I stick my tongue into the tight space between her legs. She steps out a little, just enough to make room for my mouth. Using my hands, I spread her open and I graze my teeth gently over her core. *How the hell did I manage to make this woman mine?*

"I love how you're always so ready for me, baby." I slip my tongue deep into her and taste the sweet warmness around my mouth. Circling my tongue at her center, I look up at her. Making eye contact, she tightens her thighs around my head and her fingers claw through my hair.

"Do it," she begs. "Please."

I know what she wants and savor what I'm able to do to her. I bring my mouth down and tease her my tongue. She lets her head fall back and whimpers. Using handfuls of my hair as leverage, she pulls my head into hers and starts to move against my tongue's assault. Her body finally gives in as her scream echoes against the tiles of the bathroom walls.

She holds me in place as she trembles. Coming down from her high, she clutches my face with her hands and leans down, breathing heavy across my cheek, "Now, it's my turn." A sensual smile spreads across her face as she taunts me with hooded eyes.

Shit. I'm about to explode.

Needing to be in her, I carefully carry her to bed.

Laying her down, I hover above, placing my weight on my elbows next her head. I lean in and declare my love. "The way you love me...makes me want to be a better man. You're everything, *everything* to me, Mrs. Stevens."

Her eyes darken with desire and that sexy grin appears once again. She pushes my elbow and escapes from under me. Pushing me back, she climbs between my legs. Trailing kisses down my chest and stomach, she wraps her lips around me. Taking all of me, her head moves up and down. Her hands reach for my chest as her nails graze over my nipples.

Feeling the intensity rise, I groan, "Oh Cam...Oh my God." I teeter close to my own climax, and then she pulls away and crawls up my body. Without any hesitation, she sits on me, taking it all in. Nothing feels better than the very moment our bodies entwine and fit perfectly together. It's like we are designed for each other. As she rides me to our peak, I pull her body against mine and hold her in my arms, grunting loudly as we explode together.

****

Forty-five minutes later, I'm still in bed, cuddled with Camryn. She lays in my arms, as I rub my hand over the very small swell of her stomach—the bump from growing our baby. I lean down to her belly, and place a kiss over the slope. Her hands glide through my hair, and she tilts my head up to meet her gaze.

"A penny for your thoughts." Her fingers move to the ends of my hair to twirl it around.

I had always kept my hair short, not much longer than a buzz. But after being unconscious in the hospital for a week, it grew out much longer than ever before.

When we came home, Camryn begged me not to cut it. I'd do anything to make her happy, so I kept it. Besides, it's such a fucking turn-on when she tugs it during sex.

"I was just thinking—" I kiss her stomach and move up to tickle her neck with my lips. "—our baby is so lucky—" I reach her mouth and plant a deep kiss. "—to have you as her mom." Never being able to resist her mouth, I kiss her again with more intensity.

"Do you really think our baby's a girl? If so, she's going to be a daddy's girl."

"Maybe. But no doubt she'll have her mom's beauty." I steal another kiss.

She squeezes right above my hipbone, the only person to know my ticklish spot. As I jump, she escapes and stands next to the bed. Amused by the girly sound that escapes my mouth, she places her palms on my cheeks.

"As much as I would love to spend the entire day in bed with you, I have to get to the hospital. Remember, my dad and I are meeting the potential partner who will possibly help fund the cancer clinic. And you have to meet Dusty and Gav at the beach." Camryn shakes her head from side to side. "I still can't believe I'm allowing this. He's going to catch pneumonia."

I stand up and wrap my arms around her waist. "He'll be fine. I bought him the best winter wetsuit you can find—it's actually heated. And you know I'd never put him in harm's way." I place a delicate kiss on her cheek to comfort her worries. "Besides, you can't be a surfer here, unless you're willing to winter surf. And trust me our boy has the skills to be a true east-coaster."

Camryn's eyes well up with tears.

Startled by her onset of emotion I pull her into an embrace. "Baby girl, what's wrong?"

Pressing her face into my shoulder, she sniffles, "Sorry. It's just, when you refer to him as your own, I still can't believe it's real."

As soon as Camryn walked back into my life, I instantly loved the kid. He was able to fill a void left by my Rose. Gav officially became mine one month ago, when his asshole of a father finally signed the adoption papers. It took us three months to find Todd and when we did, he dragged his feet with the paperwork. It was his final 'fuck you', since his revenge plan went awry. Thankfully, he stopped being a stubborn prick and signed away his rights, granting me a son, who would ultimately carry on the Stevens name.

I stroke her cheek, wiping a stray tear. "Not only is it real, sweetheart, it's forever...*our* forever."

"I'm so sorry. This pregnancy is making me crazy. I feel like I'm on an emotional roller coaster all day long." She straightens up. "But Cole, you handle my mood swings so well. You really are true perfucktion."

We laugh at the word Lila coined for our relationship.

I stand up and whisper into her ear. "I have a son to train and you have a dad to meet." With a delicate lick over her ear, I continue. "Meet me here, tonight. Wear nothing, but those red lace boy shorts."

Leaving her flushed, I saunter to the board closet in Gavin's room, in preparation for my morning surf. Humming a tune, I think about the old me. In the past, I would've found someone to punch after the incident at the doctor's office the day before. But now, it's all different. I am with a woman who is able to reach in and revive me. She blows life into my empty soul and gives me a reason to live. She makes me believe that maybe, just maybe, *perfucktion* can exist in my life.

Chapter Three

Past

"Happy birthday to you, happy birthday to you..."
My mom's hushed melody filters through the bedroom,
slowly waking me from a deep sleep.

Peeking through one eye, I see her contagious
smile approaching. She balances a vanilla-iced cupcake
on a plate, topped with a one lit candle. A small grin
spreads across my face. I wipe the sleep from my eyes
and sit up against the Cherrywood headboard.

"Mom, you don't have to do this. I'm not a little
kid anymore."

She finishes the song and places the plate in front
of my face. "Happy fifteenth birthday, sweetie. Now
make a wish."

I cock my eyebrow and stare at her, as if to say *are
you kidding me?*

Still beaming with pride, she nudges the plate
closer and pleads, "Oh, come on, Cole. It's your special
day. And remember, you're *never* too old to wish for
something."

With a short, quick puff, I blow out the candle.

My mom shakes her head from side to side, her
mouth tense in a tight line. "Really? That's all you
have? That was a sad excuse for a wish." She grins.
"You owe me a real one tonight, when you get your

birthday cake."

Unable to disappoint her, I hold up my hands. "All right, all right. I will. I promise."

My mom sits down on the edge of the bed and pulls me into an embrace. "Remember, no matter how old you are, you'll always be my baby." She sighs loudly. "One day, Cole, when you have children of your own, you'll understand what I'm talking about."

Embarrassed by her sentimentality, I pull back and flop down on my pillow. "Whatever you say, Mom. But I'm not really interested in being tied down like that. Ever."

She grabs my chin. "Mark my words, sweetie. One day, a very lucky woman will walk into your life, and you won't know what hit you."

"Okay, Mom. Whatever." I roll my eyes.

With her tone turning more serious, she continues. "Listen to me, honey, because I may not always be around to give you this advice."

Interrupting her all-too-familiar life lectures, I lighten the mood with a joke. "Not around? What? Are you planning your escape?"

Tilting her head, her death glare bears down on me. "I'm being serious, Cole. I'm getting older, and so are you. You need to be prepared for this."

I wipe the smirk off my face and nod for her to continue.

"You'll know when you find *the one*. But the best part is, she'll use her power to save you."

I stare at her as she unleashes these prolific words. My teenage mind is really only able to comprehend what waits for me on that day—hopefully a kickass birthday party and a brand-new skateboard.

She winks and kisses the top of my head. "Enough of my pep talk." Standing up, she walks out of the room. "Hurry up and get ready for school."

I throw the pillow over my face and groan, "Aww, mom. It's my *birthday*. Don't I get a day off?"

She shouts from the hallway, "Nice try, but aren't you a little too old to celebrate your birthday?"

Smiling into the pillow, I appreciate my mom's ability to shut me down. I snatch the candle from the cupcake and lick the icing off the end.

No matter how old I am, my mom will continue to be the driving force in my life. She has the ability to free the obedient little boy that thrives deep within.

Mama's boy? Hell-fucking-yes.
****

Once school ends, I rush home to the smell of lasagna and homemade rolls wafting through the house. I can picture my mom, in her frilly white apron, slaving in the kitchen all day, making my traditional birthday dinner. When I was a kid, she insisted lasagna was only made on special days and for only the most important people. For years I believed it, and she continued to serve it every year. I didn't have the heart to tell her that I'm too old for all of it; I know it's just her attempt to hold onto my childhood. Instead, I let her cling onto the memories of the past. It's the least I can do for her.

After dinner, I disappear to my room with a pair of headphones and a new punk mix CD my best friend, Liam, made for me. He'll be over soon since we have plans to go out for my birthday tonight. I have no clue where we're going, but Liam has a wild streak, especially since he's free to roam the city throughout the nights. His mom died when he was a baby, and his dad owns a number of boxing gyms across town and is always out late working the fights. The matches attract gamblers, and Liam somehow makes connections with the high-rollers who later become his ticket to the nightlife. With one long, badass night in front of me, I lay my head on the pillow and doze off to the sounds of The Offspring filtering through my ears.

Shortly after I fall asleep, the throbbing in my arm from a punch suddenly awakens me, and my body jolts beneath the sheets as I attempt to take cover underneath the comforter that is hanging loosely over the side of my bed. Awakened by the attack, all I can do is endure the pain from this tradition that Liam and I began when we were kids. Every birthday, since we were seven years old, marks is an occasion for what we call the "dead arm." It's blows to the arm that match your age, and always one extra for good luck. It isn't a typical punch. Somehow your arm loses every bit of feeling within the first few points of contact. It's excruciating if you are the one receiving, but funny as hell if you're on the other side of the punch.

I'm only halfway through Liam's assault when my arm goes completely numb. He managed to sneak into my room and jump on top of me, pinning me against the mattress. He never goes easy on his attack; it's always ruthless. I'm convinced he's trying to compensate for his size. Although Liam is a year older, I tower over him. He'll never admit it, but I know he sometimes feels insecure about it, like he has to prove his toughness.

"Nine, ten, eleven…." Liam, with a wide grin across his face, counts down in my ear.

Jokingly, I grunt, "Cheap shot. You attacked me

when I was asleep. It was complete sucker punch."

Liam halts and snorts out in amusement, "Not my fault you put your guard down, pussy. Thought I forgot about it when I didn't attack you at school today?" He continues to laugh as I wince in pain. "You're the dumbass who fell asleep." He tilts his head to look at me. "Why the hell are you *napping,* anyway?"

"Dude, we have a long night ahead."

Liam rolls his eyes and blurts out, "Really? A fucking *beauty* rest? Aww man, that calls for a hardcore ending to your birthday punches." He winds his arm back and releases again.

After he delivers the sixteenth punch, I roll out of bed and crouch down on the floor as I rub over my tender arm and smirk at Liam. "Good thing it's less than a month until your birthday, prick." I raise my fist in front of my face to act as if I'm inspecting it for his impending doom.

Reading my thoughts, he jumps up on the bed, leans over the side, and brushes his hand through my buzzed hair.

"Don't worry, pretty boy; I'll be ready for you." He grins and shouts out in excitement as he jumps off my bed.

As he celebrates his battering of me, I launch a pillow at his face and jokingly yell out, "Don't get too cocky, asshole." However, the pillow skims past Liam and hits my sister square in the face.

Heidi squeals out, "What the hell, Cole?" She tosses the pillow back, but it whizzes by my head and, instead, hits the horizontal blinds on my window. "Mom said to wake up and come downstairs for cake." She gazes at Liam, and I notice her cheeks instantly flush. "She wants you too, Liam."

Liam runs his hand through his wavy hair and tilts his head toward Heidi. He pretends to clear his throat, and in a low, raspy voice adds, "Is she the only one who wants me?"

Heidi, now a deep shade of crimson, sinks her gaze to the floor and quickly turns to leave the room. Amused by her flustered state, Liam calls out, "Heids, you can run now, but you won't be able to stay away forever." His cackle carries across the room as she disappears down the stairs.

I grab the pillow my sister threw at me and drill it directly at Liam. "Stay the hell away from my sister." I laugh as he throws his hands up in surrender. "She can do better than some short prick who thinks he's got major game."

"Whoa. Settle down, Coley boy. I may not be as pretty as you, but I am one sexy motherfucker with skills." He walks toward the door and turns back around to me. "And I think I'll go work those skills on a certain someone downstairs." He leaves my room singing some made-up song about being sexy down the hallway.

After splashing water on my face, I descend the staircase to the dining room. Looking around the room, my gaze locks onto the batch of colorful balloons that float above my head—sixteen blue and red balloons, to be exact. My mom always insists on adding one above our age for good luck. The chandelier is draped with streamers of the same color combination that stretch to each corner of the room. As my eyes return to the center of the table where the cake is displayed, I can't help but smirk at the iced Spiderman in the center of it. Although she swears it's a joke, I know it's also her way of trying to keep me young and innocent.

"I can't believe my baby boy turned fifteen years old today." My mom, who is carrying a platter of cookies to the table, begins to well up with tears. "Where'd the time go?"

Embarrassed by her reaction, I shake my head and continue to stare at the cake. "Come on, Mom. You say that every year."

"I know, sweetie. I just can't believe it. I mean look at you. Those stunning blue eyes, and you've gotten so tall and handsome. You've grown from a boy to a young man so quickly." She wipes a stray tear falling down her cheek. "I bet all the girls are after you. You won't be able to keep them straight."

As my face flushes, Liam walks past my mom, grabbing a cookie from the plate she is holding and mockingly chimes in, "Yea, handsome Coley. *All* those girls…you can't even keep them straight."

I playfully push him as he is hysterically laughing at his own humor.

"Dude, shut up." I turn toward my mom. "Can we just get the singing over with? We have places to go tonight."

My dad jumps in and corrects me as my mom searches the drawer of the china cabinet for matches. "Cole, show some respect. Your mom cooked that delicious dinner then baked this cake for you. No reason to rush through it."

My mom reveled in making our birthdays a big deal when we were younger. She threw us crazy parties, inviting all of our neighbors and friends within a ten-block radius. One time, when I was four years old, I begged my parents every day to go camping. Since we lived in the city, you couldn't just pitch your tent in your concrete backyard. So, at my fifth birthday party, my mom rented a bus and carted every single boy on our block to the mountains to have our very own campout. I still have the sleeping bag she surprised me with that day.

Blatantly annoyed by my earlier hint at after-dinner plans, Heidi snarls, "Where do you think you're going, anyway? I hope you don't think you're coming out with me."

As I flip Heidi the middle finger, my mom scolds me. "Cole David Stevens, don't you dare point that finger at your sister."

I flash my mom the most innocent grin. "Oh sorry." I raise my middle finger on my other hand, aiming it at Heidi. "I'll point this one instead."

With Liam trying to hold back his laughter and Heidi sulks, my dad shakes his head at our banter while he dims the lights. The entire table belts out the words to "Happy Birthday," my mom adding a few "cha-cha-chas" where she feels necessary. As the song ends, my mom yells for me to close my eyes and make a wish. Keeping my promise to her from the morning, I do as she says.

What the hell can I possibly wish for? I have it all. I open my eyes to everything I'll ever need—my parents, my sister Heidi, and my best friend Liam. I never even imagined that I could lose it all, that this very moment would stay frozen in my mind. I never thought that one day everyone that matters to me could be so quickly erased.

If only I could get back that one fucking wish.

Chapter Four

Present

The icy winds whip around stinging my face as I stand on the desolate beach and stare out to the rolling waves. Even with freezing temperatures, the ocean has a way of instantly warming me. In the past it was my escape from life, but now it's my place of solace, my home. I grip my board with one hand, secure my wetsuit hood with the other and then look next to me at Dusty and Gavin.

"You two ready for this? The storm left some pretty powerful swells out there." Crouching down to Gav whose body seems tense, I comfort him. "Don't worry, buddy. I got you out there. No need to be scared."

Confusion spreads across his face as he looks at me. "What are you talking about, Daddy? I'm not scared. I'm just freaking cold."

Dusty laughs out loud, while I attempt to hold in my own laughter long enough to correct him.

"Gav, lose the potty words that Aunt Lila teaches you. Or your mom's going to do something drastic."

A toothless grin spreads across his face knowing my threat is weak and he mocks me. "Oh yea? Like what? Wash my mouth out with soap?"

I shake my head at my too-smart-for-his-own-good

son. "No, worse. She'll have Aunt Lila come over and cook for you."

His smile disappears and morphs into a disgusted look. "Ewww…you're right, Daddy. That's way worse."

"Our little secret this time, but next time I'm turning you over to Mommy." I wink at him as his pinky twists with mine.

The three of us trudge down to the water's edge ready to conquer the remnants the Nor'Easter left behind from a few days ago. Because of the storm, we couldn't surf for over a week. The conditions before it were too dangerous, and there was no way I was allowing Gavin near the rough surf. However, the after effects are six-foot waves, bitter water temperatures, and strong offshore winds—some badass conditions.

After the initial blast of ice-cold water, Dusty paddles out and I stay close to shore with Gavin while he practices his form of popping into standing position on his board. I'd occasionally push him into the smaller waves that form closer in and watch with pride as he skillfully surfs them. I can't help but think back to last summer when the waves bonded us, and now we thrive in them together.

After some time, Dusty surfs in to switch places with me. I've been training for the upcoming qualifying competition that would determine my spot this summer at the largest surfing competition on the East Coast, The Atlantic Classic. Since Dusty won it the previous year, he's guaranteed a place in the next one this summer. So, he's spent the last few months strengthening me from my injury that forced me out of the competition and helping me to sharpen my skills on the board.

Although, if I make it again, we'd be competing against each other, Dusty never lets up on me, just grateful that I'm able to come back after the stabbing.

After an intense session in the ocean, we drag our boards out and trek up the beach. I notice Gavin's chattering teeth and pull him close to my body to try to keep him warm. He gazes up at me with a contagious grin, and I'm unable to resist returning one to him.

"So, what'd you think of the winter waves, buddy? That's the first time you ever experienced the ocean after a major storm. Pretty awesome, huh?"

In his signature lispy way, he answers, "Coolest day ever." He throws his hands up in the air. "The waves were huge and they didn't even feel cold. Well, not *that* cold."

I smile at his excitement, while Dusty reaches his hand down to him for a high-five. "Congrats, little man, you are officially a true east coast surfer." Gavin directs his wide smile toward Dusty, sticking his tongue through his missing tooth.

While Dusty continues to pump Gavin's ego, I catch sight of someone ahead of us on the beach. I squint my eyes to try and recognize the person who seems to be staring back at me. She's wearing a puffy coat over tight black pants and furry boots that go up to her knees. Once I notice the short, blonde hair that sticks out from her winter hat, I prepare myself for another Tara encounter.

With a noticeable huff, I interrupt Dusty's surfing talk with Gavin. "Do you mind going ahead and bringing Gav back to the house? I have to take care of something." I nod my head toward Tara when I see the confused look Dusty's face.

Figuring out who it is, Dusty nods and yells out, "Last one to the house has to carry all the boards to the beach tomorrow." Gavin gets a head start by sticking his surfboard in front of Dusty's legs and darting out in front of him. Dusty quickly catches up to him laughing and tugging on the leash on Gav's board to slow him down. I wait until they are close to the path of our house to approach her.

Annoyed by her presence, I snap, "Tara, what the hell are you doing here? This time you're definitely following me."

Ignoring my icy greeting, she steps toward me. "You look amazing out there." She points toward the ocean. "It's like the old you is back." She leans her mouth to my ear and whispers, "I still love to watch you surf."

I back away and bite back at her, "Tara, the old me doesn't exist. At least not the one you remember. So, maybe it's time you let go of that memory and move on."

Her lips quiver and her voice trembles. "I…I can't. I love you, Cole. I tried to forget about you so many times and I've hurt people because of it. I…I hurt you." Tears trickle down her cheeks into the crocheted scarf around her neck. "We went through so much, know everything about each other, and were together through hardest times of our lives. How can you just throw that away for some daddy-seeking bitch?"

I immediately raise my defenses and clench my jaw. "Don't ever refer to my wife as that or I swear to God I'll…"

"I'm sorry. I didn't mean it. I'm just so alone and feel like I'm falling apart." She reaches for my hand

and I instantly swat hers away. "I really miss you."

I loosen from my threatening stance and turn away from her. "Tara, you have to move on. Do yourself a favor and forget about me." I begin make my way to the house. "Go live your life and let me live mine."

She stops me in my tracks when she blurts out, "It was supposed to be us living our lives together. The three of us—me, you, and our Rosy girl. Cole, I need you. I need you more than ever."

I turn around and notice the agony in her face that wipes away her cold, bitchy exterior. I motion to her to stop moving closer to me. "Tara, I'm sorry. I really am. But it's not my problem anymore. I can't help you now." I turn again and begin walking back toward my house.

Between her sobs she cries out, "But you're the only one who can. You'll always be the only one."

Tara is manipulative, but she also had to overcome a dark past at the hands of her father. Her mom turned her cheek to it as she played the role of Stepford wife perfectly until their divorce, and her brother, Brady, just got tired of the shit and left home the first chance he had. I was the only person she could depend on. But, I can't let my guilt overcome my dedication to my own family. She hurt the one woman who means everything to me, and that scar runs deeper than any other on my body. I turn down the path that leads home knowing Tara is alone as she watches one more person walk out of her life.

The warmth of the house welcomes me as I step in from the frigid February air. Even though shutting down Tara has to be done, for some reason our conversation lays heavy on my mind. Her pain is evident and I wonder, after all she has suffered and all the suffering she's caused, if she'll be able to move on with her life—if she'll ever be able to find the same type of peace that I found with Camryn.

As I lean my board against the wall in the closet, I can't help but think of the part I played in Tara's problems. I found her when I wanted to cause more pain for myself, and then I kept going back to her to numb it. I used her as my escape from everything wrong in my life and held on to her as she fell in love with me knowing I could never return the same affection to her.

Dusty breaks in to my guilt-stricken thoughts. "You all right, dude? That one scares me. She's a crazy bitch."

I nod and continue to wrap the leash around my board. "Yeah, no doubt."

Noticing my discouraged reaction, he yells out, "Oh shit…what's wrong, man? What'd she do now?" Dusty closes the closet door to avoid anyone from hearing our conversation.

"Nothing really, but I can't get it out of my head that I made her that way." With shame lowering my voice, I mumble, "I was a dickhead. I fucked with her. You remember, man. I was toxic back then."

Dusty grabs my shoulders and shakes them. "Dude, man up and grow a set of balls. Ain't no way she wasn't nuts before she met you. That kind of crazy is in the blood." He backs toward the door turning around to open it. "Stop beating yourself up. Remember what you have upstairs. Now that's some special shit." As he inches out the door, he adds, "I gotta go, but think about what I said." He throws his hand up to wave while he walks out. "Can't save them all, buddy. Especially when they're not worth saving."

His words sink in, but I can't help but think that maybe she is worth saving. That somehow it will help me to finally move on from the grief that I continue to tuck away and ignore. That maybe in some way I need to go back in order to move forward without everything to weigh me down. However, at what risk will that put the future of my family in, and would I ever be willing to take it?

After I peel off my wetsuit and take a hot shower to clear my jumbled thoughts, I throw on a pair of lounge pants and a T-shirt. Climbing up the stairs to the kitchen, Camryn and Gavin are a welcome sight sitting at our kitchen table sipping hot chocolate. Gavin's mug overflows with marshmallows and he is giggling as Cam dots whipped cream on his nose with her finger. My eyes scan to an empty seat with a steaming mug placed in front of it. At that moment, two heads turn to face me.

Gavin squeals out, "Hey, Daddy. We made you some hot chocolate with lots of marshmallows. Just how you like it."

Camryn's eyes swallow me as she stares straight into mine with a smile that stretches across her face. I stand in the doorway of the staircase staring at my family, hoping I'll never do anything to erase those smiles from their faces.

Her sweet voice breaks me from my silence. "Everything all right, babe?"

I walk to the table placing a kiss on Gavin's head, and then wrap my arms around the top of Camryn's shoulders. "Nothing could feel more right."

Chapter Five

Present

I carry a snoozing Gavin to his surfboard bed and place him in the bottom bunk wrapping him in blankets. He's never actually experienced winter, since he spent the last five years of his life in California. So, he insists on piling blankets on his bed to try to stop the constant chatter of his teeth. Every morning, I walk into his room, and he asks the same question, *"Is it still dorky wetsuit weather, Daddy?"* I just shake my head and laugh at his image of the hooded winter wetsuit we have to wear in the cold weather—something he never saw on the other coast.

However, despite his rush to get through the winter months, I'll always remember the morning Gavin woke to see the first snowfall of the season. His face pressed against the window staring at the heavy flakes blanketing the sand. He turned to me and with wide eyes and a huge grin he leaped into my arms and begged to go outside. With only an inch on the ground, I bundled him up in a snowsuit, and we spent hours throwing miniature snowballs, making snow angels, and attempted to build a snowman that ended up looking more like a bumpy pancake. After that day, I was sure this small beach town was winning over my little man's heart, just like it did for me.

Once Gavin is tucked away in his bed, I return to my spot on the couch with Camryn crawling into my arms and resting her head on my chest. As we continue to watch *Wreck it Ralph,* the movie Gavin chose, I place one hand on her stomach and the other strokes through her long, smooth hair. I can't help but feel grateful for these small moments, the ones where our unspoken words convey more meaning than our declarations of love. There was a time when I never thought I could feel this way again, and I still don't think I deserve to.

Even the very first day I saw Camryn, she had a way of drawing me in, and when she showed up again on the beach last summer she instantly took control of every part of me. Despite the pain she had to endure as she faced the hardships of her past, I knew I had to have her. And when she became mine, I finally no longer wanted to escape, but instead, stay and live again.

She looks up at me with concern in her eyes and asks, "Are you ready to talk about what happened on the beach today?"

My hand freezes in her hair startled by her knowledge of my encounter with Tara, only bringing me to one answer—Gavin. Lifting my hand from her stomach to caress her cheek, I assure her, "Baby girl, it was nothing you need to worry about. I handled it."

She sits up and pivots her body toward me. "That's the problem, Cole. You *handle* everything on your own." With frustration in her voice she continues, "I just don't get it. When it comes to her, you shut me out like you're trying to hide me from something."

I pull her back into me attempting to quell any irritation she is feeling. "Not hiding but protecting. I think Tara put you through enough shit over the years. And with the condition you're in, I want to make sure she never hurts you again."

Camryn grabs my face and tilts it down toward hers. "I'm pregnant, Cole, not broken." She places a delicate kiss on top of my head. "I just want in here, that's all."

I bring my lips up to hers and I steal a soft kiss. "Don't you know you're already in there, every single second of the day."

A grin spreads wide across her face as she wraps her arms around my neck and hops on top of me pushing me back down on the couch. Her mouth covers mine. Our kisses grow deeper with passion. My hands drop down to the slight bump of her stomach and, at that moment, I pledge to myself that I'll do anything to protect my family. Anything.

****

The reflection of heavy falling snow shines through the tall windows of our recently renovated beach home. Camryn's toned legs are still weaved through mine while my hands cup the curve of her sexy ass. Even though you can barely tell she's pregnant, curves appear in different places on her body, which makes me crave her even more. Her kiss last night led to hours of pleasure that left her exhausted and me in need of more as my morning wood presses against her thigh and begs for her to wake up. I'll never get enough of her, and I know that only our two bodies together can create a feeling like this.

Placing a kiss softly on her cheek, I slowly untangle myself from her body being careful not to wake her. Even though it kills me, and I'll be walking around for a while with my dick protruding out of my pants, I know she needs her rest.

Once up, I put my boxers and lounge pants back on and then slip Camryn's boy shorts back on her. Even in the dead of winter, she wears shorts and a tank top to bed. From the very first time we slept together, she told me she was a hot sleeper and was nervous that she'd sweat on me all night. I laugh at the memory because there is nothing better than her sweat all over my body.

Unable to get her tight tank top back over her head without waking her, I opt to use my T-shirt instead. When she is what we call "Gavin-acceptable," I pull the blanket up to her neck and tuck the hanging sides under the couch cushion. Traipsing to the kitchen to start a pot of coffee, I know it's early as the darkness still hides behind the brightness of the white snow. The clock reads five-thirty and I shake my head. *Who the hell wakes up at five-thirty on a Sunday morning?* I look down to the protrusion still in my pants and smirk knowing it's Camryn's fault. But there's no way in hell I'd have it any other way.

After I pour the much-needed liquid in the oversized mug that says *"Life is Good"* on it, I walk to the sliding glass door that overlooks the ocean. The view always amazes me, especially when the waters are left untouched. Our beginning here was tough after my dad just left Heidi and me at our grandparent's house without even saying goodbye, but somehow the ocean pushed me to keep going, especially once I began surfing. And then some time later, I saw Camryn in the cafeteria, and I knew she'd eventually be mine.

As the falling snow grows heavy and the view of the ocean becomes murky, I catch sight of a figure sitting at the top of our entrance to the beach. Squinting to get a better view, I can never mistake the short blonde hair that is flipping up against the scarf winding around her neck. Tara just refuses to leave me alone, despite the years of shit I put her through. I turn back toward a sleeping Camryn on the couch, and then a throw on my sweatshirt that is draped over a kitchen chair and my fleece that hangs on the coat rack next to the door. Stepping into my work boots, I open the sliding glass door and march toward my ongoing nightmare.

I stop behind Tara and angrily retort, "What the hell are you doing here, Tara? Didn't you take the hint yesterday? Or did I not make myself clear when I told you to forget about me?"

She continues to sit with her knees pulled up to her chest as she stares ahead. Ignoring my question, she speaks lacking any emotion in her voice. "I've spent my whole life looking for something, some kind of affection, a sign that someone loves me. But I keep screwing up somewhere. You want to know how I know this?" She turns to face me and I grimace at the sight of her black eye and split lip. She reaches into her coat pocket and pulls out a small orange bottle. "Because I keep going back to these hoping that they'll somehow fix me. Somehow make me worthy of love."

My eyes lock on the prescription bottle in her hand as the sight of them brings me back to the day the doctor prescribed me those same pills to get through my mom's funeral, then to the days Tara and I found comfort using them, and finally to the times she'd chase dealers down to score as many as we could get our hands on.

"Tara, your face—what happened?" I step toward her as my concern grows.

Was this dramatic Tara trying to pull her shit again, or was this a real call for help?

Continuing to ignore my questions, her voice remains monotone as she listlessly stares at me. "But they don't do that. They just help me forget, let me live not feeling anything but numb. On them, I can't feel when guys promise me the world and then kick me out after they fuck me. Or the ones that slap me around when I say no to them. Even my father couldn't hurt me when I was on them. I could always see his fists coming at me but I felt…nothing."

I kneel down in front of Tara and grab her shoulders to try to shake her out of her drug-induced tirade. "Who did this to you? Tara, you're not a kid anymore. Call the police. Do something. You don't have to take it anymore."

Her gaze lifts over my shoulder back to the vast stretch of sand and water in front of her. "But for some reason, when it comes to you I can still feel. It's like you're immune to the control everyone else has over me. I can still remember our bodies pressed together and how your lips explored every part of my skin, and the way you felt inside of me." She tears her eyes away from the water and looks at me again. I notice how bloodshot and glassy they are as they struggle to focus. "Just answer me one question, Cole. Did you ever love me?"

I back away from her as I try to figure out how I'll answer her. If I tell her the truth when she's high, there'd be no telling what she'll do to herself. But, if I lie to protect her, I'll risk giving her false hope of us ever being together again.

"Not the way you wanted me to."

She continues to stare at me as if she can't quite grasp the depth of my confession. Nodding and lifting herself off the ground, she tucks her hands into the pockets of her coat and stumbles away. In the past, we'd drown ourselves in alcohol and sex, refusing to face anything head on. We used each other as an escape from our realities, and it worked until we lost Rose.

Tara turns around with a stoic expression etched on her face. "One day you'll wake up and realize you're exactly like me—only good at breaking the ones we claim to love. People as fucked up as us don't deserve to be loved." She steps back to close the space between us and snarls, "That's why Rose is dead. We never deserved her. She was too good and pure for us."

Then Tara turns away and disappears into the falling white flakes, while I stand alone living in my past again, wondering if it will ever leave me the fuck alone. I look up toward the house that's supposed to mark my new beginning, our forever, and through the blanket of white notice Camryn, wrapped in her mom's afghan, standing on the deck with her gaze set on me. And in some way, I feel forever slipping out of reach.

Chapter Six

Past

After I shovel chocolate cake down my throat, I nudge Liam up from the table and we begin to approach the door. Before we can make our escape, my dad asks, "Where are you two off to tonight anyway?"

I begin to stutter unsure on how to answer but knowing that whatever Liam planned won't be parent-approved. "Um...ah...you know..."

Liam quickly jumps in to save me. "Don't worry, Mr. S, we're just gonna catch one of those shows at the park and then go check up on Heidi." He winks at my sister and she looks down with flushed cheeks.

My dad just nods at Liam probably not believing a word he said, but before he could pry a little further, my mom chimes in, "Why don't you two just stay here? Cole, you can open your gifts, and then we'll throw in a movie, just like old times. I'll even make you that popcorn mix you both love. You know, the one with M&M's?" She looks at us pleading with us to stop growing up.

Liam swings his arm around my mom's shoulder. "You almost had me with the M&M's, Mama S, but a few of the guys are meeting us. So, I think it's our responsibility to follow through with our plans. Don't you think?"

Conceding to Liam's charm she says, "All right, all right. I get it. It's not cool to hang out with us anymore. Just thought I'd give it a shot."

Noticing the disappointment in her tone, I try to comfort her. "How about tomorrow night? I can open the gifts and you pick the movie."

A genuine smile returns to her face and she pulls me into an embrace. "It's a date, Cole." She extends an arm toward Liam and scoops him into our hug. "And of course, you too, Liam. It's been a while since you spent the weekend with us. We all miss you."

Liam jokingly replies, "You twisted my arm. You know I can't resist a weekend in the Stevens' house. Mostly because of the chocolate chip pancakes on Sunday mornings."

She continues to hold us tightly against her as she seems unable to let go, or maybe just unwilling to move forward. My mom is always emotional on birthdays, so I don't resist it or roll my eyes, but rather let her have this moment to relish in what used to be.

Pulling away, she wipes a stray tear from her cheek and takes a deep breath. "All right, go have fun with your friends. Be safe and remember to stick together." She plants a soft kiss on top of both our heads as we turn and head out the door.

Liam grabs a duffel bag from the front stoop and leads me down the brick walkway pushing through the wrought iron gate that stands at the entrance of my house. While cab drivers impatiently weave through the standstill traffic of a Friday evening in the city, I follow Liam as he briskly trots down the sidewalk to maneuver through the crowds of people that populate the outdoor seating of the many bars and restaurants that line the street. As our pace picks up after a few blocks, I yell to Liam, "What the hell, dude? What's the rush?"

Darkness begins to set in as the sun sinks low behind the skyscrapers that brush the sky above us. The warm air of late May breathes life back into the outdoor squares and parks throughout the city. I check out a few girls who are beginning to wear less in short skirts and tit-hugging tank tops.

"Don't you worry, pretty-boy. We'll be there real soon." Liam turns to look at me with a wide grin on his face. "And trust me, you're *never* gonna forget this night."

I nod to him but can't fight the small wave of anxiety that spreads through me. Liam doesn't believe in boundaries. *Live for the moment* is the motto he follows, and although I admire that, it also annoys the shit out of me. I am the one left to cover his ass when his 'moments' don't go as planned.

Finally, as we reach our destination, painted pavement appears under our feet and the deafening sounds of vehicles race along the highway above us. The lights from the distant sports stadiums cast a faint glow across the concrete paradise. Girls with color-streaked hair and caked-on makeup are hanging on shirtless guys, whose tattoos seem to be an extension of the graffiti beneath them. The smoke from charcoal grills fog the air and empty beer cans litter the bare patches of grass that surround the skate park, while punk rock blares through the speakers of car stereos.

Liam ignores a group of girls in cut-off T-shirts and ripped jean shorts that barely cover their asses who are calling him over. His head remains fixed on a souped-up Dodge truck that doesn't seem to fit in with all of the rusted-out Volkswagens parked next it. As we approach the bed of the truck, a guy with dark spiked hair stands up lifting a girl who is straddled over his lap off of him. His plaid button-down shirt is unbuttoned exposing the tattoos that cover his stomach and chest. His jeans hang low on his waist with an overly large silver-buckled belt holding them up. He pushes his aviator sunglasses to the top of his head and shouts over the music to be heard.

"Well, well. I see you decided to show." He nods toward me. "And you brought my supposed golden ticket with you?"

Liam drops the duffel bag he is holding and extends his hand out. When the guy returns the high-five, Liam greets him, "What's going on, Johnny?" He moves to the side so I'm in plain view. "This is Cole. And it's green you're gonna be counting, not gold."

An obnoxious laugh bellows from him as he draws his arm to me. "Hey kid, Johnny Jax. I hope for your friend's sake, you're ready to tear it up out there."

I stand motionless as I stare at his hand waiting to meet mine. Anger begins to boil inside of me and my head snaps back to Liam who has a cocky smile plastered across his face. I stumble back to escape whatever shit Liam is getting me involved in. Just as I turn to flee, a hand grabs the fabric of my shirt and drags me away to a hidden spot behind a concrete post.

I push his hand off with force and grit my teeth, "What the fuck, Liam? Who the hell is this Johnny Douchebag?"

"Cole…relax. Just calm down."

Feeling the blood pound against my temples, I snap, "Just fucking spill it, Liam."

He takes a deep breath and shoots his expression to the ground. "Umm, well...ummm. He's a pretty big bookie that comes to my dad's matches. I placed a few bets through him and won some good money. Well, that was until a few weeks ago." His voice becomes hesitant as his confession began to emerge.

"So, what does that have to do with me and why the hell are we at the skate park?" I fear his response already knowing what he's going to say.

He holds out the duffel bag that he carried from my house in front of me. "Well, I owe him some money and told him I have a sure bet for Skate Wars." He drops his head to avoid my stare.

Skate Wars is an illegal skateboarding contest, a showcase of unthinkable stunts that take place every Friday night at a different location. Switching skate parks is supposed to deter the cops from breaking it up. However, most of them just turn a blind eye to it since they have bigger crimes to deal with in the city.

With rage building in me, I push Liam up against concrete post behind him and snap, "Are you fucking crazy? I can't compete with those guys out there." I point toward the ramp that everyone begins to surround. "They'll tear me apart."

Attempting to soften my mood, he places his hand on my shoulder and squeezes it. "Dude, you are better than half those guys out there. And the other half...well you have one thing they don't."

I step back as the tension in my body eases and wait for his answer. He leans in to close the space I just created. "No fear."

A sarcastic laugh resonates from my throat because he's right. I'll try anything on my board, but that doesn't mean I can compete with the guys here tonight. They are years ahead of me and newcomers just don't win Skate Wars. It's unheard of.

Over Liam's shoulder, I catch glimpse of Johnny walking toward us. His sunglasses are covering his eyes even though darkness has fully set in, and the tight line of his mouth only expresses his frustration with us. He isn't the type of guy that takes well to being played, especially by a bunch of teenagers.

He speaks directly to Liam but never lifts his gaze from me. "So, what's it gonna be? Is he ready to ride or are his panties still in a bunch?"

Liam draws his eyes to mine as if he was willing me to accept the challenge. Bitterness begins to wrap itself around me, suffocating me, as I can hear Liam's silent pleas. It's always been the same with him. He fucks up, and I'm the one left to clean up his mess.

I tear the duffel bag from Liam's grasp and can hear a sigh of relief escape him. Without speaking to either of them, I traipse away toward the park. I have to fight my way through a crowd of people who are shoving each other to get a better view of the action that is about to begin. After I submit my name to the judges, I stand on top of the ramp and eye the eleven-foot wall that I'm about to ride. My breath hitches as I struggle to calm my nerves. I catch sight of Liam who has squeezed his way through to the front of the crowd, while Johnny remains close behind. Liam owes me. *Motherfucking big.*

When my name is announced, I stand immobilized at the top of the skate ramp. I peer down the steep slope as my nerves begin to take control of me. I can feel the eyes of the crowd bearing down on me along with a few jeers from some drunk assholes. I tilt the skateboard up, take a deep breath, and hop on my board as it cruises down the concrete. Through the chants of, *"choke, choke, choke,"* I reach down deep and pull out my craziest tricks. No way I'm going to lose this. No. Fucking. Way.

****

I battle through the swarms of people who are trying to meet the new kid who somehow beat out the competition. With a wad of cash in my pocket, I push through a few girls who are flashing their tits at me and approach Johnny, who's wearing a smug smile across his face.

"Well, well, boy wonder came through." He taunts.

I pull the cash Liam owed him from my pocket and drop it in his lap. Before I can escape the scene, he yells out, "Whoa, what's the rush? We have some business to discuss."

Over my shoulder I shout back, "Business was already taken care of. Now leave us the fuck alone."

With his sarcastic cackle bellowing across the parking lot, he cries out, "You'll be back, wonder boy. You'll be back." His laugh shoots through me as I race to get the hell away.

I rush across the street hoping the sounds of the skate park will soon fade along with the memory of the night. After I won, I made a point to avoid Liam and once the crowd began to huddle around me, it wasn't difficult to lose him. As cobblestone sidewalks and brick faced homes come into view, I can hear footsteps behind closing in on me. I stop in my tracks and turn around to meet the huge smile of Liam. His wavy hair is all over the place as a few pieces had dropped in front of his eye. The buttons of his army green button-down shirt are wide open, a few of them torn off of the shirt. Smudged next to his lip is bright red lipstick that looks like he tried to wipe away.

Anger filters through my body and I snap, "Are you fucking serious, dude? You drag me down there to clean up your gambling shit and you don't even have the courtesy to watch?"

He smirks and jokingly answers, "Listen. When a girl wants some ass, you make yourself available. It's that simple." He shrugs his shoulders. "Besides, I saw your entire ride. I took care of business after your run. It was my own personal victory party." He playfully jabs me in the ribs with his elbow. "I knew you could kick some serious ass out there."

I glare at him loathing every part of him at the moment. "Don't ever put me in that position again."

Blowing me off he answers, "Yeah, yeah. But one thing—how does it feel to be the shit out there?"

"I fucking mean it, Liam." I'm done cleaning up your stupid-ass messes. You're on your own with your shit going forward." I lean into him to make sure he understands. "You got me?"

Probably ignoring my threat, Liam just nods as I turn back around to leave. He shouts to me, "Wait, where you going? Don't you want to go celebrate victory and your birthday?" Without turning to face him, I yell back, "You're on your own tonight. And don't call me to bail you out of whatever shit you get into." I pick up the pace as he continues to beg and plead. But I am done playing his games for the night.

****

The shrill of Heidi's sudden cries wake me from a

sound sleep. She had been out at some party or something, so I didn't realize she was home and she startled me. I had finally turned off my cell phone after I ignored a shitload of calls from Liam. He left messages, but I wasn't in the mood to listen to them, so I threw on my headphones and fell asleep. I'll deal with Liam tomorrow. Now, I need to see my sister. With only the reflection of the city lights shining through the darkness of my room, I know something has to be wrong.

Darting out of my bed toward Heidi's room, I find her slouched on the floor with her knees pulled up to her chest. She's still wearing the same clothes she went out in, except now the strap of her tank top looks ripped off and she's only wearing one of those pointy shoes she swears are comfortable. Tears flood her cheeks, while she gasps for air between her screams. Her cell phone is next to her still flipped open, and I can hear the echo of my dad's voice calling her name. Reaching down to the floor to retrieve her cell, I put it up to my ear, my hand trembling with impending fear.

I choke out my words, "Da...dad it's me. What's wrong?"

It's evident that he is holding back sobs, and there is no mistaking panic in his voice. "Cole...son...I need you and Heidi to get down to the hospital now."

I stumble backward and catch my weight on the wooden footboard of Heidi's bed, fearing the answer to my next question, "Why? What happened?" I am met with silence on the other end and shout louder while Heidi's continues to weep into her hands. "Dad, tell me. What the hell happened?"

"The...there's been an accident." His words shake

45

with terror and drip with regret. "She's gone, son…mom's gone."

I drop the phone unable to endure the piercing pain that runs through me. *I didn't hear him say that. He's lying.* She can't be gone. I rush out of my sister's room and burst through the closed door of my mom and dad's room. I tear all the pillows and blankets from their bed desperately trying to find her asleep. *She's supposed to be here. She has to be here.* As my dad's words replay over and over again, I fall to the floor and hold my head in my hands. I can't breathe, I can't move. All I can do is feel my life being stripped away piece by piece. All I can see is my forever changed.

Chapter Seven

Present

The cutting winds prickle my skin while the heavy falling snow stings my tired eyes. I have to squint to see my wife, who waits on the deck for me to come to her, to explain why Tara was out on the snowy dunes of our beach entrance. She deserves to know everything—the impact of my mom's death, my downward spiral after she was gone, and the effect Tara's accusations have had on me. But I can't dampen that spirit I spent months building back up in her. She is my angel and I sure as hell won't drag her down to the depths of hell with me.

I creep past the dunes, my eyes unable to leave hers. As the conversation with Tara echoes through my mind, all I can grasp is the truth in her words. Over and over again we'd just raise our middle fingers and tell the world to fuck off. She's right—everything about us is destructive and as I climb the deck stairs to my wife, I wonder when I'll eventually destroy her.

Camryn extends her hand out to me, "Everything okay?"

I shrug my shoulder and take her small hand into mine. Forcing a smile, I assure her, "I am now."

Her lips curl down and tears well in her eyes. Her pain is evident, pain caused by me. She wraps her arms around my waist, draping the blanket over me. Resting her head against my chest, she pleads, "Cole, please let me in. I can see you're hurting."

I dig my face into her hair inhaling that oh-so-familiar strawberry scent. She is begging me to let her into the darkness and all I want to do is push her toward the light. I'll be damned if I ever ruin her.

Anything to protect her.

I drag my hands up her back and caress her cheeks with my thumbs. Tilting her chin toward me, I whisper, "Baby girl, *she* doesn't mean anything to me. She never did. You're the only one that will ever matter."

A ghost of a smile appears on Camryn, yet the worry still hides within her eyes. She grabs my wrists and starts to walk backwards toward the glass door. With one hand, she blindly reaches behind her and slides open the door tugging me through it. Her previous concern is replaced with lust, and desire reflects in her eyes.

"I need you, Cole. Right now." She stops us in her tracks and stands on the tips of her toes to reach me and whispers, "Can I show you just how much I need you, how much I want you?"

I smile at Camryn, trying to erase the worry that I hear in her pleas. Grabbing beneath her ass, I hoist her up into my arms. "When it comes to you I can never say no."

I whisk Camryn down the stairs to our bedroom latching the door behind us. I toss the blanket draped over her shoulders to the floor and peel the clothing from her. Stepping back, I take in all of her as my eyes travel down her naked body. I pause at the swell below her belly-button, and Tara's toxic words flood back to me for the moment. I have to find a way to keep them away from the mistakes that I have to live with, the poison that's defined me for so many years.

The darkness has begun to resurface, but I vow to tuck it away for Camryn. I sink my hand into her tangled hair as I cup the back of her head and draw her toward me. After I place a delicate kiss on her lips, I drag my hand down her body my thumbs circling her hardened nipples. Her head drops back with a slight moan exposing her neck, and I lean into it gently sucking and biting until I can feel her knees weakening. I lay her on the bed and lean over her.

"You are so beautiful, Camryn."

Her cheeks flush at my compliment and a wide smile spread across her face. That's enough to erase the pain, for the moment, to block out the darkness that's begun to wrap itself around me again.

****

While Camryn is in my arms, I am able to forget about Tara. After a sweaty lovemaking session and then a steamy shower to follow, we end up drifting back to sleep until Gavin darts into the bedroom squealing in excitement. He leaps on top of the bed and bounces by our feet as he begs to go play in the snow. I can't help but jump out of bed to satisfy his wishes.

I grab Gavin and throw him over my shoulder, while his feet dangle in the air, "What did you say, buddy? You want to go where?"

His infectious laugh carries down the hallway. "The snow. I said snow, Daddy."

I open the front door and pretend to throw him into the snow that is piled up on the stairs to the porch. Gavin chokes from his laughter as I draw him to me and hold him in my arms. "You ready for the craziest snowball fight of all time?"

Gavin's mouth drops open and his eyes are wide with surprise. "Are you serious? Can we, can we?"

I place his feet on the tiled hallway floor and lead him to his room. "You bet, little man. We have the whole day to play in the snow."

He claps with excitement and races to his dresser and begins to layer himself with warm clothes. Needing to get dressed myself, I sneak back to my bedroom and find Camryn standing in front of the sink in the bathroom. Wrapping my arms around her waist, I rest my chin on her shoulder and speak to her reflection in the mirror, "You up for a pretty insane snowball fight today?"

A mischievous grin spreads across her face. "There's nothing else in the world I'd rather do today." She spins around to face me. "And don't think for a moment I'm going easy on you." She leans into my ear and whispers, "You see I plan to have no mercy when it comes to you.

I lift her and murmur, "Well that's good to hear because when it comes to you tonight I plan to have no mercy either."

I lean down and tilt her chin up toward me. Our lips meet with the same spark they've always carried. However, our moment of passion is quickly broken up by the whines of our five-year-old.

"Grooosss! Do you *always* have to do that?"

I smile into Camryn's lips before I separate from her. Brushing my hand over the top of Gavin's head, I assure him, "One day you'll understand, buddy. You'll want to kiss a girl too. Lots of them."

"Uhhh…okay. Whatever you say?" Gavin looks at me like I'm crazy and I can't help but laugh remembering the advice my mom used to give me that I would blow off.

Once we are all bundled up, we head out back to our own winter play land. While Camryn and Gavin are busy gathering their ammunition, I stare out toward the dunes where Tara had torn open my wounds earlier in the morning. For years I shoved away the pain from loss and the guilt that came with it. But this time it's different. This time I have my family.

Anything to protect them.

Just as my regrets begin to consume me, a packed ball of snow whizzes by my head. When I turn around to duck for cover, a cold shot smashes into my face and uproarious laughter follows. I wipe the icy drops from my eyes and reach down to scoop up my own handful, packing it tightly between my palms. I dash toward Cam and Gav and unleash my own fury as the snowball smashes against the top of Gavin's leg. At that moment, I am smothered in a barrage of white while they throw snowball after snowball at me. In dramatic fashion, I drop to the ground in defeat. When Gavin stands over me and claims victory, I pull him to the ground and roll him in the snow. Camryn lays down next to us and we laugh until it hurts.

We are still outside when Lila and Carter show up for family dinner. They always come early, usually spending the entire afternoon with us. Lila and Camryn get lost in the kitchen as Camryn cooks and Lila gossips, and Carter, Gavin, and I usually waste the day away in the game room as they attempt to beat me at *Transworld Surf,* in which they have no shot.

I am shoveling the snow from the walkway and porch and Camryn and Gavin are putting the final touches on the snowman they built when Lila's shrieks out, "You best be taking that hideous plaid scarf off that snowman." She unravels the scarf from her own neck and hands it to Gavin. "Here, use this one instead. It's much more stylish."

Gavin holds up Lila's scarf and looks to Camryn for approval. Camryn's stares at Lila in shock and says, "Are you crazy? That's a designer scarf you're putting on the snowman."

Lila shrugs her shoulders, "Oh it's just a scarf. Besides you can't have that dingy old one on a snowman on this block. We don't want the neighbors complaining about the eye sore."

I look at Carter and just roll my eyes at the incessant giggling that always seems to happen between the two of them. But, regardless, I will be forever grateful for Lila and Carter. They took care of Camryn and Gavin before I was around and supported her through the most difficult years of her life. And I know Camryn and Gavin will always have them for the rest of their lives.

Once the snowman is fashionable enough for Lila's standards, Camryn and Lila drag our blue-lipped boy into the house, while Carter and I stay outside to clean up. He grabs the extra shovel on the porch and starts pushing the snow off the stairs.

"So, man, I heard you're cranking it in training." He looks up and points out to the falling snow. "Don't know how you guys train in this shit. There's no suit warm enough to get me out there. That's for sure."

I joke, "I'm disappointed. Thought that pansy ass

west coaster would be out of you by now."

He flips some snow up at me and defends himself. "Nah, dude, West Coast for life. I'd much rather rake in the cash from you crazies who have to buy a new wet suit each time the temperature changes."

"Can't argue with that. But I'll never give up the winter surf. Empty beach, powerful swells—there's nothing like it."

"According to Dusty, the beach hasn't been all that empty for you." Carter stops shoveling and waits for me to answer.

I'm not surprised that Dusty told Carter about Tara's visits to the beach. He was always there to watch Tara fuck with my head, and then it was him who was left to deal with my mood swings that came from it. But what Dusty didn't see was what I had done to Tara. I used her when I needed to feel something and let her believe we could be something more.

"Yea, I guess Dusty let you know we've had a little audience when we train." I return my gaze to the walkway I'm shoveling to avoid more of the conversation.

"Sounds more like a big ass pain. Just be careful, Cole. That girl can do some serious damage. You and Camryn don't need that shit right now. And you definitely don't need Lila *dealing* with it."

"I know, man." I grab his shovel and lean them both up against the porch railing. "Let's go in. We've done enough work for the day."

We are hit with the aroma of garlic as soon as we walk into the house. Once I change into jeans and thermal shirt, I meet Camryn in the kitchen who is chopping vegetables for a salad. Lila hurries out of the kitchen to meet Carter in the game room for an intense game of *Mrs. Pac-Man* while Gavin is knocked out on the couch. He is snuggled underneath a blanket with a trail of slobber down his chin.

I grab a spoon and stir the pasta sauce sneaking glances over to my wife. She has her hair plaited to the side in a braid, exposing the smoothness of her neck. Some strands of her hair fall into her face, which causes her to have to blow them out of her way. Her mouth has the slightest tilt upward as she lip-syncs the words to the folky song that plays in the background. She peeks up from the cutting board and catches me staring, which causes her cheeks to flush.

I place the spoon on the counter next to the stove and stroll over to her. I pull her into my arms and delicately kiss her lips. "I just can't get enough of my wife."

She stands on the tips of her toes and wraps her arms around my neck. "And what's going to happen when you've had enough of me, Mr. Stevens?"

"Impossible, baby girl. I will never have enough of you, Mrs. Stevens." I pull her waist into me and cover her mouth with mine.

Just as our kiss is deepening, a high-pitched voice suddenly stops our passion, "Eww...really? Are you always groping each other like that?"

I look over Camryn's shoulder to see Heidi and Dusty standing in the entrance of the kitchen. Camryn rushes over to give them a hug while I sarcastically add, "If you would've come five minutes later you could've seen me take my wife right here on this counter."

Camryn screams my name in embarrassment, while Heidi just stares at me in disgust. I hand Dusty a beer while he holds it up to salute my humor. Before she drags Dusty out of the kitchen, she yells over her shoulder, "You're disgusting, Cole. Way too much information."

I pop open a beer for myself and continue to stir the sauce. A few minutes later, Camryn's dad, Jack, walks into the kitchen. He races over to Camryn and hugs her.

"Hey, Goldfish. It smells delicious."

Once she greets him, he walks over to me and does the one-armed man hug. "Hey Cole. I'm hearing some great things about your training. Sounds like you'll be a major contender in the Qualifiers this year."

"I hope so. I'm trying to focus pretty hardcore on getting back in."

Jack pats my shoulder. "Well, it's just great to know your back out there doing what you love."

I smile at his enthusiasm and ask, "So, what about you? Cam told me that you guys found a partner for the clinic."

A month after our wedding, Jack told us his plan for a cancer clinic was approved by the hospital. He asked Camryn to be a part of it. Not only would she be a partner, but she'd work as the head nurse once it opened. After watching her mom suffer from cancer for so many years, she jumped at this opportunity. She said it was a way for her to keep her mom's legacy alive. And I am damn proud of her for it.

"We did. He's going to be a financial partner. You know, the numbers expert." Jack beams with pride while Camryn jumps into the conversation.

"Cole, you're going to love him. Has the same business sense as you."

I grab Camryn's apron tie and drag her to me. "Oh yea? Love him? Just as long as he keeps it strictly business with you."

She playfully swats at my face. "Is that jealousy I'm hearing?" She places her palms on my cheeks. "Because you have absolutely nothing to worry about." She reaches down and rubs her stomach. "We totally and completely belong to you."

I bend down and place a soft kiss on her lips. Jack clears his throat to interrupt our intimate moment. "Well, if it's okay with both of you, I told him to swing by for dinner. I mean he just got here and doesn't really know anyone."

Camryn quickly nods to appease her dad. "Of course, Dad. We'll make him feel right at home.'

Jack grins at his daughter and walks toward the family room. "Well, I have a little shark to wake up. Call me in if you need any help with dinner." Camryn gives him a thumb's up as he walks away to find his grandson.

When I return to the stove to stir the sauce, the doorbell rings and I notice Camryn's body jerk at the sound of it. "The doorbell? Don't think I ever heard it. Everyone else just walks right in."

"Hmmm…I think you're right. Maybe we should start walking around the house naked. That will get them to ring the doorbell." The sound of Camryn's sweet laughter fills me as I leave the kitchen to answer the door.

Once downstairs, I swing open the door and feel my body instantly tense at the sight of who's on the other side. My hands, now tight fists, drop to my side and I clench my jaw with force as if I'm prepping for battle. While I stand in the doorway, I can only hear the echo of my heart beating against every vein in my body. The sight of him only draws heavier breaths from my lungs as past memories flash through my mind.

With my mouth rigid, I snap, "What the fuck do you think you're doing here?"

He takes a step toward me, half of his foot landing in my house. "What's wrong, *Coley*, not happy to see me?"

I inch closer to dominate the space between us, and demand, "I've already warned you before. Stay the hell away from me, Liam."

His cocky smirk only reveals that he has no intentions of heeding my warning this time. Liam is here for a reason, which leaves me to wonder how I can save my family from his impending destruction.

Chapter Eight

Present

I stand rigid in the doorway with an icy glare that matches the frosty winds that whip between us. I search his face, covered in scruff, for his reason to find me, but all I can see is the aloofness of his stone-gray eyes and sneer of his smile taunting me. He runs his hand through the sandy-colored waves on top of his head and just shakes his head in amusement. As he continues to silently mock me, I shudder with desire to hurt him, to make him suffer from the same pain he's caused me for so many years.

He stretches his neck to peer over my shoulder and scoffs, "So are you going to invite me in or what?"

I pull the door toward me to close Liam off from seeing in the house and threaten, "It's time for you to leave. You're not welcome here. Ever" My jaw grinds harder with each word I speak.

A haughty laugh escapes from him and he steps closer to me. Broadening his shoulders, he looks up, his eyes set on mine and reveals, "I don't think *Camryn* would agree with you. Especially since I'm the one in control of whether her beloved cancer clinic happens or not." He backs away with an arrogant smugness beaming from him.

My chest constricts at his confession, as if he has

just sucked the air from me. To hear my wife's name, leave his lips feels like the biggest act of betrayal from someone who once was a brother to me. But ever since that one night, everything he's done was against me, like a sick act of revenge. I thought he was gone—that he finally accepted his responsibility in everything that went down. However, as he calmly lingers in the doorway, I realize he had no intention of leaving forever.

Rage over his knowledge of Camryn, I shove him out onto the porch. Grabbing him by the wide collar of his wool coat I pull him close to my face. "You can try to fuck with me, Liam, but not with my wife. Touch her and I'll fucking end you. It's that simple."

Liam pushes my wrists away and readjusts his jacket. Still wearing a stupid grin, he places his hands up in front of his body, his palms facing me. "Whoa, settle down, pretty boy. I have no intentions of hurting your wife. I want nothing more than for her and Jack's clinic to be a success. It's just a shame for you that I'm the one person who can make that happen, which means you'll be seeing a whole lot of me."

My anger begins to take control of my body and just as I ball my fists and prepare to lunge at him, a soothing voice brings me out of my fury. From atop the stairs Camryn is calling down to me. "Cole, who's at the door?" I can hear her footsteps descend down the staircase.

I attempt to compose myself as I steady my breathing and try to erase the previous few seconds from my head. In just a matter of minutes, Liam is able to drive that person out of me again. The one who does nothing but damage others. The one who I thought was buried so deep with no chance of coming back.

Camryn inches in next to me as she hooks her arm around my waist. A broad smile stretches across her face at the sight of Liam. As she gazes up to me, I notice a flash of concern hiding within her expression. Camryn can always read my thoughts, even when I try my damnedest to hide the pain. To erase her worry, I fake a smile and assure her, "Liam and I were just getting acquainted before I brought him upstairs."

She nods at me with confusion, as if she could see right through my lies. I continue my phony act as I open the door wider to let Liam in. Before he walks through, Camryn greets him with a hug and exclaims, "I'm so happy you could make it. You get to meet the whole gang tonight. They're all upstairs waiting for me to put dinner on the table."

Liam replies, "Can't wait. I'm looking forward to a home-cooked meal. It's been a while since I've had one of those." His glare tears right through me as if I'm the reason for his lack of dinners over the years.

Camryn motions for Liam to come in and she begins to lead him up the stairs. I close my eyes for a second and repeat our mantra in my head, *"Own your breath, Cole. Do it for her."* Once a bit of calm levels me out, I follow Camryn and Liam up the stairs, my eyes directed on him, and I'm left to wonder why the hell my past is walking into my dining room right now.

Everyone is seated around the table as loud conversation fills the house. Gavin looks half-asleep, probably from Jack waking him up from his nap, but he's still able to entertain Lila and Carter with one of his famous joke sessions. Dusty and Heidi are entrenched in one of Jack's many surgeon stories, which are always so uncomfortably graphic. As the three of us approach the table the conversation abruptly stops, and all heads avert to the new person who is in front of them.

I first hear a gasp from Heidi and then see her leap up from her chair, her eyes wide and watery as she throws her arms around Liam's neck. Liam hesitantly returns her affection as he notices Dusty's glare settled on him. She pulls away from his body and tilts her head as if she has to confirm he's real. "Oh my God, Liam. What are you doing here?" I pick up on the hint of regret in her voice. "I never thought I'd see you again."

He clears his throat, "You know I never wanted that, Heids." I reach for Camryn's hand to stop me from tackling the asshole. He continues to explain, raising the volume of his voice for everyone to hear but keeping his eyes locked on Heidi. "Well, I was lucky enough to meet Jack and he had a great business opportunity for me with this clinic that he and his daughter are starting. So, I decided to finally leave the city and head for the small town of Sea City. I mean it just seems like the perfect place to start brand new and forget about everything." He clears his throat and looks behind him straight at me. "Don't you agree, Cole?"

If not for Camryn's hand entwined with mine, Liam would be flat on his back while my fists rearrange his face. Instead, I just eat his shit as I tightly nod at his very revealing question. Noticing my struggle to remain calm, Heidi quickly blurts out more questions to Liam to cut the tension between us.

"So, are you here for a while or just until the clinic opens?"

I squeeze Camryn's hand tighter as the

conversation leads to the direction of Liam's future here. However, I already know his answer. Liam always has a plan, and it's never short-term. As the pressure builds inside of me, and my body grows stiffer, I can feel Camryn's eyes on me studying me.

Jack stands up and pats Liam on the back. "Don't worry, Heidi, he's here to stay." Jack turns, faces the table, and jokes, "Anyone else know Liam from a past life?" While he manages a laugh from the all the ladies, he continues, "For those who don't know him, this is Liam Duffy, our new partner for the clinic." He pats Liam's back with pride while everyone welcomes the asshole to our family dinner.

Liam sits across from Heidi, as I take my seat at the opposite end of the table next to Gavin. Everyone is focused on him throughout dinner with Lila trying to recruit him as a client at the salon, Carter comparing Los Angeles and Philly night life, Dusty staring him down every time Heidi talks to him, and Gavin entertaining him with his knock-knock jokes. Throughout dinner, Heidi continues to look in my direction, her nerves obvious in her expression. I try to remain focused on my plate, moving my food around it with my fork. Aware of my lack of appetite, Camryn leans into my ear and, with concern, asks, "Cole, what's going on with you? Are you all right?"

I can only nod and kiss her cheek being careful not to spit the venom that is rising in me. She reluctantly accepts my gesture and places her hand on my thigh. Her touch manages to calm me, but it will never last—not with him sitting across the table from me.

Gavin tugs on my shirt's sleeve to get my attention. "Daddy, how do you, Aunt Heidi, and Mr. Liam know each other?"

Heidi's head quickly turns toward me, and fear registers in her eyes. I focus on Gavin and his innocence as I explain, "Well you see, before Aunt Heidi and I moved here, we lived in a really big city not too far away and so did Liam. He went to the same school as us."

Thankfully, Gavin doesn't pry for more. "Oh, okay. Cool. So, can I go play now? I'm finished my dinner."

I manage to smile at Gavin and pull his chair out from the table. "Sure thing, buddy. Save me a game for later tonight." He flashes me a double thumbs-up and skips out of the room.

"So, Coley, now that the little guy's not here you want to tell everyone how we know each other?" The iciness in his tone shoots through me. "Why don't you tell everyone the truth?"

Everyone around the table goes silent, except for Heidi, who quickly interjects, "Hey Liam just let it go for now."

Liam ignores her and continues to jab at me as everyone stunned to stillness. "Go ahead. Tell them every little thing. Every. Little. Lie."

As Jack attempts to pacify Liam's hostile accusations, Dusty hops out of his seat and walks around the table toward Liam while Lila grabs hold of Carter's shirt to stop him from getting out of his own seat. Rubbing over my white knuckles, Camryn leaps from her chair to stop whatever is about to transpire. "Liam, that's enough. Nobody needs to know anything or even *thinks* anything. We just want to have an enjoyable dinner with a new friend, that's all."

Liam erupts in laughter, "Friend? Camryn, that's the last thing I am to your husband." Still focused on me, he digs in deeper. "Doesn't your wife deserve to know? And all your *best friends*?" His voice begins to quake. "Come on, Cole. Paint me out as the bad guy, tell them I ruined you, go ahead tell them…"

Before he can finish I launch out of my chair and yank him out of his seat by the collar of his shirt. Camryn tugs on the back of my mine pleading for me to calm down, while Dusty and Carter race over to pull me off of Liam. With Dusty holding me back and Carter guarding Liam, I grit my teeth and spat out, "I don't have to tell them a damn thing. They'll see who you really are on their own." Over Liam's shoulder I catch a glimpse of my scared son in the other room, who is gaping at me in terror. At that instant my heart shatters, so ashamed that I can't tame the beast inside of me for his sake. I shake Dusty's grip from me, and race down the stairs out of the house. I have to get out of there; I need to somehow find my breath. I rush down the sidewalk ignoring all of their pleas being shouted from the porch as I disappear into the darkness to find some form of solace.

Once I'm a few blocks' distance from the house, I stagger through the door of *Twisters* instantly surrounded by the oak-paneled walls that adorn the place. I sit on a vinyl-topped stool that faces the fish plaques hanging around the glowing red wall clock. The town is dead during the off-season so only a few locals are scattered around the wood-topped bar. I stare out the window toward the bay that always seems to inhabit a different type of calmness from that of the crashing waves of the ocean. But nothing can settle the turmoil that rocks me tonight. I throw my wallet and cellphone on the bar in front of me and noticed missed calls and texts from Camryn. I can't face her right now. I just can't.

The bartender throws a coaster in front of me and asks, "So what's it gonna be tonight?"

"Two shots of Jack." I keep my eyes focused on Camryn and Gavin's picture flashing on my cell that continues to vibrate with each ring.

He slides two shot glasses in front of me. "That kind of a night?"

I throw back one shot and nudge the glass toward him. "Just keep them coming, all right?"

He fills the glass again adding more. "Yes, sir."

After polishing off half a bottle of Jack, I finally uncover the numbness I am so desperately seeking. Each time the night replays in my head I see Gavin's face, his frightened look, and down another shot. Liam was able to tear down everything Camryn built up, drudge up every demon that still haunts me, and reminds me of the person I really am.

As I continue to stare at my phone wrestling with my conscience, another shot is placed in front of me and a voice tears me away from my self-loathing. Tara stands next to me holding a glass of her own. The bruises on her face are faded from her make-up, but the slash on her lip is still evident. However, it's the emptiness in her eyes that startles me, as if I'm staring at a reflection of my own eyes. She tilts her glass toward me and proposes, "Bottoms up? For old times?"

I mumble out, "I think I've had enough of *old fucking times* for one night."

She places her glass on the bar and climbs onto the

stool next to me. "Cole, what's wrong?"

I know that if I answer her I'm inviting her back into my life, but I'm too drunk to care at that point, "Let's just say an old friend of mine decided to pay me a visit tonight."

Tara stares at me as she tries to register my drunken thoughts. She gasps in surprise, "Liam. Is it Liam you're talking about?"

I nod as I take a swig of the beer the bartender just set in front of me. "And he's not leaving anytime soon."

"Why is he back?"

I stare at my shot glass twirling it around in a circle and shrug my shoulders.

Our attention is suddenly drawn toward the vibration of my phone against the top of the bar. Guilt floods me as I eye the picture lighting up with each ring: Camryn's and Gavin's heads both tilted to one side sticking their tongues out.

Anything to protect them.

I grab my phone and Tara watches as I push the silence button on the side. Shame wraps around me as I begin to shut them out. But I will never let them endure my pain, not after what they have been through already. Raising my glass, I tilt it toward Tara, "To old fucking times."

A smile creeps across her face and she clanks her glass against mine, "To old fucking times."

Chapter Nine

Past

The city skyline disappears behind the gray fog looming overhead. Thunder rumbles amidst the high-pitched squeals of sirens racing through the streets. Wiping the large drops of rain trickling down from my eyes, I focus on the seventy-two stone steps below me leading to the entrance of the stoic art museum. Every day you see tourists running up these stairs reenacting Rocky Balboa's famous climb. But I've never never seen anyone attempt to skateboard down them—not until now.

A small crowd gathers at the bottom, all staring at the crazy ass sixteen-year-old who they probably think has a death wish for himself. What's the big deal about death anyway? I'd never take my own life on purpose—that's too fucking easy; but you can't stop or hide from it, so why not challenge it? My mom never had the chance to a year ago. It just swooped in and claimed her. It took her away from my sister and me without giving us a chance to say goodbye. It left us with a checked-out father and a house full of empty liquor bottles. So, every chance I have, I'm going to challenge death for her and if I end up losing, who the fuck will care anyway?

Tilting the board up from my foot, I eye the first

landing, the one with the most jagged edges and loosest stones. If I can make it past that one, I'll have a real chance to reach the bottom in one piece. After I kiss up toward the sky, a gesture for my mom, I lunge down and pivot my front foot, slamming the board down to the ground. As I begin my bumpy descent, I raise my two middle fingers and yell out, "Fuck you, death!"

I skim across and down the steps with my skateboard, able to hear gasps from onlookers. Their comments flood my thoughts. *This kid's crazy. He needs help. He has no respect for himself or public property.* But the judgments don't bother me anymore. I hear them from teachers, neighbors, and counselors—people who all promised over my mom's dead body that they would stand by me. People who I haven't seen since the day of her funeral. Well I don't give a fuck what they think about me. They're not paying the bills while watching the house they grew up in slip into foreclosure, or seeing everything their mom worked for fall apart, or wiping puke from their father's mouth while he's passed out on the bathroom floor. When their time comes and are given a shitty hand, they'll turn their backs against life, just like I am.

Once I pick up speed halfway down, I manage to maneuver swiftly over the rough terrain even able to throw in some tricks with my board for show. Grabbing the edge of my skateboard, I jump the last set of steps and land in front of a group of my classmates. While they surround me with cheers and high-fives, a squeaky voice breaks through the crowd and pain begins to splinter through my arm.

"Why would you do that? Are you trying to kill yourself? Are you insane?"

Heidi's voice rises with each punch into my arm. While my sister has watched my transformation since our mom died, she refuses to accept it. She still clings on to hope for the old Cole to return. Since she's the only person who means anything to me, I let her hold on to that even though what I used to be died along with my mom. I detain her wrists to stop her assault on my arm and lift my petite sister off of me.

Grinning at her attempt to punch me with her arms locked in my grip, her expression grows angrier at my amusement. "You're just an asshole." Tears well in her eyes. "You can't die. I need you here. I'm not going to lose my brother too."

I loosen my grasp and pull her into an embrace. Her reaction to my shithead antics cuts me to shreds and guilt drapes me like a suffocating blanket. Trying to calm my sister and make light of my actions I joke, "I'm sorry, Heidi. But you gotta admit my skills are pretty sick. That was one badass ride."

Heidi swats at me missing my face with her palm but catching her nail on my chin. "We all know you're hard core, Cole. Can't you just tone it down a bit? If not for you, then for me?" She gazes up to me with soft blue eyes that match mine, which are now wide and pleading.

Unable to disappoint my big sister, the girl that stepped into my mom's role only a year ago, I squeeze her tightly against me. "I'll try." I lower my voice and mumble to myself, "But it's only for you."

At that moment, slow, exaggerated clapping breaks through the crowd that surrounds us. When I hear the voice attached to it, I quickly push Heidi behind me so that my body blocks his view of her. I straighten my shoulders and step toward him, swallowing any space that is between us. Once we are face-to-face, I speak in a low, threatening voice. "Didn't I warn you to stay away, dickhead? Or do you need to taste my fist one more time to be sure you heard me correctly?"

Liam smirks at me with amusement and shoots back, "Nah, *Coley*. Think I missed that. Guess my head was between your sister's thighs." He glances at Heidi and winks at her while her head drops to the ground in embarrassment.

I was pissed that Heidi began to date Liam after that night. She would deny it when I brought it up, but she always had a problem hiding her feelings for him. So, he was able to slither back into my family as he made Heidi believe in his bullshit regret. For a while, I hung close by to watch him with a careful eye. He knew I was hovering and he played the role of perfect boyfriend. But once I backed off, he found a way to break another person in my family when I found him slouched against my mom's headstone in the cemetery with some half-naked girl sprawled across him. My fist immediately met his jaw without any chance for him to defend himself, and I couldn't stop pounding him until my dad's arms locked around me and dragged me away. It was the first time I wanted to kill someone, and probably would have if my dad didn't jump in.

My eyes glare into his. "Short-term memory?" I lower my voice so only he can hear. "Because the next time, I'll fucking finish what I started that day in the cemetery. And then afterward I'll lick your blood right off my knuckles."

Liam backs away, his smugness disappearing. "You're fucking insane, dude." He mutters out, "Bat shit crazy. Just like your old man."

No longer able to control myself I leap on top of him slamming him into the pavement. Mounted on top of his chest blow after blow escapes from my fists to his face. Heidi's piercing screams slow me down, allowing Liam to sneak in a crack to my jaw that sends me to my back. Before he can launch more punches, I feel a trembling body covering me. Heidi, refusing to move, begs Liam to leave. While I mumble to her to let us finish, she slaps her palm over my mouth to shut me up. Liam easily gives in to her pleas, but leans down close to my ear and whispers, "One. Day. I. Will. Fucking. Ruin. You."

When Liam walks away, the crowd dissipates realizing the show is over. Leaning up on my elbows and rubbing my bruised jaw, Heidi reaches out her hand offering to help me off the ground while she shakes her head. "Are you ever going to let it go? And just leave him alone?"

The bitchiness in her voice is irritating and I snap back, "Nope. Not until I wreck the asshole." I push her hand away and pick myself off the ground. "So, just back off, *Heidi*. You, of all people shouldn't defend him after what he did to you."

She opens her mouth, probably to defend Liam's actions. But, before I let her sputter more meaningless bullshit, I clutch my skateboard against my hip and start walking briskly away from the scene. Crossing the parkway, I hear my sister's quick steps behind me. Still annoyed by her reaction, I pick up the pace to try to lose her.

"Cooooole. I'm sorry. Just stop. Come on, puhlease talk to me." Her whininess drives me to escape even faster.

Everything that went down with Liam that day in the cemetery was because of Heidi. To protect her from him. To make sure her reputation stays solid and pure. I'd never be able to live with myself if anything happened to her because of that shitbag. He doesn't deserve a girl like Heidi anyway. He doesn't deserve anything from us ever again.

Just as I'm about to head over South Street toward my family's brownstone, I am stopped in my tracks by the sound that rips me apart. The sound that makes my stone exterior crumble to the ground. The sound of someone I love crying because of something I did. Turning around, I spot Heidi hovered over on a porch stoop, her shoulders trembling as her blond ponytail hangs close to the ground. She holds her face in her hands, while the sobs that wail from her are gaining attention from a few passerby's.

I sprint over to her, pick her up into my arms and hug her. Letting my prior irritation melt away, I pat her upper back to comfort her. "Please don't cry. I'm not mad at you. It's him. He turns me into this person, that's all."

After sniffling into the shoulder of my *Misfits* t-shirt, she looks up to me with painful eyes. "I just feel like the old Cole is slipping out of reach. That he'll be gone forever." She sinks her head back into my arm and releases more of her tears.

Hushing her cries, I whisper, "Maybe he'll come back one day. Maybe someone will save him." Not able to sound the least bit convincing she digs her face deeper into me and holds me tighter like she's grasping onto whatever is left of the old me.

****

Bursting through the heavy, metal doors of the school to the start of vacation, I am met by a fog of haze that blankets the skyscrapers in the city. The humidity of Philadelphia summers is setting in early this year. While people rush pass me celebrating and littering the sidewalks with the contents of their schoolbags, I lean against the sign of the subway entrance, the same one I stand at every day to wait for Heidi. For me summer break just means more time around the house to clean up my dad's shit

Staring across the street I catch glimpse of Liam readjusting his shirt over the waist of his jeans as he hurries away from the park with the giant sculpted board game pieces that seem to be plopped in random spots—the park where teenagers go to get some ass. I'd occasionally ditch class and meet my friend Cassidy in between the standing dominoes. She's always good for a decent blow-job, and we have an agreement of no-strings, just strictly friends-with-benefits. She's seen as a slut for it, but never seems to mind, and I'm able to actually feel pleasure once in a while.

The sight of Liam's smirk makes me want to dart across the street and drop him, especially since he probably just took advantage of a girl after I'm sure he promised her the world. As if he senses my eyes burning through him, he looks directly into my glare and smugly nods to me. Clenching my fists and raising my foot to go after him, I am stopped dead in my tracks by the short, blonde girl who scurries from the park a few steps behind him. She is smoothing the skirt of her dress as she frantically runs across the street searching around and eventually landing on my stare. My expression softens a bit at the terrified look on Heidi's face, the one where you realize you've been caught red handed. My head jerks back to Liam whose smirk turned into a full smile. As Heidi notices our exchange, she runs up to me before I can make a move toward him. Greeting me with a hug, I watch Liam grab the crouch of his jeans to adjust his dick sending me the message that my sister just had it. Heidi drags me down the subway tunnel before I have a chance to retaliate the only way I know how.

Even within the noisy subway, my silence is deafening, causing Heidi to fidget in the seat next to me. Out of the corner of my eye I can see her twisting her ponytail, a nervous habit she's had since we were kids. Enjoying the anxiety I'm causing her, I remain silent, staring ahead. I know if I open my mouth now, I'll say something I'll regret, and it'll most likely send her to tears. As the subway train approaches our stop, she finally breaks the silence between us.

"I don't know why you're so mad. We were just talking." Her voice is blanketed with guilt.

I continue to stare ahead as the anger in me begins to boil over. Not only is she fucking around with him, she's lying to me about it. Noticing that I'm not answering back she continues to defend herself.

"Anyway, even if we were doing more, it's my choice, not yours. You act like I'm fooling around with your best friend." She stops, realizing my face is turning more crimson at her empty words. "I'm sorry, Cole I didn't mean to say that…I mean I'm not doing this to piss you off. We're just friends, that's all."

Unable to listen to another word from her, I leap out of my seat and stand at the pole across from her facing the window. My sister, the only person I have left in this world, wants the one douchebag who I want to destroy. And what pisses me off the most is that she buys into his bullshit. Just like he's done before, there is no doubt in my mind that he'll hurt her again. And that means, this time, I'll have to kill him.

Heidi grabs above my hand on the pole and lays her head against my arm. I want to rip my arm away, actually I want to punch her in the face, but I can't. No matter what, I'll always take care of her, I'll always have her back, and I'll always believe that you protect your own blood. And she is just that—the only normal functioning blood I have here.

Realizing that my body is beginning to relax and my silent treatment is wearing off, Heidi speaks up. "I'm sorry, Cole. But you have to let me make my own decisions in life. You have to stop protecting me."

I tilt my cheek and rest it on the top of her head. "Never, I promised her I'd never stop."

With a heavy sigh she nods and accepts the fact that I'll never break a promise to our dead mom.

****

Heidi furiously knocks on the door of our shared bathroom screaming at me to get out. Grinning at the frustration I'm causing her, I slow my actions just to make her suffer a little longer. Although she promised to stop seeing Liam, I still think revenge is necessary. Not only am I hogging the bathroom and making her late, but I'm also about to break the news that I'm going to the same party as her.

After I run my hands through my newly buzzed hair, I reach for the knob and open the door to a pissed off Heidi. She stands in front of me wearing pajamas with her hair wrapped in a towel and her blow dryer in one hand and hairbrush in the other. She stares at me with flushed cheeks, indicating her anger at me.

"What the hell, Cole? I was knocking for like an hour." She attempts to push passed me, but I keep shifting in the same direction to block her. She huffs in frustration.

In a sarcastic tone I say, "You haven't said the magic words. You think I'll just let you pass without them? Now where's the fun in that?"

She pushes my shoulder and as she passes by me. "You're such an asshole. Why do you need to be in here anyway? Just to torture me?"

I shrug my shoulders and answer back, "Nah...I'd never do that to you, big sis." I peek in the mirror once more. "I just want to look good for all the older chicks at Brady's party tonight." I can't hold back the playful smirk spreading across my face.

"What do you mean Brady's party? You're going?" Heidi's eyes are wide with surprise.

"Yeah. Why the hell not? I could use a night out with *friends*." My tone drips with sarcasm.

"Cole, tell me what you're up to? You're not even friends with Brady, so obviously he won't want you there."

"Why the hell not? Brady doesn't have a problem with me. Anyway, I saw him today and he told me to stop by. Think it's about time I kick start my social life again. Don't you think?"

Dismissing me, she flashes a fake smile. "Sure. It'll be fun." She's trying to cover-up her annoyance, but there' no hiding her tense expression.

I grab my cologne bottle and leave Heidi in the

bathroom. Feeling satisfied that I succeeded with pissing my sister off, I enter my bedroom and throw on a NOFX T-shirt, jeans, and my favorite black Vans. Looking at my naturally dark complexion in the mirror, a smile spreads across my face. It's turning out to be the perfect night to wreak some havoc. No way in hell I'll ever let Liam wreck my family again—*never* again.

****

Brady lives a few blocks from us in a gated community. His dad does something with finance making a boatload of money. His parents are always taking trips out of the country or spending weeks at their Jersey beach house leaving Brady home with his twin sister. His parties are legendary with kids from different high schools coming and the festivities always lasting to all hours of the night. Because his dad donates a shitload of money to the city cops, there's never a worry about his parties being shut down.

The stench of spilled beer and weed permeate through our noses as we walk into the private terrace behind his house. There's a group of football players surrounding the keg lifting the kicker head first into the spout while they chant out the seconds he's able to drink. A few girls occupy the patio furniture taking body shots off of a guy who is shirtless on the recliner. Brady's manning the bar in the corner as Cassidy, my friend-with-benefits, licks his ear and neck. With her hands somewhere down his pants, she just nods when she sees me.

Heidi rolls her eyes at Cassidy and mumbles something that sounds like *slut* under her breath as she makes her way to a group of her friends, while I venture into the house to grab a bottle of the good beer that always seems to be stashed in the back of refrigerator. Lifting my head as I close the fridge door, I meet Liam's glare. His wavy hair is falling into his stone-gray eyes as he leans against the cabinet with his leg crossed over the other.

"Why are you here? Thought you were more a stay-at-home kind of guy?" He crosses his arms over his stomach.

I step toward him, towering over him, to suffocate the space between us. "Yeah, well I've been thinking about getting out more." I scope the kitchen to make sure my sister isn't there, and I lean in close to his face. "So, get used to seeing me around *all* the time."

A smug look appears on his face. "I'm looking forward to it. I know your *sister* will be happy that you're back out. She talks about it all the time."

I scowl at him and clench my jaw. "Stay the fuck away from my family." With my resentment boiling over, I raise my voice over the small crowd gathering in the kitchen. "You've already shit on us enough. Just stay the hell away!"

Liam backs away grabbing a full bottle of beer from the counter and tilts his head back to gulp it as if he's drinking it with a purpose. He tosses the bottle aside and spews out, "When are you going to accept the blame? That if not for what you did it never would have happened?" He snatches another beer from the refrigerator and tosses the bottle's cap at me as he stomps out of the kitchen.

After Liam tears open the wound that will never really heal, I leave in search of Heidi. As I make my way to the French doors that lead out to the terrace, I bump directly into Brady's sister. Although she's his twin, they can't look more opposite of each other. While Brady, with his jet-black hair, has a short, stocky build, his sister has long, blond hair that tops her tall, slender body. The twins are good looking, popular, and rich—qualities that make them wanted and desired by everyone.

"Hey, Cole." She inches closer to me. "I saw you walk in and was waiting for you to finally come my way."

Confused by the attention she's showing me, I take a step back. "Hey." I scan the room for the football jock she's supposedly dating. "Not sure if Riley would appreciate you *waiting* for me."

She giggles at my obvious sneer. "We're nothing. You buy into the gossip too much." Her tone turns seductive. "So, I can *wait* for anyone I want."

I peek over her shoulder through the glass panel of the French doors and notice my sister creeping alone toward the dark path that leads from the terrace to the front door of the house. Knowing exactly where she's sneaking off to, I push past Brady's sister and dart outside. I rush to catch up to Heidi as I follow the paver walkway to the front door. Running up the staircase to the second floor of the house, I open every door in search for her but each room is empty. After I discover a staircase that leads to a third-floor loft, I climb up and burst through the entrance. I walk in to a shirtless Liam, his jeans hanging open, as he hovers on the bed over my sister. His hands stroke up her shirt and their lips are molded to together so as never even noticing me in the doorway. With fire burning through me, I charge at Liam and, before he has a chance to jump off of Heidi, I have him in my grasp and am landing punches on whatever part of him I can reach. He attempts to fight back, but my rage is too strong for him. Heidi's screams only fuel my assault, until those words leave her mouth. Words that feel like salt pouring into my open wounds.

"Cole, Stop! Please. I love him. I love him." Heidi's desperation bleeds through her screams.

Paralyzed by her confession, I toss Liam back onto the bed and back away from both of them. I stare at them in silence only able to see betrayal. Liam rubs the bruise forming on his cheek, while Heidi kneels down next to him holding a T-shirt to the cut on his lip. Backing out of the room I punch the door and slam it shut. I make my way down the stairs toward the kitchen and grab a bottle of Crown Royal from the buffet cabinet in the dining room. Searching the room, I spot her in the same spot I left a few moments ago.

Forcefully making my way toward her, I bitterly ask, "You still waiting or what?"

She grabs the bottle from my hand and takes a swig as a smile forms behind the top of the bottle. "Actually, I think I just found who I was waiting for."

Reaching for her empty hand, I lead her to the stairs as we make our way to her bedroom each taking swigs from the whiskey bottle. Closing the bedroom door behind us, my mind screams that this is no doubt a bad idea. It's dangerous to get involved with Tara Chambers. However, with the way I feel tonight, nothing can feel more right.

Chapter Ten

Present

I bury my face underneath the comforter as the blinding sun creeps through the thin opening in the curtains that hang over the double-paneled window. I can't open my eyes, or maybe I just can't bear to face my family. They deserve an explanation, a reason why I ran out and didn't show up until after two in the morning. The pounding in my head doesn't even come close to the sickness I feel for being a fucking coward.

My actions from last night begin to play out through the fogginess of my mind. The bile in my stomach rises to my throat as I recall the lack of control I had with Liam, and then running away to drown my regret in a bottle of Jack with Tara. But nothing can damage me more than that terrified look on Gavin's face when I had Liam in my grasp, the look I'm responsible for.

As I lay awake in bed fighting the throbbing in my head, I reach next to me to find her spot still smooth and untouched. Her body not next to mine is a sign that I hurt her, abandoned her, which only makes the sickness spread through my body.

I throw off the comforter and stumble out of bed with the need to find her and somehow salvage what I ruined last night. After I tighten the drawstring on my sleep pants and throw a T-shirt on over my bare chest, I venture out of the bedroom and follow the sound of Camryn's soothing voice that leads me to Gavin's bedroom. I peek through the slightly cracked open door to the sight of Camryn squeezed next to Gavin in his bottom bunk. She is turned on her side, propped up on her elbow, and stroking through his hair with her open hand. Her words to him are those of comfort, but they only rip through to my soul knowing I'm the reason he needs consoling.

"Gav, just close your eyes. I promise you when you wake up you'll see him." She leans down and places a delicate kiss on the tip of his nose. "He would never hurt anyone, sweetie."

Gavin gazes up to Camryn, his cheeks blotchy from crying, voice hoarse from a restless sleep, and asks, "Then why would he do that to Mr. Liam? Why would he try to hit him?"

Camryn sighs and readjusts our son so that his back is against her body. She wraps her arm around him and pulls him tight against her. "No matter what Daddy does it's only to protect you…to protect us. And that's all you really need to know."

I watch as a stray tear drips down Gavin's cheek and he wearily nods into his pillow. The shame tears through me as the realization of my true self begins to resurrect. All I've ever done is hurt people then hide from the truth, drowning myself in this world of make-believe. Camryn and Gavin are my chance to move past the person I once was, to prove that I'm better, but I somehow find a way to fuck that up.

I tap on the door and slowly push it open. The worry in Camryn's eyes only strengthens at the sight of me, and Gavin covers his face beneath his blankets unable to look at me. I creep closer to the bed and gently sit on the edge with my back facing them. I can't bear to see their disappointment, especially since I'm the reason for it. Turning toward Gavin, I run my hand through his hair and clear my throat, "Hey, buddy. Maybe it's a good idea that we talk. What do you think?"

Gavin ignores me as he wiggles further beneath his blankets and digs his face deeper into his pillow. *What the hell have I done?*

Unsure of whether to pursue a conversation with him, I look to Camryn who nods to me, coaxing me to continue. I clear my throat and begin to explain my thoughtless actions to my son.

"What you saw last night...what I did...it was wrong. And I'm so sorry." I drop my head and place the palm of my hand on the blanket that covers his back. "I never would hurt you buddy. You need to know that."

Tears well in my eyes as I feel his body move to the rhythm of his own sobs. He's hurting because of me and that alone crushes me. I'm supposed to be his superhero but after last night, he sees a villain.

I surrender to his silence and lean over to place a kiss on top of the blanket that covers his head. I shrug with defeat at Camryn whose own teary gaze bears through me begging me to fix what I've broken. But what she doesn't know is that I'm better at breaking.

Forcing myself off the bed, I traipse back to the doorway to leave them alone. I glance back to see my exhausted wife whispering to Gavin through the blanket. I can only imagine how much hurt I've caused her and know we'll have to face that soon. But how will she ever understand that my actions are only to protect her and Gavin?

Just as I reach for the brass doorknob, Gavin's voice floats to me giving me back some semblance of life.

His small voice cracks between his tired cries, "Hey Daddy." I turn back around to face him. "It's okay, you know. Even Batman makes mistakes."

An effortless grin spreads across my face at his simple words that hold such deep meaning. Gavin is always able to look past the negative and somehow find the natural beauty of a person. I'm convinced that's Milena shining through him.

Agreeing with his rationale, I answer, "You're right, little man. Even your favorite superhero makes mistakes."

He reaches his arms toward me inviting me in for a hug. I rush to him accepting it with my own open arms. As I hold him tightly against me, he whispers, "Don't worry. Batman's nothing. You're still my favorite superhero."

I pull him closer to my chest and bask in the depth of his understanding. His heart is good and pure and there is no way in hell I'll allow someone to taint him ever again. Even if it means protecting him from myself.

"That's funny, bud. Because you see, you're by far the best superhero I know."

His disappointment fades as his toothless smile returns and he leaps from the pile of blankets he's hiding under. He quickly dresses in his soccer pants and hooded sweatshirt that he usually wears over his wetsuit. He disappears from his room and yells to us from the hallway, "Come on slow pokes. I'm not missing the bus again because of you guys."

Noticing the glassiness of Camryn's eyes most likely from the exhausted night she endured, I lead her to our bedroom and tuck her into bed. I place a kiss upon her head and whisper, "Get some rest. I'll take care of Gav and get him on the bus."

"But we need to talk this out, Cole. We need to face what happened last night." Camryn pleads.

I place a kiss upon her head and whisper, "We will, I promise. But you need some sleep."

She exhaustingly gives in and nestles further into the abyss of sheets and blankets on our bed. I stroke her cheek until her eyelids can no longer flutter to stay open. I steal a few moments to admire my wife—the darkness of her lashes that line the top of her cheek, the perfect slope of her delicate nose, and the peace that has somehow found its way back to her. I struggle as last night replays over and over in my head realizing that as I come face to face with my past, I can destroy the only person who brought me back to life.

I tiptoe out of the room and shut the door behind me before heading upstairs. I meet Gavin in the kitchen, who is standing atop a stool at the counter attempting to pour milk into an overflowing bowl of cereal. I quickly reach my arms around him and help tilt the heavy bottle into the bowl. Once his cereal is swimming in milk, he grabs another bowl, dumps some cereal in and passes it to me.

"This will help your sad heart, Daddy."

Confused, I ask, "What do you mean?"

He shrugs his shoulders and replies, "That's what it said on T.V. This cereal makes your heart healthy."

I laugh at his innocence and slide the milk carton to the bowl. Hopping on the stool next to him, I tilt my spoon toward his, "To happy hearts."

He clanks his spoon against mine and we gulp down our breakfast together, while for the moment, I live in my son's purity. As I watch Gavin slurp the milk from his bowl I can only wish that life could be that simple, that hearts could be that easily put back together. Even one as damaged as mine.

****

Gavin rides on my back to the corner of our street to wait for the school bus. Although Heidi is his teacher and offers to drive him to school, Gav refuses saying he doesn't want to be the new kid and the "kiss-butt." I understand his reasoning, honoring his wishes. So, he takes the bus every day and sits with the new friends he made at Heidi's summer camp.

It doesn't take long for the bus to arrive when we reach the corner. I pop Gavin off my back and give him a high-five before he climbs on the bus. Hugs and kisses are off-limits in front of his friends, so I respect that even though on most days I am tempted to just pull him against me and never let go.

Pressing his nose against the window, he waves out to me and that sadness from the morning has completely erased, leaving me grateful for his resilience. In his short years of life, Gavin has been dealt so much between the death of his grandma, the move from the only place he ever knew, and the actions of his shitbag birth father. I could never live with myself if I added more, which makes me even more determined to keep him from feeling the effects of my past choices.

I watch the yellow bus disappear down the street before I begin to make my way back home. I know what awaits me and I'm not sure I'm ready to face it. I've spent so many years tucking away the denial somehow convincing myself that I overcame it. But the minute I laid eyes on Liam, the memories wouldn't stay buried, they'd never leave me the fuck alone. But Camryn deserves to know. She needs to see how toxic I was.

In the distance, I notice the porch swing swaying back and forth and see Dusty, his hands in the front pocket of his hoodie and his slouchy beanie hat hanging off the back of his head. Dusty was the first real friend I made here, so he was with me as I dealt with some shit. But I never really talked to him about my life before we left the city. It was like I just locked it away hoping it would never break out.

I climb up the first two porch stairs and turn around, plopping myself on the top one. Staring at the dirt and snow that gathered in the corner of the step below me, I begin to nervously brush my foot over it spreading it across the top. Dusty is the first to break the awkward silence that was ensuing.

"I wanted to pound his face too, but for different reasons obviously. So, what's the deal, man?"

I groan out struggling to explain my darkest secrets. "Liam and I have a complicated past." I roll my head in his direction. "There's a lot of twisted, fucked-up shit and it's hard to explain."

One side of Dusty's lip curls up. "Oh yea? Try me. Because it looks like this fucker isn't leaving anytime soon, and now I have you going into crazy-fighter mode and Heidi's just acting weird."

Concerned with my sister, I ask, "What do you mean weird?"

"I don't know, man. She's just seems so distant since dinner last night. She faked being asleep today when I tried to wake her up for a morning happy."

"Dude. Leave the details out. The last thing I want to picture is that."

He laughs at my reaction, but his humor quickly fades and his expression turns more serious. "So, explain to me who this Liam guy is. Because Heidi sure as hell never mentioned him and she seemed pretty damn excited to see him last night."

I sigh not really wanting to get into it with Dusty, especially before talking to Camryn. "Liam was an old friend we grew up with. My parents practically raised him." My voice fades out not wanting to continue.

"If this guy is practically family, what happened last night? Because if that's what you call family, you're pretty fucking dysfunctional."

I shrug my shoulders and reply, "Just talk to my sister about it. She can fill you in."

Dusty nods accepting my reluctance to reveal everything. One thing about Dusty is he never pushes or prods. He always has my back, no questions asked. And I'd do the same for him.

He stands up from the swing and squeezes past me down the stairs. "All right, dude. I just stopped by to make sure you were all good. It was an ugly scene last night, especially when you ran off. Where the hell did you go anyway?"

I drop my gaze again to the dirty snow I smoothed out on the step as regret trickles back through me. "You don't even want to know. Big. Fucking. Mistake."

He shakes his head from side-to-side. "Awww, man. Don't even tell me you ended up hanging with that mental case?"

I hang my head farther in shame and Dusty warns, "I'm telling you. She's nothing but trouble. Cut her completely out of your life." He grabs my shoulders and with his two hands and gave them a shake. "Listen, man, she's too far gone to be saved."

"I know. I know. She just showed up at the bar on her own. It was a drunken mistake. That's all."

"Let's not make any more drunken mistakes, okay dude?" He lets go of my shoulders, extends his one hand to mine for a high-five handshake before he starts down the walkway.

Lightening the mood, a smile stretches across his face and he shouts back, "At least I have time to for an afternoon happy. Maybe catch her after she's home from school."

I grab a handful of snow and fired it at him pelting him in the shoulder and shout, "That's my sister, asshole!"

He raises his hand up to me and flashes the peace sign before he hops in his truck and heads out. I watch as it disappears down the street and then slowly stand up and turn toward the house. For a few moments, I stare at the solid wooden door knowing that when I walk through it I'll have to relive the parts of my life that I fought so hard to forget. Every ounce of pain I once felt will rise to the surface ripping my wounds wide open again. And all I can do is hope that Camryn will be able to stop the bleeding.

Chapter Eleven

Present

The stillness of the house only makes me more unhinged with what I'm about to reveal. Opening up my past secrets will wipe away the peace that I promised Camryn and expose the person I used to be, or maybe the person I still am. But my wife deserves to know. She has the right to know all parts of me, even those that only live in my mind, tucked away from the rest of the world.

I amble down the hallway toward our bedroom trying to steady my breathing and find the courage I seem to lack since Liam walked through my door last night. He holds the key to all of my secrets and has the ability to ruin me and the life I was able to find when Camryn walked into it.

Peeking through the crack of our bedroom door, Camryn is laying on her side, her head propped up on two pillows and another pillow squeezed between her legs. The sheets are scrunched up on my side of the bed with only a small portion covering her arms. Blankets really never have a chance to stay on Camryn.

When I notice her body begin to rustle, I push open the door and move toward the bed. Her eyes slide open as I stand next to her and, despite the pain I caused her by running out last night, she's still drawing me in, begging me to open that part of me that still remains locked up. I reach down to rub my thumb over her cheek and tuck a piece of stray hair behind her ear. Her mouth opens slightly, and she squeezes her eyes shut as if she is savoring my touch—a touch that can be so destructive.

I sit on the edge of the bed next to her and she repositions herself up against the headboard. I take a deep breath and sensing my anxiety, she reaches for my hand and cups it between her palms. With her eyes refusing to leave mine, she reassures me, "Cole, it's okay. I'm here. I'll always be here."

I pinch the bridge of my nose and shake my head from side-to-side. "I'm sorry, Cam. I promised you I'd never let you down." She squeezes my hand tighter and I continue my confession. "But I lied."

Camryn leans toward me and presses her forehead against mine. "Cole, what are you talking about? What's going on?" The concern in her voice strangles me, never wanting to expose her to this truth. But I no longer have that choice.

"Liam was like a brother to me. He practically lived with me. You see, my mom was best friends with his mom while they grew up in the city. When Liam was born, his mom died shortly after...complications after labor or something. My parents kind of took him in as their own, especially my mom. Liam's dad owned boxing gyms across the city and ran all the fights, so he was always there, working throughout the night. Liam and I were fucking inseparable until..."

My voice begins to quiver as my mind is flooded with memories, the ones that I have run from for so many years. Camryn unclasps her hand from mine and climbs on my lap, hooking her arms around my neck. She whispers to me, "Baby, I'm right here."

I wrap my arms around her waist and pull her closer. I need to feel her, smell that intoxicating strawberry scent from her hair.

"Inseparable until my fifteenth birthday. Liam planned this big night out for me. I was fucking stoked all day. He had connections because of his old man and could get us into any club or bar despite our age. But Liam was also notorious for getting himself into shit and dragging me in to clean it up for him. Well, that was what happened the night of my birthday. He entered me into this illegal skateboarding contest so that I could pay back some douchebag bookie he owed money to." I can feel the anger pour out of me as I get closer to the part of the memory that rips me to shreds. "So, I fucking did it. I won the contest, paid his debt, and then walked away from him. He tried to call me all night long, but I turned off my phone and went to bed. I just couldn't deal with him. I needed to cool down."

Camryn's fingers stroke the back of my neck attempting to calm me, but just reliving the story is excruciating.

"Heidi woke me up in the middle of the night and she was hysterically crying. My dad was trying to reach me first, but my phone was turned off, so he called her. He left his bar that night when he got a call from the hospital. My mom was in an accident, only a few blocks away from our house. The other car just blew through the intersection claiming to never see her car turning. And she was fucking dead…not even a chance to survive."

At this point, I'm shaking as Camryn's tears drip

down on my arms. She pulls me into her, embracing my pain and softly speaks, "It was an accident, Cole. There was nothing you could do to save her."

My own cries unleash from her words because she has no fucking clue about the guilt that drowns me. It's becoming impossible to bear this secret any longer.

I choke out my next words, unable to recognize my own voice. "But I could have…I could've saved her. Because it wasn't supposed to be her out that night. It was supposed to be me."

Camryn holds my face and wipes the tears streaming from my eyes as remorse pours from me. "I turned off my phone. I fucking turned it off. If I 'd answered it, he wouldn't have needed to call her . She wouldn't have gone after him, and she'd still be alive."

Camryn's eyes are wide as she connects my confession to the animosity between Liam and me. She opens her mouth to talk, probably to try to convince me that it's not my fault, but I don't want understanding or comfort. I don't deserve it and Liam sure as hell will never get it. Liam called her when I refused to answer, knowing she'd help him out of whatever shit he got into. That is as unforgivable as my own ignorance.

Camryn continues to hold on to me as every emotion that's been bottled up inside me breaks free. I mourn the loss of my mom all over again as my blame comes to the surface. If Liam wasn't such a selfish asshole, she'd still be alive. But if I just accepted that side of Liam, which I had for so many years, I would've bailed him out of trouble myself, and she wouldn't have been in the car that night.

I sink into her as she hugs me against her chest and strokes through my hair. Her soothing voice reverberates through me. "Cole, you can't do this to yourself. You can't keep holding onto this. It's not your fault. It never has been."

Although Camryn believes in her words, I'll never be able to embrace their meaning. I was the reason Liam got shitfaced at some dive bar and started a fight with some gang thugs. I was the one who ignored his calls for help. I was the reason he reached out to my mom instead. I may have driven her to that box in the ground, but Liam slammed closed the top.

The need to somehow mask the pain, to feel something other than this unending ache rushes through me. Camryn can always take me out of my fucked-up thoughts and I want her, need her. I drag my hands down to her ass and press her body to mine. Her head rolls back coaxing my mouth in as I feverishly explore her neck, tasting every inch of her skin. With her hands stroking through my hair and twisting the ends around her fingers, I shift my body from her and guide her down on the bed.

Crawling over top of her, my hunger takes control as I rip off her sleep shorts and tight little T-shirt tossing them to the floor beneath us. Dragging my hand up her thighs I circle my fingers over her pink lace panties, craving what's underneath. Her eyes, full of both desire and concern, draw me in as I yearn for more of her, selfishly taking to numb my own pain.

I slip my fingers into her, her back arching and pushing me in deeper. As I lean closer to claim her mouth, I moan out, "I want you to take it away. Just make it all disappear." As the desperation begins to strangle me, Camryn slams her lips into mine attempting to answer my pleas.

Sliding my fingers out of her, I inch her panties down her legs and toss them off the side of the bed. I unclasp her matching lace bra, and, for a moment, I admire the swell of her breasts and the curve of her body, still slender and smooth. *She is fucking breathtaking.*

Her urgent hands tug at the white T-shirt and warm-up pants I threw on earlier, and I help her work them off my body. Our naked bodies tangle together, like they are somehow complete. A perfect fit. But how could they be when I'm so damaged?

I lose myself inside of Camryn, the swell of her wrapped around me, and my body slowly floating on top of her. Her cries grow louder, syncing with my needy moans, as we rise to the peak of our desire. My hands travel up her body greedily taking to ease the heartache, only knowing it will return when we leave this moment. As Camryn's breaths quicken, I thrust into her with more force helping her to climb faster. When her body begins to tremble, I hold her face between my hands, her eyes burning through mine, and I lip to her, *"Save me,"* right as we both tumble over the edge of our passion.

****

I wake up an hour later in Camryn's arms, her fingers repeatedly tracing the lines of the tattoo on my arm. The broken heart with the rose weaved through the cracks is a reminder of what I lost in my life, what I helped to destroy. But the dark-haired angel wrapping her arms around it, embracing my faults, show me what I've overcome because of Camryn. She is gazing down on me, her expression loaded with questions and her eyes filled with comfort.

"It just doesn't represent Rose, you know." I nod my head toward my tattoo. "After I lost her, I broke down again blaming myself for everything. All the memories of my mom came flooding back and I was drowning in it all. So, I went out and branded myself— a permanent reminder of my sins. A rose for my baby girl and my mom, Clara Rose, weaved through my own cracked heart."

Camryn's lips tilt up into an understanding smile. "It's not sinful, Cole. It's a beautiful memory of those who were taken too early from your life. You have to stop living in this world of regret. You're not responsible for any of it."

I sigh. "I wish I believed that, but too much shit has happened to people I love, people who I'm supposed to protect."

She rests her cheek on top of my head and rocks my body in her arms. "Cole, I know you have this constant desire to protect me, but you have to promise me to never do what you did last night again. Don't ever run out like that. No matter what it is, I can handle it. We can handle it together."

I caress her cheek with my finger. "Everything I ever do is to protect you and Gavin. I will *always* do what keeps you safe until the day I'm taken from this life. Do you understand?"

She smiles at my pledge to her and our family. No way in hell will I destroy them too. I'll give up my own life before that will ever happen.

I climb out of bed to head for the shower. I catch Camryn's eyes admiring my naked body. Noticing that I caught her, she blushes. I can't help but grin at her innocence, something that drew me to her in the beginning. It made me want to shield her even more.

Turning on the steamy shower, I yell out to her, "I have to work on some leasing contracts at the office, so I'll pick up Gavin from school later."

I hop in, close my eyes, and let the water rush over my head holding my body up with my one arm flexed on the tiled wall. The sound of the glass shower door startles me as it opens. Camryn slips in under my arm and she wraps her arms around my waist. The water floods down her body, matting her hair against her back. Droplets stick to her long eyelashes causing her to blink quickly. A playful grin spreads across her face while she teases, "I hope your clients aren't in a huge rush for their contracts." She circles her nails around the small of my back. "Because you see, you have some unfinished business with me first."

She shyly giggles at her forwardness causing me to laugh and remember back to one of our first days together. She thought she could beat me at a flirting contest, and still swears she did. But the truth is I let her win. I just wanted to find a way in, chip away at the protective wall she built around herself. And it worked because that night she held my hand as we walked to dinner. In a way, that day was the beginning of our forever. I could only hope that I'd be able to hold on to it.

I pull her closer to me, my hardness evident against her body, and lean into her ear. "I think they'd understand that I can't possibly turn down my amazingly sexy wife who is tempting me with her incredible naked body." I look up and down her dripping wet body. "Besides what if I told you I didn't really give a shit if they did care?" I grin at her before I tilt my head and meet my mouth to hers, our tongues instantly connecting. We again find ourselves in each other as the steamy water flows down over us. The anguish from before slowly pours away, leaving me safe—for now.

Chapter Twelve

Present

I slam the top of my laptop down with force and sink my face into my hands. I can't focus, unable to get my head out of the past. I thought I put it all behind me, that finding Camryn somehow helped me to move on from it all. But who am I fucking kidding? I don't deserve a second chance, not after the people I've hurt.

The images from that night play on a continuous reel in my mind: the terrifying screams from my sister, my mom's lifeless body on the hospital bed, the emptiness in my dad's eyes as he stands in the corner of the hospital room watching the doctors cart her away. I leap up from my rolling leather office chair and angrily shove the papers off my desk to the floor. I can't fucking bear my sins any longer. If I would've just answered my phone that night, if I would've stayed in when she begged me to, she wouldn't have left the house, my mom wouldn't be buried in the fucking ground.

My cell phone rings, startling me from my self-destructive thoughts. I dig into my pocket and pull it out glancing at it. Sliding my finger across the screen, I lift it to my ear and greet my best friend.

"Hey, man. I called your house and no answer. What do you say we hit the surf later? High tide's gonna kick in some crazy shit."

I crack a smile knowing the waves are his way of keeping me straight. Dusty has seen me at my worst when Heidi and I first moved here. He witnessed my short temper, my lack of control with my fists, and my self-blame. He'd be the one to pull me away from a fight and drag me to the beach to find solace within the waves. After the way I acted last night, there's no doubt that he's worried that I'm falling back into my old ways.

Desperately wanting to control my own behavior this time around, I answer back, "I'm game, bro. I'll meet you after I grab Gav from school."

After we hang up, I toss my phone on the desk and notice something sticking out from under the calendar. As I slide it out, my knees buckle, and breath catches at the sight of Rose, living on machines, but pink-skinned and wide-eyed. *Alive*. She's wearing a diaper that is way too big for her miniature body and a tiny T-shirt with *Shore Memorial* etched on the front of it. The sleeves are long and folded over her nails so not to scratch the delicate skin on her perfect face. As she lays in the incubator, her knees are pulled up toward her chest and her thin arms are sprawled out next to her. She has dark fuzz peeking out from the pink striped knitted cap she's wearing. I remember how I would slide the hat off and rub the top of her head laughing how my daughter managed to have such dark hair.

Pain from the memories splinters through me leaving me to wonder if they'll ever stop haunting me. My choices, my actions, take people I love away from me. Will I ever be free of this guilt or am I to be punished with a life of regret?

I tuck Rose's picture in the back pocket of my jeans, grab my coat and dash out of my office door locking it behind me. I need to clear my mind somehow, find a way through this, so I head straight for my place of healing.

The waves crash fiercely against the flattened sand, matching the turmoil of my thoughts. Snow is still piled up on the dunes, but none of it remains on the areas touched by the churning tides. The wind stings my skin and I tuck my hands deeper into the pockets of my jeans. I creep closer to the edge of the water craving the sound of it, the roughness somehow with the power to always calm my rage. Staring out into the eerie vastness I wish it would somehow engulf my past mistakes and hold them forever beneath its surface.

My body jolts when a bitter voice invades my silence. "You're never gonna let it go, are you?" Liam creeps next to me his arms crossed tightly in front of him. He stares ahead stealing my ocean—my peace. "You want me to suffer for the rest of my life, don't you?"

I continue to gaze ahead hoping to find the strength to shut him out, to fight the desire to beat the shit out of him on my own hallowed ground.

Liam inches closer and rambles on, "I'm here to tell you I'm fucking done. Done accepting your blame. Done believing it was my fault." The strength in his tone fades and is replaced with emptiness. "You're not the only one who lost. Because of you, I lost too. Everything that matters."

Refusing to give in to my fists that are now tightly clenched in my pockets, I glare ahead in silence grinding my jaw with each word of bullshit that pours out of his mouth.

A sardonic laugh escapes from him. "All of sudden, Coley-boy goes silent. Well, we'll see about that. Remember I made a promise to you that day your dumbass decided to skate down those museum stairs." Out of the corner of my eye, I watch his head turn toward me. "Remember it? Or should I remind you?" Still grasping hold my silence, I feel his breath against my ear. "I. Will. Fucking. Ruin. You."

Liam backs away and turns his back to the ocean. As he begins to walk away, he pats my shoulder and says, "It's just too bad your selfish ass destroyed your wife's dream. I was really hoping sweet Camryn wouldn't be affected by our *history.*" Hearing him even mention Camryn's name unleashes the rage I am so close to controlling.

I lunge at him, tackling him to the freezing sand below us. Pinning him down with so much force, he has no ability to wiggle out of my hold. Leaning into his face, I shout, "What the fuck are you saying, Liam? You drag my wife into this and actually expect that I won't fucking kill you?"

His mouth tilts up as he grins humorously at me. "There's the Cole I know and love. You're just too easy, pretty-boy." He laughs at himself. "I knew it would be practically effortless to shatter you."

My lips still tense, I spatter out, "What do you really want, Liam?"

All the humor melts from his expression and he sets his eyes directly on mine. "I already told you. I want redemption."

I press his wrists deeper into the sand. "You'll never fucking get it. Never. Not while she's lying in a wooden box underground. A box you put her in."

Through his clenched teeth, he mutters, "And you think you're innocent?" His eyes turn to stone gray. "Why don't you ask your family who's to blame?"

My eyes widen and my fury takes control of my body. Before I can react to my hungry fists, slender arms wrap around me and are trying to pull me off of Liam. My head snaps back to see Tara who manages to pin my arms back, so I can't swing them in Liam's direction. I try to shake out of her grip, but she somehow immobilizes me making me surrender to my desire to hurt Liam. Standing up frees Liam who is beneath me. He gets up and brushes the sand from his hair with that fucking smirk still plastered across his face. God, I want to end him right here, but Tara has me trapped.

He straightens his pea coat and readjusts the collar up to cover his ears. When he turns away, a mocking laugh escapes him. "Just like old times, I see. I wonder what your wife would think if she knew your ex was here to save you from yourself."

Tara bites back, "Liam, cut the shit."

I jerk my hands free and traipse over to him. Tara is yelling at me to calm down, but her words are drowned out in the sound of the waves. My focus is Liam, and, at this point, I don't care if I'm acting reckless.

I grab his collar and jolt his body toward mine. "You don't know shit about me or my wife. So, I suggest you keep your fucking mouth shut."

He glances down to my hands that are holding him and continues to taunt, "You suggest? Well you got me now, Coley. Hit me. Come on, just do it."

As I pull my fist back to swing, I catch a glimpse of the red and blue threaded bracelet tied around my wrist. Instantly, my rage subsides as I remember what it represents. Camryn and Gavin had planned me a surprise party as a good luck thing for the Atlantic Classic. That night was agonizing because Camryn had walked away after a fight broke out between Todd and me. She thought she was saving me by letting go of our relationship. Later on, Heidi showed up at my house with a pile of gifts and told me that even if I didn't want to I had to open the tiny gift bag on top. After she left, I took it off the top of the pile, pulled out the crumpled tissue paper that was inside and this bracelet fell out. A yellow sticky note was inside the bag that said,

"Best superheroes for life. Love, Gavin"

A few days later I showed up on the beach to check up on Todd and make sure Gavin was safe. He ran up to me and flashed his own black and yellow bracelet toward me. I lifted my arm for him to see mine secured around my wrist. His smile stretched clear across his face and his eyes lit up with an excitement, a sight that's still ingrained in my memory. He then touched his own wrist to mine and said, *"Best superheroes."* I repeated the same phrase back. It was a symbol of the bond we formed with each other. From that day forward, the bracelet has never left my arm.

As thoughts of Gavin rush through me, I shove Liam away and drop my fists to the side. I rub the yarn of the bracelet as if it somehow gives me the strength I need to conquer the demons that are creeping back into my life.

Liam stumbles backward away from me, his head shaking side to side, as laughter bellows from him.

"Almighty Cole can't even settle this the way he knows how. No need to fight it. You destroy everything you touch. No matter how hard you try, you can never be more than that."

As he backs away toward the top of the beach he yells out, "Oh yeah, thanks to you, Camryn backed out of the clinic. She told her dad she couldn't do it knowing how you feel about me. I heard she was crying but refused to reconsider because of you. You, Cole. You shattered your own wife's dream. Like I said, you destroy everything you touch, you selfish bastard."

His words break me, cutting through me like jagged glass. He's somehow able to tear open my wounds and I'm left to find some way to stop from bleeding out.

I jolt when Tara grabs my elbow, forgetting she's still here. She drags me away from Liam just as he backs his way off the beach.

"Don't let him win, Cole. Beat him at this sick game he's playing with you." I can't tell if her words are genuine, or if it's just one of her games.

Still annoyed at the encounter with Liam, I snap, "What the hell are you doing here anyway? You just always seem to be around lately."

She sinks back away from me, almost like a scared child. "I just needed to find you today. Actually, I need to give you something."

With my frustration eating at me, I reply, "Well, you found me, didn't you? You seem like you're pretty damn good at that."

Tara takes a deep breath and stumbles over her words, "I...I just...found a box of Rose's things, some gifts given before she was born. And, I, well, I thought you should have them, with all that's going on for you now."

The mention of my baby girl instantly weakens me, erasing the harsh feelings. Aside from all these negative feelings toward Tara, I still respect the fact that she brought Rose into this world. And that will be the only lasting connection we have to each other.

Grateful for her offer, I walk with her off the beach to grab the box. When we reach her car, she turns into a sobbing mess of tears, and begs me to grab a drink with her. Feeling guilty about removing a few more of her memories with this box, and not wanting to leave her in hysterics, I hesitantly accept, despite Dusty's warnings ringing in my head.

Chapter Thirteen

Past

The early morning sun blinds me as I slip through the heavy, black door of my house. Avoiding the possibility that my dad who is slumped on the couch nursing his daily hangover, I keep my head straight and dart up the wooden stairs hoping to reach the confines of my bedroom before I hear evidence of the shit that now defines my life. Kicking my door closed, I hop into bed, hoping sleep will cure my aching head and erase the images of my sister and Liam from last night. Instead, the silence of the house just makes me even angrier.

There was once a time when I didn't want to hide, when being home meant family dinners, gathering around the fire pit on the back patio, and friends always crashing overnight and never in a rush to leave. The aroma of homemade chocolate chip cookies seemed to be a permanent staple throughout the house and laughter could be heard as soon as you stepped up on the front stoop. When you walked through the doorway, my mom would be standing there with a plate of cookies in her hands and a huge grin on her face. Definitely June Cleaver shit, but I loved it. However, now this house just represents pain, faded memories, and everything that should have been.

Smashing the pillow over my head, attempting to drown out the deafening silence, I search for a peaceful sleep, and wonder if that even exists anymore. I just stopped hoping things will change, that any remnants of my life before my mom died will come back, because hope is for the weak, for those who believe that life can actually be fair. I'm over hope and succumbing to this everlasting feeling of emptiness.

As I begin to drift off, the creaky bedroom door swings open and familiar sounding footsteps scurry across the wooden floor. With no energy to face my sister and her bullshit drama, I clutch the pillow tighter in hopes she'll leave me alone. Instead she rips the covers off and yanks the pillow from me launching it across the room. I pretend to adjust my eyes, focusing on the noticeable scowl on her face.

"Wake up *now*, Cole." Her voice tightens displaying even more annoyance. "When your phone rings like twenty-five times in a row, maybe you could take the hint and pick it up. I don't understand why you even have it if you're not going to answer it." She takes a breath to calm her rant. "I really need you right now."

The urgency in her voice drives me out of bed, awakening my defenses. Standing over her, I grasp her shoulders and crouch down to eye-level with her. My overprotectiveness trumps my raging anger at her, and in a serious tone, I ask, "What the hell did he do to you? Did he hurt you? I swear to God, Heidi…I'll…"

I back away from her as she puts her hand up to my face and interrupts my tirade. "Cole, just stop. This isn't about Liam." She hisses in frustration. "He was the one there for me last night, not you. Just remember that."

I flinch, her harsh words piercing me. "There for

you? Are you serious? He'll fuck you over the minute you're not looking, and you think he's *there* for you?" I shake my head in disappointment. "You better wake the fuck up soon." I traipse back to bed plopping back into the mattress as my previous anger returns.

Ignoring my warning, she quickly changes the subject. "We're not going to talk about Liam. Dad needs us right now."

Resting the back of my wrist across my head, I roll my body in the opposite direction of my sister. Uninterested in finding out the latest on my dad's drinking problem, I hope she takes the hint and leaves me alone.

Yanking my body back toward her, she raises her voice. "Stop being selfish and help me get Dad home. Andy, his bartender, called me and said he was passed out and unresponsive at the bar. Liam helped me get him out of there and back to his house. But he's still out cold and we have to get him home before Liam's dad gets back. You know dad would go crazy if he knew he was there. So, we have to get him out."

Casually, I draw the blanket back up and reach for another pillow on my bed. Before I smother my face beneath it I brush Heidi off, saying, "Well, maybe since that *douchebag* is there for you, he'll help you do just that."

With the pillow covering my face again, I hear her feet stomping away from my bed. "You're a class A dick, Cole." She slams the door and her footsteps continue down the stairs leaving me to wallow in my misery again.

****

The sound of Heidi's voice coaxing my dad to

open his eyes and to walk straight startles me from my sleep. His incoherent mumbling only proves that he's drowning deeper in his addiction, which makes me angrier that he is taking the easy way out. I can do the same thing, and there were many times right after my mom died I thought about downing half the bottle of anxiety pills the doctor prescribed me. I still fight the urge to just pop them in my mouth and let the medicine numb my body, but I just can't seem to do it. I feel like it would disappoint her somehow.

Sinking deeper beneath my blankets, I attempt to ignore the shit-show my life has become. As Heidi shrieks at my Dad, my door slams open banging into the wall behind it. Peeking out from my comforter, my eyes rest on Liam's glare.

Instantly on guard, I jump out of bed and my body stiffens as I stare back at him. Liam hasn't stepped foot in my room since the night my mom died. At one point, we practically shared a room, even having his own bed across from mine. But now the sight of him in it makes me want to tear him apart.

Clenching my teeth, I threaten, "Get the fuck out or I can end it right here for you." I close in on him, taking away any empty space he's trying to preserve around him.

Still continuing to glower at me, he calmly says, "Go to Heidi. She needs you. She can't help your dad by herself. And I know you don't expect her to."

I push his shoulders causing him to stumble back a few steps, and shout, "You don't know a goddamn thing about me anymore. So, stay the fuck out of my face."

I turn away from him stomping back toward my bed when Liam stops me in my tracks.

"You're gonna lose her too, you know." Liam's voice grows louder as he moves closer to me and he slowly speaks each word. "Just like everyone else." His warm breath stings the side of my face. "And then you'll be left to fucking rot all alone in your pathetic excuse for a life."

My body stiffens as I grit my jaw. This indescribable urge to hurt him consumes me, and I reach behind me clutch his throat in my grip. Throwing him up against the wall, all emotion drains from my body leaving me hollow, void of any feeling but rage. Squeezing tighter and tighter, I can feel the desire to end his life take over. Liam is the reason my family is falling apart, why I am ripping open at the seams, why life just doesn't matter anymore. And he sure as hell doesn't deserve forgiveness or any second chances.

With my hold continuing to tighten, Liam begins to gasp for whatever air he's able to suck in. I glare into his pleading, my hatred for him inescapable as it rises to the surface and bleeds from my pores. I want nothing more than to end his life so he can no longer breathe the air that he took away from my mom.

A scream sounds across my bedroom forcing me to loosen my hold. Just as my eyes avert to my sister darting toward me, I'm knocked off my feet from a blow to my cheek. Liam unleashes more punches as I lay immobile on the floor underneath the weight of his body. Behind his fury, I can see a touch of regret as if he really doesn't want to be hurting me like this, but I quickly push it out of my thoughts.

My head shifts side-to-side with each crack to my face. The numbness begins to set in with each contact of his fists. It should hurt, but it doesn't. Maybe it's because pain is the only thing that makes me still feel alive. It's the only thing I've felt since she died, since the phone call about the accident, since I saw her lifeless body in the hospital bed. With my eye swelling shut, I concede, waiting for the one strike that will take me out of consciousness.

As Heidi's cries grow closer, I feel Liam being lifted off of me, and I turn on my side hugging my knees up to my chest. As I lay still catching the blood dripping from my gashed lip, Heidi attempts to calm Liam. I need to get out of here. Rolling onto my knees I struggle as I crawl to my closet and grab a pair of jeans and T-shirt that are balled up on the floor. I stuff them in the half-full duffel bag that's at the bottom of my bed, the one that still holds clothes from our last family vacation together. I force myself to stand up despite the piercing pain through my ribs and the fogginess caused from my pounding head.

With the bag over my shoulder, I limp my way toward the bedroom door and growl back to Heidi, "As long as he's in your life, I'm fucking out."

Despite her pleas for me to stay, I continue down the staircase through the front door and head back to the one person who can help me forget.

Tara's house remains motionless even after I push the front door open. Bodies are passed out in all rooms, while the smell of skunked beer and stale cigarettes filters through my nose. Stepping onto an empty condom wrapper, I trip over a couple cuddled together under a small blanket. The burn of my injured ribs slows me down as I climb up the back staircase to her room.

Entering her light pink room that displays her

childhood dolls and stuffed animals, I can't help but smirk at the irony of it. Her bedroom is a little girl's dream that screams innocence, but after last night the only side of Tara I met was wild and reckless. She is lying naked underneath a thin sheet that barely covers the forbidden places of her body—ones I came to know last night. I lift my bloody shirt over my head and toss it into the trashcan next to her desk. Crawling up her bed I turn onto my side in the same spot I left earlier and face her. Tara's eyelids flutter open as she focuses on my swollen eye, and she grazes her thumb over my cut lip.

"Oh my God, Cole. What happened to you?" Her hoarse voice is laced with concern. "You want to talk about it?"

Brushing her hand from my face, I answer, "Nah. I don't need to talk. I just want you to help me forget."

She sits up and pushes me back on her bed. Unbuttoning my jeans and dragging them off my body, she lets them fall to the floor. She lifts her one leg over my body and straddles me, ignoring the moans of pain from me.

Pinning my arms down above my head, Tara leans down to my ear and whispers, "I have a better idea. Let's *forget* together."

****

I manage to avoid pretty much everyone for the next three weeks, but it's not like anyone is searching real hard for me. I don't give a shit, though. With Tara, I have a place to stay, alcohol, and plenty of sex to help me escape my reality. I only venture home when I need to switch out clothes or grab some money from the stash I keep in my bedroom hidden from my dad. In the past I'd do small chores for the neighbors, like walking their dogs, shoveling snow, or staining their decks and balconies and, in return, they'd pay me. However, since I stopped doing that, my cash flow started getting low. So, I occasionally drop by whatever skate park is hosting Skate Wars and enter the contest. Johnny Jax would always be there staring me down from the edge of the skate ramp trying to intimidate me into working for him, but I won't give in. I'm not looking for big money, just enough for the basics: food, condoms, and beer.

While at Tara's house, we never really stray too far from her bedroom, thanks to her parents' month-long excursion to Europe. I guess I keep her satisfied because she never complains, even when we missed the biggest party of the summer at some new club in Old City. But I have a feeling she's hiding from something too. I just don't care enough to ask her about it.

Hearing Tara's shower water still running, I kick off the covers and stumble over to the windowsill where my phone is charging. My head is aching, probably from the numerous games of beer pong last night. Tara and her twin, Brady, decided to have a few people over, but as always it turned into a party with a shitload of people showing up. I was surprised Liam didn't come, being that he's a friend of Brady's, but I guess Heidi's keeping him away to avoid me.

Scrolling through the plethora of missed calls from Heidi over the last few weeks, I come across a number I don't recognize. Not only are there incoming calls from it but outgoing as well. Wondering who it is, I click send and place the phone to my ear.

After two rings some guy picks up and blurts out,

"Well, well, you may be my best customer. The stash from last night already gone? Ready to move on to something stronger? I would tell your hot, little ass to slow down, but I gotta say, I like the money too much." His annoying cackle forces me to lift the phone from my ear.

The morning after the fight with Liam, Tara cleaned me up, wiping the blood from my cuts and icing my bruises. I fell fast asleep and when a I woke up a few hours later, I noticed my bag was opened and some of the clothes were pulled out from it. She had put a new shirt on me, but I also noticed a few of my pills were missing from the bottle. The doctor prescribed them after my mom died, but I never touched them. I guess I thought it was the easy way out, besides I deserve to feel the pain without masking it since I'm part of the reason she's not here anymore. The pill bottle would empty out and then mysteriously be filled again. I knew it was Tara, but I didn't care. Who was I to judge? I was using her just like she was using the pills as a way to escape.

Figuring the guy on the other end of the call to be Tara's dealer, I decide to fuck with his head a bit. Placing my hand over my mouth to muffle my voice I shout into the receiver, "You are surrounded. One wrong move and you will be shot. Lay down on the ground and put your hands on your head."

Heavy breathing fills the earpiece as he begins begging and pleading, claiming he's innocent. Humored by how the tough drug dealer shattered in an instant, I continue to bark orders. "You have the right to remain silent, everything you say…"

My phone is jerked from my hand and I turn

around to see Tara glaring at me as she panics into the phone. "Nate. Nate! There are no cops. It was just a joke. I swear…you're fine."

I howl in laughter while Tara attempts to calm the jackass who is now yelling obscenities at her through the phone. Not amused, Tara frowns at me as she stands in a short bathrobe and a towel wrapped around her head. Her slender legs seem to travel for miles up to her flat stomach that's accented with a small pink-stone piercing. Her robe hangs loosely open exposing her cleavage, tempting me to pull it off so I can get the full view of her round breasts.

Wanting to soften her obvious anger at me, I slip my hand through the opening of her robe and slowly drag my fingers over her breast. Her head falls back while her mouth gapes open. I take her hardened nipple between my fingers and pull, causing a slight moan to rise from her throat. I know I have her as the previous irritation with me melts away. I grab the phone from her hand and interrupt the tirade that's still spewing from the guy's mouth.

"Tara will have to call you back. She's a little busy right now." I snap my phone shut and toss it on the floor behind me.

I slide the robe off her and pull the towel from her head combing my fingers through her wet strands. Pushing her down to the bed, I crawl up her body, my mouth teasing her breasts and my fingers sliding between her thighs. As lowers her hands down on me, I know we're headed to the one place where I can forget everything, where I can finally hide and not be found.

****

Tara's screams and a piercing pain that's running

116

down my spine wakes me up. We fell asleep naked and tangled up with each other in the silence. Now, I'm being dragged out of Tara's bed by the back of my neck and am smashed face first into the side of her dresser. I fall to the floor as the sting of the contact with the wood jolts my body alive, while threats and obscenities are being shouted at Tara.

I look over my shoulder to see Tara sitting up in bed with the sheet tightly wrapped around her body and her dad, his veins pulsating through his neck and eyes glazed over with rage. I won't be surprised if he starts to foam at the mouth. He's shouting over Tara's desperate pleas throwing out words like whore and slut while his glare remains fixed on me.

Derek Chambers holds a lot of power in this city and he's never shy about flaunting his money, especially when he needs something to go his way. *A complete pretentious douchebag.* Tara never talks about him, but I figure they have a strained relationship since she always shuts down when I ask about him or her mom. She's quick to change the subject or avoid any questions about her family. I don't push her to talk because I have enough shit of my own piled up and sure as hell don't need to add to it.

Every time Tara begs her dad to stop, he just kicks me again, harder in the gut. I curl up bringing my knees to my chest as I attempt to block his foot from my body, but he just continues to attack any vulnerable part of me that he can reach.

Tara cries out, "Dad you're going to kill him. Stop. Please stop."

"Awww the little whore doesn't want this useless piece of shit to be hurt." His assault on my body momentarily stops as he taunts her, "Does my little princess want me to stop hurting her Prince Charming?"

I roll over and crawl to my clothes while his focus turns toward Tara. I slip on my boxers and jeans and slowly stand up rubbing the welt that is forming on my stomach. I listen to the abusive words spewing from his mouth and watch as Tara just takes it in, not even attempting to fight back. Tears stream down her cheeks and she struggles to hold back her sobs.

Her dad rants on, "Tara, what is it about this scumbag that you want? Or will you let anyone stick his dick in you, you fucking little slut?"

She winces at his harsh words and he snaps his head back to me. He glances up and down me and a sinister smirk spreads across his face.

"Oh, it's the Stevens kid. I'm surprised at you, Tara. Thought you were worth more than this trash." He turns his back around to face her. "I mean can't you find someone whose dad isn't a waste of life? I mean his mom had to die just to free herself from them."

The second he mentions my mom, I launch at him and leap on his back pushing him to the floor. My fury trumps any rational thinking and I begin throwing punches and screaming, *"Fuck you,"* over and over at him. One mention of my mom seems to click a switch of anger and wrath on in me.

Tara jumps from the bed and pulls back my hands to stop me, but they just flail around unable to find any sense of control. As she struggles to trap my arms, her dad crawls out from under me and leans in close to my face.

"You're done in this town, kid. You have no idea what you just started." He stands up over us and smoothes the suit pants he's wearing. "Now get the hell out of my house."

He storms out and slams the door against the wall causing a piece of the drywall to crumble to the ground. I jerk my arms from Tara's grasp and grab my duffel bag and black T-shirt that's hanging over the desk chair. I throw on the shirt and hurry out without even as much as a look to Tara. I probably should stay and make sure she's okay, but I can't control the rage that's rushing through my body.

As I shove my way through the crowded sidewalks to reach the gate that leads to the entrance of my house, the misery begins to set in and this time, there's no pushing it away, no one to hide behind. I am empty, a fucking hollow shell that is slowly being chipped away. I pause in front of my door and reach into the front zipper of my bag that hangs from my shoulder. With the small, orange bottle in my grasp, I twist open the top and dump two pills in my hand. Ashamed that I'm resorting to this, masking the pain from the sins I bear, I close my eyes, throw back my head, and pop them into my mouth. As the numbness begins to set in I revel in it, finally surrendering and letting the darkness take control.

Chapter Fourteen

Present

The bar is just steps off the beach situated on the corner of the main street that leads through town. From the second I walk off with Tara, the self-hatred begins to take over. *How could I lose myself again so quickly?* I spent years learning to control that side of me, the side where the anger drives me straight to aggression. I had it in my grasp. I thought I was healed. But it took Liam one day to unravel it and expose me for the person I really am. *One motherfucking day.*

I dig my hands deeper into my jeans' pockets and tuck my face into the collar of my jacket as the bitter winds swarm around us. The warmth will never be achieved anyway, not after the coldness that's building inside of me. I follow Tara through the double-paned glass door into the bar. The small opaque square windows that line the one side wall give no way to the bright light of the sunny day outside. A few patrons hang around the various bars that occupy the space next to the dance floor. I trap the smell of stale salt air in my nose as we approach the smallest bar next to the entrance, and hop up on a wooden stool that lines it.

I order a Jack on the rocks, and Tara gets some fruity drink for herself. I just stare across the chipped countertop bar wondering how I got to this place again, the state of constant guilt and responsibility for others' actions. And now, here I am having a drink with the person who tried to destroy my family only a few months ago. The one person who took so much from me. But didn't I ruin her too? Didn't I take and take from her without giving a shit about how I damaged her? These murky thoughts only draw me to my glass as I drown myself in the whiskey.

Tara takes a sip of her drink and places her glass down closer to mine. She inches her hand to my arm and lightly drags her nails up to my elbow. Her intimacy makes me uncomfortable and I jerk my arm from the bar.

"Oh come on, Cole. You can't tell me you stopped liking that? You always loved when I'd tickle you with my nails." She's talking in a sweet, innocent voice with, of course, no sign of the sobbing she did to get me here.

Annoyed with her constant games and manipulations, I spit back, "You're right. I love it, but only when Cam does it." I hold my left hand up to flash my ring at her. "You remember her, right? My wife?"

She rolls her eyes and pushes my hand back down to the bar. "Oh please Cole. Stop the chivalry act. Does *your wife* know you're with me right now? Does she know you were with me last night?"

I feel the rage building back in me. "There's nothing to know."

I grab my drink and take another swig, refocusing my attention back to the small stage that's against the center wall. It's empty, desolate, just like me. Tara's right. I didn't tell Camryn that she was at the bar with me last night when I ran out of the house for hours. And I sure as hell didn't tell her I was grabbing a drink with her today.

Tara continues to talk as I stare ahead, my fingers fiddling nervously with my glass, as my thoughts jumble together. "Why is Liam even here? It has to be because he wants to hurt you. He knows your weakness is your mom and that you partly blame yourself for everything. I mean look at everything he did to you after she died."

I cringe at the memories she's bringing back to life and find comfort in the whiskey that burns as it trickles down the back of my throat, only compelling me to drink more. I motion to the bartender for another glass.

"He turned everyone against you after she died. Brady told me about the scene he made at her funeral. It was like he was the victim in all of it. So, he knows what he's capable of and probably gets off on it too." She breathes a heavy sigh. "I wonder how Heidi's doing since he came back. I mean they claimed they were so in love, right?"

The mention of my sister cracks my daze and I spin my body around on the bar stool to face her. Defensively, I answer, "What are you talking about? Heidi? That was some high school bullshit between them."

Unconvinced she retorts, "Whatever you say, Cole. But can't you remember the way they were with each other. It was her and Liam against the world." She sarcastically laughs. "Face it, he turned her away from you. I wouldn't be surprised if she blamed you for you mom's death just like he did."

And just like that, the conniving, manipulative Tara is back. The one who sucked me in at sixteen-years-old and used my weaknesses to her advantage. The very same way as today, with the bullshit sobbing act. It doesn't take away the fact that her words sting though, that they cut straight down to the bone. I spent the last ten years doing the same thing I'm doing this exact moment with Tara—hiding from the truth. It's easier than facing it, easier than coping with the grief, easier than admitting who I really am. I pass the blame on to others, but in reality, the guilt I have is mine alone. And the more I run, the more I hide from it, the more I lose along the way.

I lift my glass and tilt my head back to help the liquid pour down. Interrupting Tara, I blurt out, "You need to go. Take your fake act and find a guy who believes it."

Tears well up in her eyes, but I don't care at the moment. My irritation swells and through gritted teeth I continue, "Just go the hell away." I slam my glass down on the bar, causing a thud. "Tara, I need you to leave me alone."

She slowly gets up and begins to shutter away. I see her stop and look back, like she wants to say something or comfort me, but she knows better with the state I'm in and continues out the door. I welcome the fogginess that begins to set in from both the Jack and the anger. Just as I'm about to order another drink I am nearly pulled off the stool. I peer behind me to see Dusty grabbing the back of my shirt. He throws cash onto the bar and drags me toward the door. Trying to balance myself on my feet, I shout out, "Yo, Dus. What the hell is wrong with you?"

With obvious frustration, he raises his voice loud enough to cause the other customers to stare. "What's wrong with me? With me? Don't you answer your goddamn phone?"

I feel over my pocket but am surprised when I don't feel my cell phone. Remembering that I threw it on my office desk, I shake my head and in an apologetic tone answer, "Sorry. I must have left it in my office."

Dusty, his hand still gripping my shirt leans in and whispers, "I'm not the one you need to apologize to. It wasn't me you had to pick up from school."

I gasp and drop my head in shame. *How could I forget Gavin?* From the first time I met him, I knew I never wanted to disappoint him. And I failed—I failed my son again.

Dusty continues raising his voice louder, "I told you, man. Poison. That's what *she* is. Fucking toxic."

I concede as the whole scene sobers me, "It's not what it looked like. She gave me some of Rose's things and then pulled the crying act. I just kicked her out a few minutes ago."

Dusty grits his teeth and snaps back, "She fucks with your head and makes you feel guilty for all of the shit *she* did." He raises his voice a bit louder, definitely generating more stares, "She's nothing but a selfish bitch."

I am startled by Dusty's outburst, which is completely out of character for his usual laid-back way. I put my arm on his shoulder and say, "Dusty, I know. You don't need to tell me twice. But the blame is on me. I'm the one who fucked everything up today." I lower my voice in disappointment, "But, right now, I need to get the hell out of here so I can see Gav."

I rush Dusty with me through the exit, focused on salvaging whatever is left of my son's trust in me. *How the fuck could I forget him?* My head spins from everything that just went down, but I begin to dart down the sidewalk in the direction of Dusty and Heidi's place. Dusty stops me, pushing me up against the brick front of the bakery that is a few doors down from the bar.

Dusty, with a fury I have never seen in him, has my back pinned to the wall. "Gavin's has no clue what happened. He's out with Heidi and is fine. And you're not going anywhere, dude." He relaxes his shoulders and loosens his grip. "Not until we erase that whiskey smell from your breath." He nudges me toward the entrance of the bakery and reaches around me to opens the door. "You need coffee and we need to talk."

His tense eyes and the edge in his voice overshadow his usual easygoing nature. So, I follow him through the door and plop down at the small bistro table closest to the entrance even though all I want to do is get to my son. While Dusty is at the counter I peer around the place staring at the pictures that line the walls, all photographs of cakes they've made for different occasions. My gaze lands on one that shows a white one trimmed with light blue icing on the edge of each tier. It reminds me of the one Camryn and I shared only a few months ago. She insisted that blue icing had to be on ours and not just the trim, but the entire thing. She kept saying the color reminded her of the ocean and the ocean was me. So, of course, we had a big blue cake that day and it was the best one that was ever smashed into my face because it meant so much to her.

A large steaming cup of coffee appears on the table in front of me while Dusty sits on the chair across picking off the chocolate chips on top of a muffin and tossing them on the plate next to it. I watch in confusion as they pile up. "What the hell are you doing with the chips? They're the best part."

"Nah. All the chocolate just globs together and it doesn't taste like a muffin."

"That's the point. It's the best part. Definitely not the muffin part."

He shrugs a laugh, "Sober your ass up with that coffee and leave me to my chipless muffin eating, okay?"

I roll my eyes, "Whatever, dude. But you're missing out on the finer things in life." I take a sip of the coffee and flinch as it burns through my body reminding me again of why I'm drinking it.

In a stern tone, Dusty asks, "Shouldn't I be saying that to you? I mean what the fuck's going on? You actually went out for a drink with that psycho? And then forget to pick up your son?" He leans over the table closer to me. "What about your *finer things*, man? You know your wife, your son, your baby that's on the way?"

I drop my head and stare at the thin red stirring stick that's floating in my cup, while the stabbing pain of guilt returns with a vengeance. With a deep sigh, I say, "I don't know, man. I always seem to fuck things up."

Dusty slams his palms down on the table causing some of my coffee to spill out. He gains attention from a few of the workers behind the counter but still pushes his chair from under him, stands up and leans over the table toward me. With a tensed jaw and hair falling in his face, he clenches his jaw, "It's her...it's Tara. She fucks with your head and you let her. And then this mysterious-practically-family-used-to-be-best friend guy shows up and you're throwing down again. What the hell, man?" He takes a deep breath that seems to calm him a bit and sits back in his chair. "I can't get a straight story from Heidi, so it's on you. What the hell's going on, dude?"

I stare at Dusty while I gulp down my coffee trying to regain my composure through the whiskey fog. I don't feel like talking about it, not with Dusty. He'll just try to tell me that everything was an accident, that I wasn't to blame. But I don't want to hear it—not anymore.

A server from behind the counter comes to our table and fills up my cup with more coffee. I rip open a sugar packet and swirl it around the cup attempting to avoid the confession Dusty is waiting to hear.

He tosses one of his chocolate chips at my face to get my attention. "You realize that the Winter Qualifiers are two weeks away. *Two weeks.* If you want to make the Classic again you have to be on your full game. You can't have this shit on your mind. And you can't have that bitch messing with your head, making you forget about your family responsibilities."

I slowly nod in acknowledgement of his concern as I try to find a way to explain everything to him. "Liam was the one who called my mom for help the night she got in the accident. He got in some trouble with some gang guys and needed someone to come get him out. He was trying to get through to me, but I was pissed at him and turned off my phone." I take a deep breath as I relive the night again. "It should've been me there with Liam, not her. She should've never left that night to get him."

Trying to understand, he asks, "So you blame Liam for your mom's accident?"

I shake my head from side to side. "No, I blame myself for the accident. I blame him for her death." I shift in the chair and continue as the memories begin to sober me. "The day of her funeral, Liam came whacked out of his mind on something and made a scene. He was screaming at me, blaming me for ignoring him when he needed me the most and some bullshit about shutting him out. So, I tackled him to the ground and delivered blow after blow to him until my dad was able to pull me off. But the damage was done. My mom's funeral was a spectacle and Liam managed to get everyone to see me as the villain."

Dusty lifts his foot and rests it on top of his planted leg. He listens to me, nodding in understanding as I continue to divulge my past.

"After that day, Liam was determined to bury me. Turned old friends against me and I swear he even made Heidi believe I was the reason our mom was gone. I don't know…it was like he just snapped." I took a long sip of coffee as I try to recover from my confession. "And as for Tara. She was just there for the taking. I could hide when I was with her, never having to face the truth."

Dusty interrupts, "You hold some heavy shit, man. But what you just said…it's not the truth. You let your mind interpret your guilt. You didn't kill your mom that night. Another car did."

And there it is—the consolation, the letting me off the hook. To me they are just words that are supposed to be said at a time of tragedy. I've heard them so many times and they never work, never leave me unbroken.

As the fog in my head begins to clear, I stand up from the chair signaling to Dusty that I'm done, done with the coffee and done with the confession. Dusty follows me out the door and we turn in the direction of his house. I dig my face into the collar of my jacket as the air grows colder with the setting sun. Dusty's texting someone on his phone while he walks next to me. Once he's done, he tucks his phone back into his pocket and says, "All right, we're meeting everyone at Mack's for pizza. Heidi and Gav went to that indoor haunted mini golf place. Camryn called Heidi concerned that she couldn't reach you and Heidi covered your ass and said you left your phone at the office while me and you went out to talk about the qualifiers. So, you're all good."

Ashamed that my best friend and sister have to cover for my stupidity I mumble out, "Thanks, man. I owe you for this."

Dusty lets out a deep breath. "You know I always have your back, but don't ever put me in this fucking position again."

I nod to him and pick up the pace as the feeling of need sets over me. I need to see my son, need to hold Camryn in my arms, need my family's instant healing. But as my past is holding me down, slowly drowning me, I wonder if they'll be able to keep my head above water.

Chapter Fifteen

Present

Since most places on the boardwalk are closed during the winter months, it' eerily quiet when Dusty and I follow the dimly lit block that leads to *Mack's Pizza.* The sun had set while we were at the coffee shop clearing the grogginess that had set in from my afternoon at the bar. The guilt of forgetting Gavin lingers in my mind and I can only suffer in my silence as we make our way down the creaky wooden boards.

As we pass by the darkened amusement area, I glance up toward the towering Ferris wheel reminding me of the night last summer when I took Gavin on it. It was when Camryn found her way back to me after I told her about my connection to Todd. She had finally taken that first step to accepting her past and started to see me as her future.

Thinking back to how inseparable we were that weekend, I can't help but remember that last night as we strolled down the boards together like a family. I watched Gavin's eyes light up with curiosity as he stared in awe at the giant wheel that remains a focal point for the island. With the flashing lights reflected in his eyes, I bent down and whispered in is ear, *"I'll go if you go?"* A huge grin spread across his face, *"Let's do it."* He reached for my hand and I led him there, and I didn't let go if it until we got off the ride. I held onto him so tight while we went round-and-round never to think that I would ever leave him alone or forget him only to have my sister and best friend pick up the pieces.

"Snap out of whatever thoughts you're torturing yourself with now. Everyone's waiting for us already and you have to be normal." Dusty edges me back to the present.

"Yea, I'm cool." I slow down before the entrance to the pizza shop and Dusty notices and stops next to me. "Thanks, dude. You saved my ass today."

"It's cool man. Told you already, I always got your back."

We nod to each other and proceed to the doorway. The shop was empty except for our two booths and a few stragglers sitting at the counter. Gavin instantly sees me when I walk in and run up to me jumping into my arms.

"Daddy, Daddy. I got a hole-in-one. I hit it right under the skeleton bones then...BAM." He elatedly slaps his hands together. "The ball went in...it actually went in."

His excitement brings a smile to my face as I hold onto him in my arms grateful for Heidi and Dusty.

"Rock on, little man. Now tell me one thing." I lean in close to his ear. "Did you kick Aunt Heidi's butt or what?"

He throws his head back in laughter. "You know it, Daddy!"

Heidi and Camryn approach and as Heidi leans into Dusty, she shouts, "I heard you, Gav. And I'll remember that. I know a certain someone's birthday is coming up."

His jaw falls open with surprise, and he jokingly retorts, "You love my cute face too much, Aunt Heidi. Remember you told me that today?"

We all laugh at Gavin, and Camryn reaches around both of us for a hug. She stands up on her toes and gently kisses my cheek. I grin at her and search her eyes for the disappointment Liam told me about earlier. She hides it well, but I can still see it, knowing that all she wanted was to hold on to her mom's legacy through the clinic.

Camryn squeezes us tighter and says, "I missed my boys today." She looks at Gav and tells him, "Saw Pop-Pop today and said he needs to make a visit to see his little shark. Think he may have something for you."

Gavin squeals at the idea of seeing his grandpa. After the many years he missed with Camryn, Jack makes it a point to be around and Gavin has grown really close to him in the last few months. It was just one more thing Milena made possible for the ones she left behind.

As we notice the server making his way to our booths with two steaming hot pizzas in his hands, Camryn grabs Gavin from my arms and places him down next to her.

She leans down to him, "All right, buddy. You're coming with me to wash those hands before you even touch that pizza."

Gavin whines out, "Awww, Mommy, I washed them already…like a hundred times. I mean you do put wet wipes in my lunch box."

"What can I say? I'm a nurse and I like clean hands. Sorry, buddy, you're stuck with me." Camryn jokes.

I pat him on the back and console him, "Just do it, bud. We'll never win that one."

Gavin huffs and stomps away with Camryn to the bathroom, while I make my way to the table where Heidi and Dusty are just seating themselves across from Lila and Carter. As I inch into the open booth behind them, I greet Lila who oddly cold-shoulders me and then I high-five Carter. He leans over the booth and warns,

"Dude, I have no clue what you did, but she is pissed off. My advice when she's like this...Don't. Make. Eye. Contact." He shrugs and slaps me on the back of my shoulder before he turns back around in his seat.

Before I can heed Carter's warning, Lila is next to me in the booth glaring at me with a humorless look on her face. I lean back to lengthen the space between us, but it only prompts her to move closer to me. Confused by her obvious bitterness, I stare at her not knowing what to say.

Lila peeks up in the direction of the bathroom and quietly begins to rant, "You know where my salon is, right?" I slowly nod wondering where this conversation is leading. She continues, "Well, just know that I have eyes everywhere. Especially in certain corner bars." Her eyes burn through me as if she can see the monster within me. "And I have to say, I don't buy your act...not for one minute.

Fearing what Lila thought she saw, I ask, "What are you talking about Lila? What *act?*" My questions come out more bitter than I had wanted.

She squints her eyes in anger. "I'm talking about

that look on your face, you know, the I-sucked-down-three-coffees-to-sober-up-look." Her eyes avert next to me and she relaxes her stance and plasters a fake grin across her face and continues. "I don't know what you're doing, but just know if you fucking hurt them in any way, your balls are mine."

Before I can defend myself, she stands up and grabs hold of Gavin, who is just returning to the table. She takes his hand and starts twirling him around singing some Justin Timberlake song. While he giggles with Lila, Camryn's eyes are locked on me. Her head is tilted to the side and lips in a tight line while she stares straight through me. It's as if she already discovered the demon that lives deep within me, the selfish beast that has taken so much.

Before she can interrogate me, Gavin jumps next to me begging for pizza. I happily dig into the pie that's on our table and place a huge slice on his plate. His timing is the perfect distraction for Camryn's wandering thoughts, and I use it to my advantage. I have now sunk to the level of hiding behind my son.

Gavin is the dinner entertainment for all of us as he reenacts the play-by-play of his mini golf victory. His energy warms me and for a moment I can forget the reason that led him there. After we demolish two pizzas, we all go outside to the vacant boardwalk to head home. Lila grabs Carter and makes a quick escape, but not before she threatens my balls one more time. For years Lila was all Camryn had, besides her mom, so I understand her concern.

Gavin runs over to the pavilion that is lined with benches all facing the ocean. While Camryn and I watch as he hops from bench to bench, Dusty and Heidi approach us. She creeps up next to Camryn and starts telling her about some girl who follows Gavin around the playground at school.

Dusty, who is next to me, quietly speaks, "Intense session tomorrow. Pretty extreme waves rolling in." I look over to him while he stares into the distance in front of Gavin. The ocean can only be heard through the darkness of night as the rough waters of high tide rush beneath our feet and slam against the dunes under the boardwalk. He continues, "Don't forget, man, they need you as much as you need them." He returns his gaze to me.

Trying to weed through his philosophical views, I ask, "What the waves? Or my family?"

He pats my back and glanced around us. "When it comes down to it, aren't they one in the same?"

I look from him to Gavin to Camryn and my sister and whisper back, "You ain't kidding, bro."

Heidi busts in between us and grabs hold of Dusty's hand, pulling him toward the exit ramp. She whines out "Baby, are you ready yet? It's freezing up here."

Noticing they are leaving, Gavin runs up and wraps his arms around each of their legs shouting out how much he loves them. When he returns to bench hopping, Heidi leans over to me and whispers something in my ear about needing to talk. I quickly nod and pull away from her hoping that Camryn didn't hear anything. Turning my attention to Dusty, I extend my palm out to him.

He gives it a slap and as Heidi drags him out he yells, "Tomorrow. Six A.M. Not a minute later."

I grin at Dusty being Dusty and acknowledge him

with a thumbs up. When I turn back around I notice Camryn's chattering teeth and wrap my arms around her growing waist drawing her body into mine. Even through the aroma of garlic from the pizza shop is in her hair, I can still smell a hint strawberry, that intoxicating scent that hypnotized me from the first day I held her in my arms. I dig my face further into her hair, craving her, needing her. With a soft kiss to the top of her ear, I feel a shudder through her body, which lures that sweet giggle from her.

Swaying her in my arms, I smile into her cheek and murmur, "I love you, Mrs. Stevens. Always have, always will."

I feel her cheekbones rise as her smile widens. "I love you, Mr. Stevens. Never stopped, never will."

We stand together, cheek-to-cheek watching Gavin jump each bench pretending hot lava is beneath him. I envy his innocence, how effortlessly he finds happiness, as it was stripped from me after I lost my mom. Looking to Camryn, I know she's the reason for it. She made sure Gavin would never feel the pain she endured, even if it meant giving up her own desires. I watched as she struggled to let me in, felt her resistance as I slowly knocked down the protective wall she built around her and Gavin, and lived through the pain of loving her when she tried so many times to pull away from me.

The memories of the last few days flood back and the shame of who I am only grows. Camryn faced her past head on and when mine looks me straight in the face, I can only fade back into the misery. *Fucking weak.* As the sound of the waves echo through me mixed with the laughter of my son, I know it's time to face my mistakes, relive my grief, break apart all over again. I owe it to Camryn, Gavin and my unborn baby. *They deserve that much.*

I glance across the pavilion past Gavin into the blackness of the winter night sky and through my jumbled thoughts I declare, "Call Jack. Tell him to meet us at home.'

Camryn tilts her head up toward me. "My dad? Tonight? What's wrong, Cole?" Her voice shakes, evident of the worry in it.

I look into her frightened eyes and stroke her cheek with my thumb. "Because you're telling him that you're in. That you're doing the clinic."

Confusion spreads across her face and shakes her head from side-to-side attempting to dispel me. "No. I won't. Not when someone who's hurt you is involved. I can't. I…"

I catch her face in my grasp and interrupt, "Yes. You can. And you will. I refuse to *ever* be the reason that you abandon your dreams. You understand?"

With tears pooling in her eyes she grabs hold of my wrists and slowly nods into my hands. Her bottom lip trembles and a stray tear trickles down her cheek unable to control the emotions bursting through her. As I brush my thumb across her face, I know I'd do anything to wipe her tears away, even if it means that I'd have to shatter to pieces all over again.

Chapter Sixteen

Present

Shortly after Camryn calls, Jack rushes over to our house straight from the hospital, still dressed in his mint-green scrubs. While he hangs with Camryn downstairs to help finish Gav's bedtime routine, I stand at the counter in the kitchen and pour him a scotch. I hold it up and stare through the amber liquid disgusted with myself for finding comfort in it earlier. But the other side of me yearned to pour it down my own throat to savor the numbness it can provide.

Jack clears his throat as he enters the kitchen interrupting me from my inner battle. I quickly lower the glass and place it on the counter in front one of the stools on the kitchen island, although I'm pretty sure he caught me gawking at the glass. I turn around and grab two water bottles from the refrigerator to avoid the questioning look on his face. When I turn back around, Jack begins our conversation like he usually does, with stories from the ER, even though I'm sure his mind is reeling from what he just witnessed.

The one thing about Camryn's dad is that he never judges anyone. I met him for the first time after I woke up in the hospital and, despite his daughter nearly getting seriously injured in the attack, he never once questioned her safety with me. In fact, he helped bring

Camryn back to me that night. He somehow convinced her our love was real and worth the fight.

"Can you believe he wanted to just hide the key from his wife?" Jack chuckles as he is babbling through some story of a patient who swallowed a house key.

Missing most of the story due to my wandering mind I shrug at Jack. "I guess he figured it was a good hiding place for it."

"You're not kidding. He now wants to send it to his wife as a memento." He takes a sip from his glass still laughing at his story. "You see he caught her cheating a few weeks back and as she was sneaking out tonight to do God-knows-what. He quickly swallowed her house key so she couldn't get back in. I guess it worked because she came storming into the hospital screaming at him right after the nurses were able to get him to pass it. Amazing it didn't shred his insides."

I crack a smile hoping it will be enough to appease him.

Noticing my discomfort, he switches gears from his stories and ask, "Cole, you know I try not to pry but is everything okay with you?"

I lean against the kitchen island with my arms spread to hold up my weight. I look down and eye the small dark specks that run throughout the granite countertop and begin to nervously tap my fingers along the edge of it.

Before I can answer him, Jack suggests, "You know if it has to do with Liam, we are cutting him out, trying to find someone else who's willing to fund the clinic?"

Not wanting to become the problem, I cut Jack off and refuse his offer. "No. Don't even think about it.

Liam stays as partner." I run my hand through hair. "I just have lot on my mind. Nothing I can't handle."

Jack nods not pressing the issue any further. He picks up his glass and swirls the liquid around in it, staring into it like he is wrestling with his own issues.

He takes a sip and narrows his focus in on me. "Just remember that sometimes what you think you can handle becomes the one thing that destroys you."

His eyes avert behind me and his stiff shoulders loosen as his expression quickly dissolves into a wide smile that stretches across his face. I turn around and notice Camryn, who changed into a pair of ass-hugging velour pants and a tank top that accentuates the swell of her breasts and curve of her stomach. Just looking at her is addicting. She comes over to me and wraps herself into my arms. I hold her, massaging over her stomach with my one hand. While Jack's previous tension melts into his admiration for Camryn, I am left to wonder for what sins he needs saving.

After Jack and I spend over two hours convincing Camryn that she needs to be a part of clinic, she finally gives in to our persistence. She worries that, with Liam, my past will never leave, and I'll fall apart as the grip of it tightens around me. But I'm willing to take that chance for her—willing to break so that she won't feel one ounce of pain.

Anything to protect her.

As we stand in the doorway watching the taillights of Jack's car disappear down the vacant beach block, I turn to Camryn and swoop her up in my arms relishing in the sound of her laugh. Kicking the door closed behind me, I carry her down the hallway to our bedroom and gently lay her across our bed. Tucking a stray hair behind her ear I lean into her mouth and murmur, "Hope you don't mind, but I'm going to take every bit of you I can tonight."

She wraps her arms around my neck and that playful grin appears, "I hope that's not a one-time offer, Mr. Stevens."

My eyes narrow. "Definitely not, baby girl. You know how greedy I can be."

I unhook her arms from around my neck and stretch them over her head. Pulling her tank top off, I gently drag my needy hands down the length of her body savoring every bit of contact I can have. I edge her pants down her legs and toss them to the floor next to the bed. Gazing down at the slender lines of her body, emphasized by a round belly and adorn in only bra and panties, I become lost in her beauty, the pure essence that defines her. I peel off my own clothes and crawl up her body needing to bury myself in her. This has become my own personal therapy. Her eyes follow mine, hypnotizing me, as she begins to lead me to ecstasy.

****

The sound of footsteps against the wood floor grow louder as they approach my door. Glancing up to the window, the faint glow of the streetlight shining through tells me that morning is just settling in. I bury my head deeper into the pillows hoping sleep will find me again, but I know she won't let me. Not today. She always insists on being the first person and that means waking me up at the crack of dawn

The door slowly creaks open and I hear her tiptoeing across my room. The well-known tune is floating from her soft voice as she sits on the edge of my bed. Just as she finishes the last words, she rubs my back and leans into my ear coaxing me awake.

"Happy sixteenth birthday, sweetie."

Startled by her greeting, I turn around to my back and focus my gaze on her as she holds my cupcake with one candle out to me. Confused, I ask, "What are you talking about, Mom? I'm not sixteen...I can't be."

She tilts her head and softly smiles, "What are you talking about, honey?" She lifts the plate toward me. "It's time to make your wish."

I scoot away from her and begin to scream out, "You're not here! You can't be! You didn't make it...you didn't live!"

Oblivious to my outburst, she continues to smile and push the plate closer toward me. "Make a wish, honey. You're never too old to wish for something. Come on...do it for me."

My chest pounds as I struggle to find my breath. I tremble as I reach out not wanting to touch her, but at the same time needing to see if she's real. She continues to nudge the plate toward me with her comforting smile. As my eyes fall to her hands, my body stiffens and pain pierces through me like a knife as my mom holds my dead baby girl in her arms.

My body jolts awake and sweat covers me as I fight to come back to consciousness. I leap from the bed and rush to the bathroom reaching for the faucet, eager for the cold water to somehow erase the visions of them. As I splash the iciness across my face, the images from the dream begin to fade, but the guilt remains. I lean over the sink letting each drop of water trickle off my face, and I wonder if I will ever be truly free.

Unable to face the depth of my nightmares again, I leave the bedroom to head upstairs hoping some late-night television will put me into a dreamless trance. But as I creep down the hallway, I hear Gavin's voice coming from his room. I peer in through the small opening in his doorway and catch sight of his silhouette exposed by a flashlight he is shining beneath one of the sheets he made into a tent. As I slowly open the door, attempting not to frighten him, I whisper out his name. He instantly stops talking and his small head pokes out of the opening of his tent.

His eyes, evident of sleeplessness, perk up at the sight of me. "Hi, Daddy. Wanna come in my tent?"

Curious as to why he is awake in the middle of the night, I don't hesitate and I climb right in situating myself against the wall on the bottom bunk next to him. Snuggling beneath the blankets, I ask, "So what's up, buddy? Why are you awake right now?"

He nudges his face into me as I feel the wetness of his warm tears against my t-shirt. Trying to comfort him, I stroke through his hair. "It's okay. You know you can tell me anything."

Gavin peers up at me, his lips pouted, eyes glossed over and sniffles out, "Promise not to be mad at me?"

I lift my wrist up flashing the bracelet he made me. "Superheroes promise."

One side of his lip tilts up and he meets his bracelet to mine. He grabs his Batman stuffed animal that's laying against his pillow and takes a deep breath. "I pretended to fall asleep when PopPop was here."

Trying not to further upset him, I calmly ask, "Why'd you do that, buddy?"

He takes a deep breath as he wrestles with his

143

conscience. As he begins to fidget from his nervous energy, I squeeze him closer to me to comfort him. "I wanted to hear what you guys were talking about." He sighs and his voice quivers, "I—I was scared you'd leave again."

His words are devastating, digging deep into my heart. *How could I have been so careless? How could I have been so damn weak?* I rub his back and kiss the top of his head. "Gav, you have to know that I'll *never* do anything to hurt you. Everything I do is to protect you and Mommy. Do you understand?"

While his head slowly nods up and down, I continue to console him, "Buddy, promise me that you'll never worry about all of this adult stuff again, okay?"

He raises his thumb up to my face and a smile tugs at the corners of my lips at the gesture we began with each other that night on the Ferris Wheel. I meet my thumb to his and in unison we declare, "Thumbs up for a deal."

Laying him back down on his pillow, I straighten the blankets over him. I lean down and plant a kiss on his forehead. "All right, Little Man, let's try to get some sleep."

His big aqua eyes look up to me. "Can you stay with me, Daddy?"

I tap my finger on his nose and reply, "You couldn't get rid of me if you tried."

I watch as Gavin buries himself under his blankets and snuggles into his pillow. As I lay next to him, I begin to stroke his hair. Before he gives in to his exhaustion, he whispers, "Daddy, is Mr. Liam a bad guy?"

Not wanting to expose him to the ugliness of my past, I answer, "You don't have to be scared with Liam. I'll *always* keep you and Mommy safe."

He stares at me as he struggles to keep his heavy eyelids from closing. "But what about you?"

Confused, I ask, "What do you mean, buddy?"

He snuggles closer toward me and rests his face against my chest. "Who's gonna keep you safe?"

Gavin's simple words slam me square in the face as they carry with them so much meaning. It's time to realize that there is no one to bail me out of the prison my past has built around me, no place to run to escape the choices I've made. It is time…time to stop hiding.

****

After watching Gavin sleep soundly the rest of the night, exhausted and still tormented, I climb out of his bed and tiptoe toward the board closet to get ready for my training session. There is no way in hell I'm going to show up late, not with Dusty now watching my every move. I peek back to my son, who is cuddled beneath a mountain of blankets with his tiny hands curled up beneath his chin, and for a moment I revel in his peacefulness. *I never will take that away from him.*

After I dress in my wetsuit and lean my board up against the front door, I go back to my bedroom and kiss Camryn. She stirs a bit but never wakes up, grateful that she probably didn't notice that I left the bed last night. After checking on Gavin one more time, I grab my board and head outside in the frigid air toward the beach. Climbing over the steep dunes that are built up to combat the winter storms, I spot Dusty by the water's edge staring at his wrist. When he notices me approaching him, he shakes his head and points to his watch.

"One more minute and I was coming to drag your ass out here. I thought I said six o'clock last night?" He smiles, pleased with himself for breaking my balls.

I dig my board into the sand and situate the hood of my wetsuit over my ears. Rolling my eyes at him, I growl back, "You said six and according to my clock I was on time, you prick." I kick some sand in his direction to add to the amusement.

He lifts his watch to my eyes and laughs out, "Well, smart guy, you're on *my* time now. So, get your ass in the water and start paddling out."

With a sarcastic smile, I salute him and then grab my board and head to the ocean, the place that balances me. As I wade away from the shoreline and dive under the wave, I embrace that first shot of icy water letting it seep through my body, hoping it can heal my torment. Paddling out into the vast depths of the sea, which has become my home for the last ten years, I am able to slow the bleeding of the wounds that have been torn open again and again. Off in the distance the water begins to rise, and I paddle toward it, surrendering to its power and letting it take control of my board and me.

Although Dusty warned it would be intense, I didn't expect to be crawling onto shore after a two-hour session. I know it was his way of punishing me for all the shit from the day before, but it was also Dusty being a friend and actually giving a fuck about me. He sees the ocean as therapy, healing any scar that mars you and the more you're immersed in it, the stronger the treatment.

While I stay on the beach to stretch out my cold muscles, Dusty heads off so he can get back to his office in time for a therapy session with a client. Since there aren't many physical therapists in this beach town, especially ones who focus on sports' injuries, Dusty handles all the athletes of the area.

After loosening up, I put a hooded sweatshirt over my wetsuit and turn to leave, but instead I'm met by the cold stare of a pair of gray eyes. My body instantly tenses stealing the calmness that the ocean had just granted me.

Liam steps toward me while his glare remains fixed on me. "Does it ever cross you mind, I don't know, maybe a passing thought? Do you even give a shit?"

Annoyed by his mere presence and cryptic questions, I bite back, "What the fuck are you talking about?" I start to nudge past him. "I don't have time for this shit today, Liam."

He catches my elbow and I feel the blood rush to my face as the rage began to take over. Reaching in myself for the sound of Camryn's voice telling me to "*own my breath,*" I attempt to control the anger. Violently shaking his hand off of me, I take a step farther away and without turning to face him, I warn, "Just leave me the hell alone. You got what you wanted, man. You're working with my wife, *my family.* Now just walk away or I swear I'll…"

Before I could finish my threat, he yells out, "Or what, Cole? What are you gonna do? Kick my ass? Pound my face? Or better yet, how about you just take everyone I love away from me?" A sinister laugh escapes from him. "Oh, that's riiight, you already did that."

I turn around to him expecting to see a fucking

smirk on his face, but instead I see defeat. His eyes are glossed over as he peers in my direction, never locking his stare on me. He has his hands tucked into the pockets of his jacket holding them close to his body. The cocky Liam who showed up on my doorstep the other night now just seems wrecked.

Refusing to fall victim to his pity act, I take a step toward him and straighten my shoulders, towering over him. I finger into his shoulder. "You lost everyone you loved? *You*? You're fucking delusional." Liam doesn't flinch at my finger's contact as he lets me release the pent-up tension that has plagued me for ten years. "I was the one, Liam. I was the one who lost everything I loved that night. Not you." As the memories flash back, I feel the anger surge through me. "If you would've just left me alone that night…not called her for help…this wouldn't of…she wouldn't be dead."

He stares, empty of all emotion, into my eyes and in a quiet tone reveals, "I've spent so many years feeling guilty, feeling responsible. All because *you* made me feel that way. And I'm done. I'm fucking done accepting the blame for something I never did." His voice raises with conviction. "Did you hear me, Cole? I didn't do it. I. Never. Fucking. Called. Her."

Chapter Seventeen

Present

I glare at Liam as his words strangle me. His confession is false, an insincere attempt to free himself of the wrong choices of his past, but somehow it tears me further apart. As he waits for whatever sympathy he is searching for, the venom begins to spread through me and all I want is for Liam to feel pain—make him suffer for everything.

"Do you think your bullshit means anything to me? That somehow I'd forgive you for the last ten years?" I grit my teeth. "No matter what you claim, your shithead antics were the reason she was out. She fucking *died* because of you."

Liam, unaffected by my outburst, stares right at me and continues to ramble, "I felt like shit after I dragged you to Skate Wars just to bail my ass out of another gambling debt. So, after you ditched me, I stopped by a party looking to throw a few back to feel good. But those two shitbags were there, the ones who followed me out. I wouldn't let them get away with it...I wanted to kill them after what I saw what they tried to do." He squeezes his eyes closed and his voice fades as if the memory is too difficult to bear.

Unable to grasp the meaning of his story, I interject, "What the hell are you talking about? Kill who?"

Liam's eyes fly open and his body jolts, shaking off whatever memory haunts him. His smug attitude quickly returns as he snaps back, "Would you really fucking care? Are you ever really willing to see past the asshole you've made me out to be?"

Before I can get another word in, he turns around and begins to traipse off the beach. "Maybe you should ask Tara about that night. She was there."

I watch Liam disappear behind the dunes leaving me to wonder how I can survive traveling down this road again, the one that's left me weak and damaged.

****

Hunched over a stack of closing papers on my desk, the silence of my office only fuels my thoughts. The scattered pieces of my past are a jumbled clusterfuck, and I struggle to piece them together as I slip back into my old habits. Throwing my pen across the room, I grab the picture frame on my desk. As I stare at Camryn, Gavin, and me posing on the jetty at the inlet, I can't help but wonder if I can hold on to them, or if I'm just too toxic for anything so pure. I slam it face down on the papers and clutch my face with my hands.

What happened to me? When did I turn into such a pussy?

Pushing up from my chair, I snatch my phone and pace my office. My fingers toy with the screen as I debate on calling Tara. She can give me answers, but she is dangerous, a ticking bomb about to explode.

Wrestling between the desire for answers and the need to keep Tara at a distance surge through me. I never want to turn to her again, for anything, but I am somehow speeding in that direction with no way to slow down. In the past, Tara started off as a distraction for me, a place where the shit in my life would go unnoticed, and because of that, she became an obsession for me. With her I never had to feel, never had to deal with my internal suffering. I hid and pretended my life wasn't going to shit. That was until we lost Rose and every bit of sensation that I buried within me for so many years came rushing back, hitting me so fucking hard.

I look to the picture frame face down on my desk and begin to dial Tara's number. I want to convince myself this is for them, that going back to that night will somehow make me a better man. *Who am I fucking kidding?*

I am just about to change my mind and hang up after the fourth ring when I notice a strangled breath coming through the receiver. Startled, I begin to speak into the phone, "Tara? Tara? Is that you?"

A screeching sob overtakes the breathing and I begin to shout, "Tara? What's going on? Is this one of your fucking games?" I become frustrated, as her cries only grow louder. "Answer me, goddammit."

In a barely audible voice, she whispers out, "Cole, I need you. Please. Come help me."

Attempting to find out what is wrong, I start shooting questions out. "Where are you? Are you hurt? Is anyone with you?"

Before she answers my barrage of questions, the line goes dead, and I am left to decide if I should go to her aid. Not wanting more shit playing on my conscience, I grab the keys to my Jeep and rush out of my office, heading down the Drive in the direction of her house.

When Tara's mom finally left her dad, she won their beach house in the settlement and they moved here the summer before our senior year of high school. However, after we graduated, Tara's mom disappeared, leaving her a stash of cash but no hint about where she went.

Her house is an oceanfront property situated just outside of town. She happens to share the block with Lila and Carter, however they are closer to the bay. As I turn into the stone-topped driveway, I notice her, crouched down on the top deck stair with her head buried into her knees. Throwing my car in park, I hop out and race up the stairs, glancing around to see if there are any signs of a break-in. When I don't notice anything, I reach out to her and place my hand gently on top of her head. Her shoulders are shaking evident that she's crying. I lean down to her. "Tara, are you all right?"

Her one eye peeks over her elbow and once she notices me hovering over her, she slowly lifts her head from her knees. Blood is pouring out from a deep gash on her lip and the swelling around the wound is beginning to form a bruise. Her tears are pouring from her eyes as they fall into the blood-soaked towel she clutches on her lap.

I grab the towel from her and press it to her lip. Her eyes squeeze shut and she shudders at the contact with the open wound.

"Tara, we need to get you to the hospital. You're gonna need stitches. It's pretty deep."

Her head tilts to the side as if it was too much effort to hold up and her gaze shifts back up to me. It's evident that she's high but as she continues to blankly stare at me, I can only guess what may have spurred it.

I repeat myself to her and extend my hand out to her, "Let's get to the hospital and get that stitched up."

Tara looks intently at my hand before she put hers into it. The emptiness behind her eyes and helplessness within her gaze only adds to the awkwardness of the situation. I shouldn't be the one here for her, but that's the thing, I'm the only one. I carefully lead her down the stairs and help her up into the front seat of my Jeep. After I shut the door, I walk in front of the car and peer at her through my windshield. Blankly staring through the window, Tara sits with her one arm tightly wrapped around her waist and the other pressing the towel against her lip. Suddenly, my life is set on rewind and as it spins out of control, I am left trying to reach for the stop button.

****

Once the ER nurse leads Tara to an examination room, I take the elevator to the maternity floor where Camryn works. Walking through the long hallway that leads to the circulation desk, the weight of my memories come crashing down. One time when I walked on this floor, I was told that my baby girl was dead, that her tiny body couldn't sustain the trauma from Tara's fall, the fall that I caused.

I stop and close my eyes hoping the memory will go away, that these halls will just represent my future with Camryn, Gavin and our baby. But that vision is slowly fading as my past mistakes resurface.

Own your fucking breath.

My eyes snap open with my coaxing thoughts, and I push through the double doors toward the circulation desk. Behind it a short, chubby woman with red cheeks to match her hair is furiously typing on the computer. It's Melva, the head maternity nurse who helped Camryn through everything when she came back here. We've never actually formally met, but I know she's always been good to Cam.

I lean against the tall desk and clear my throat hoping it will take her attention away from her computer screen. When she looks up, her cheeks flush even more and a wide smile spreads across her face.

"Hi, I'm here to see my wife. I'm…"

Before I can introduce myself, she jumps up from her chair and interrupts, "I know who are, sweetie. And I'll get Miss Camryn for you right now." As she reaches for the intercom, I smile back to her.

"Thank you very much."

A small giggle escapes her as she pages Camryn to the front desk. After Melva places the receiver down, she returns her attention to me. Still grinning from ear to ear, she says, "Camryn should be here any minute. She'll be so excited to see you. She's had a rough start to her day."

"Is she okay?" I ask with concern and a bit of panic.

Melva waves her hand at me as to brush off the anxiety in my tone. "Oh, sweetie, no worries. She had some weird stomach bug that seemed to have stopped by lunch." With a knowing grin, she winks at me. "The virus has plagued her for the past few months."

I can only smile at Melva for discovering the pregnancy. Camryn and I are trying to keep it quiet for a bit longer, but I know she wouldn't mind Melva knowing, not after all the support she's given over the last nine months.

Jokingly, I add, "Oh yea, I heard those stomach bugs hang on for pretty long…like nine months or something." I wink back as I out our secret to the jolly red-headed nurse.

She clasps her hands together and squeals, "Oooooooohhhhh! I'm so excited for you two. I have dibs on delivery nurse, you got it?"

I nod my head. "She probably already planned on that." She squeals again in excitement.

A desperate gasp interrupts our lighthearted conversation and I swing around to find Camryn's hand covering her mouth as she stares down at my hands. When I look down, I notice blood covering the sleeve of my shirt. When I held the towel to Tara's lip, her blood must have dripped down and stained the end of my sleeve. Melva darts away from the desk toward Camryn, while I start waving my hands out in front of me.

"No, Cam, no. It's not my blood. I promise" I slow my hands to show her they were clear.

Camryn, her eyes locked on my hands, approach slowly as if she doesn't believe me. Melva returns to the desk, but chooses a computer on the other side, giving us as much privacy as she can in the center of a bustling maternity floor.

I extend my arm out to Camryn inviting her to place her hand into my open palm. She hesitantly reaches out, her hand trembling. Once in my grasp, I pull her to me and plant a soft kiss over her mouth, which causes her shoulders to relax. I press my forehead against her. "Is there somewhere we can go to talk?"

One side of her lip tilts upward as she considers where to go. "Ummmm…I'll bring you to the break room."

She leads me down the one hallway through a metal door that opens up to a room stacked with a wall of lockers. I follow her through another doorway that leads into a slightly larger space with a small kitchen in one corner and two round tables. On the other side of the room a television hangs on the wall and is surrounded by two futon sofas. After she guides me down on one of them, she peeks down at my bloody sleeve again.

I tilt her chin back up to me and comfort her. "I promise you, I'm fine. The blood is Tara's. I had to rush her to the emergency room after I found her bleeding from a split lip and completely out of it in front of her house."

Camryn takes a deep breath and presses her back against the futon. She unclasps her hand from mine and in a frustrated tone bites out, "What the hell's going on with you, Cole? When are you going to stop falling for her games?"

Her bitter tone jolts me and I attempt to explain, "She was out of it…unresponsive. I couldn't just leave her alone. I had to do something."

She lengthens the distance between us and defensively blurts out, "Why the hell not?" her voice grows louder. "She's not your responsibility. And you're not hers to lean on…you're *my* husband. Don't you see it? I mean look at everything she's done…scheming with Todd to keep us apart and using the daughter you lost to gain your attention. Yet, you still go running every time she calls for help." She takes a deep breath attempting to calm herself. "Stop trying to save her. Please, I'm begging."

As her pleas pour out, my guilt only grows stronger. I hear everything she's saying, agree with each word of it, but I know I can't leave just let Tara wither away, especially since I caused a part of her anguish. But I also can't bear this overwhelming feeling that I am abandoning my own family, that I am pushing them away while they are trying to pull me in closer. I hopelessly dig my face into my hands and shake my head from side-to-side.

Feeling powerless, I concede, "I can't. I just fucking can't. I can't be the reason for another one." Aggravated, I tug at the ends of my hair.

Camryn sighs as she shifts closer and snuggles into me. She drapes her arm across my back and I feel her breath against my cheek. "Another what. Cole?"

I lift my head from my hands and meet her concerned gaze burning a hole through me. My breath shortens and body tenses as the word slips to the tip of my tongue, "Death."

She buries her head into my neck, and I feel her tears wet my skin as she witnesses the guilt that is consuming me. "It kills me that you do this to yourself, that you blame yourself for it all."

She releases me from her hold and grasps my face with her hands. As her thumbs circle over my cheekbones, she murmurs, "Cole, I need you to try for me." She rubs her hand over her stomach, "Try for us. Try to see that none of it was because of you." She grabs my hand and presses it against her stomach. "I need you to see that you've given us life."

Camryn leans in and meets her lips to mine. The

taste of her is like a drug that numbs every sensation in my body.

She breaks apart from me. "Listen go for a surf and clear your head. If Tara's blood tests show any sign of substance abuse, they'll admit her to the hospital overnight anyway. I'll check in with her and let you know what's going on. Okay?"

Weakened by her pleading eyes, I give in to her request and then guide her mouth back to mine greedily taking more of her healing. The vibration of her pager breaks us apart summoning her back to her patients. I walk with her back to the front desk and before I turn to leave she calls out to me, "Cole, one step toward home." She etches an "X" over her heart. "I love you."

I lip back, *"Always have, always will."*

****

Before leaving the hospital, I hurry past the examination rooms in the ER to make sure Tara was admitted. Most rooms are empty, probably due to the slow winter months and lack of people living in the area. Many of the nurses are loitering the hallways. When I find the room Tara is in, I peek behind the door and see her lying on her back staring at the ceiling while a nurse tends to her lip.

I shudder at the sight of her, so frail and detached from reality. Memories begin to haunt me as I see the striped hospital gown draped over her limp body, the bloody gauze pads that litter the tray next to the nurse and the blankness of her stare. I squeeze my eyes shut as I attempt to purge the visions from my head. When I open my eyes, the nurse who was just stitching Tara is speaking to me.

"By any chance are you Cole?"

I slowly nod to her.

"Well, good thing because your name is the only thing that young lady will say."

She moves out of the doorway to allow me to pass by her into the room. Tara locks eyes with me as I tread softly toward her. The scene feels eerily familiar as if I am living the nightmares all over again. Tara's skin is beaded with moisture, probably withdrawing from whatever pills are streaming through her system. The dark circles beneath her eyes stand out from the paleness of her skin and her normally styled hair is wavy and some parts are matted down to her scalp.

When I reach the examination table she is reclined on, she stutters out, "Cole, I-I n-need you...you're h-help."

With a heavy sigh, I reply, "I know you do."

She lifts her finger and points toward the windowsill where her jeans are crumpled into a ball. Knowing exactly what she needs from me, I walk toward the window and grab the jeans from the floor digging my hand into each pocket. Pulling out the unlabeled orange bottle, I stuff it into my coat pocket and twist back around to Tara.

"These will disappear along with me." The firmness in my tone draws a cry from Tara. "I'm done, Tara. I...I can't do this again." I draw a deep breath and continue, "It ends right here, right now. You understand?" I stare into her hollow eyes hoping my message will sink in. "Tara, I'm not the one you need. I'm not the one who can save you."

Before I catch her reaction, I turn back around toward the door and walk out. Tara's sobs grow louder with each step I take away from her. Once out of her room I rush out the automatic doors into the parking lot. Leaning against the hood of my jeep, the icy air stings my throat as I struggle for air. I kick the front tire with force.

"Goddamit Tara. Why can't you just leave me the fuck alone?"

I know that's impossible. I know my past mistakes can never stay buried. I know the guilt will never subside. I know the next time she'll be bleeding out from her wrists, not from her lip—just like before.

Chapter Eighteen

Past

A week after the incident with Tara's dad, I remain locked away in my bedroom, away from the shitshow my life has become. It isn't about being afraid of Derek Chambers, but rather not wanting to deal with the repercussions of assaulting someone so powerful and well known in the city. Instead, the pills make it easy. They blur the memories and dim the nightmares. The more I pop, the farther detached I become from reality and the deeper I slip into my own oblivion.

As I sink deeper into my self-destruction I can't bear the fact that I'm masking my pain, that I somehow failed my mom by not allowing myself to suffer for her. Instead, I'm becoming addicted to this state of nothingness. With the pills I can hide in a world where only I exist, everyone else a faded memory.

Sweat pours down my body and soaks the sheets below me as the glaring sun bursts through the one wooden blind that is twisted open. I stumble out of bed tripping over the beer bottle that I used to wash down the two pills I took last night. After hearing my dad stagger in at some obscene hour and the voice of some whore he must have picked up along his drunken path home, I had to drown it all out and make it disappear.

I make my way over to the window and kneel

down on the floor where the air conditioner vent is. I lay the side of my face to it hoping to feel a cold shot of air through it, but instead feel nothing. As the bitterness streams through me, I lift my head from the floor and begin to slam my fists against the gold-plated vent until all that is left is a mangled piece of metal dangling in the hole of the hardwood floor.

Unable to find the energy to return to my bed, I stay flat on the floor and watch the blood pool on my knuckles.

"What the hell did the air conditioner ever do to you?" Heidi's voice surprises me, drawing my eyes away from my hand.

I haven't seen my sister since I left that morning back to Tara's. She continued to call and leave messages, but I refused to call her back, especially since I know she continues to see that asshole.

I answer back in a bitter tone, "What the hell's wrong with the AC? It's ninety-fucking degrees out."

She walks over to my closet doors and grabs a towel that is hanging on a hook. When she reaches me, she grabs my bloody hand and begins wrapping it tightly with the towel.

"It's not ninety degrees...not yet at least." She places my hand gently back on the floor and sits down next to me leaning her back against the windowsill. "And the air conditioner was turned off, just like the rest of the electric in this house. Dad hasn't paid any bills since you've been gone." A hint of anger etches in her tone she continues, "Guess paying the bills would take money away from the sluts he brings home."

I pull myself off the floor and prop my back against the wall next to Heidi. "When did that shit start?

I mean last time I checked it was just the drinking. Prostitutes now?" Heidi nods to me. "Man, what the fuck?"

"Yea I know. I'm not sure when it began. All I know is that one night Liam and I stopped in to pick up some of my clothes and he was on the reading chair in the den doing some things to a bleached out blonde girl."

Just the sound of Liam's name coming from her mouth sends the rage back through my veins. *How could she be with that prick? How could she go against me?* I lift my body off the floor and stomp back to my bed. As I fall to the mattress I throw a pillow over my head and shout, "Just the get the hell out, Heidi. I see you haven't come to your senses yet."

Her footsteps grow louder toward me and she lifts the pillow from my head. "You're not running away this time. I'm not letting you." I watch as she opens the side table drawer next to my bed and takes out the bottle of pills. They shake as her hands begin to flail, "You think I don't know about these…that I don't know what that stupid bitch got you into? You're better than this, Cole. You're better than that piece of trash you've been hiding away with."

Annoyed that she is lecturing me, I leap on top of her, tackling her to the floor and snatch the orange bottle from her grip. "You have no fucking room to judge. You lost that right the minute you jumped in the sack with that shithead." I trap her arms so she can't move. "Just stay the hell out of my business. Better yet, stay out of my life. Pretend that I'm fucking dead."

The tears immediately unleash from Heidi and I loosen my hold on her and roll back onto my bed. My thumb begins toying with the top of the pill bottle in my hand as the rest of my body craves the silence I know they can bring me. I twist it open and pour three pills in my hand. Heidi crawls up from the floor and grabs my hand before I can throw them in my mouth. Her eyes, watered with tears, plead with me as she squeezes her hand tighter over mine.

"Please don't do it, Cole. Please don't take them."

I close my eyes as I try to block out the guilt, the pain, the loss, but it's useless. Opening my eyes, I shake Heidi off of me and toss the pills in my mouth savoring every part of them as they hit the back of my throat. Heidi plants her face into the mattress and sobs overtake her, but I am too numb to care. Slowly lifting herself from my bed, she wipes the tears from her cheeks with the back of her hand. She stands over me as I begin to get swallowed up by the empty hole the pills create around me.

"I'm not gonna let you, Cole. I don't care what I have to do, but you're not gonna turn into dad. I'm not walking away from you." Her voice quivers with pain.

As Heidi backs out of the doorway to my room, she begins to deteriorate from my vision becoming just another one of my faded memories.

****

Days slip by as I sink lower and lower trying to reach the ultimate state of nothingness.

No feelings. No emotions. *Nothing*.

The air conditioner finally kicks back on, so I assume Heidi took care of the electric bill because it sure as hell wasn't our dad. He wouldn't be able to pull himself away from the bottle long enough to do something responsible. As I hear him bring more and more whores home with him each night, I know he is slipping farther away, unable to be reached. He has given up on life.

I haven't talked to Heidi in a week, since the day she begged me to stop taking the pills, but I know she comes in my room to check on me. I always pretend to be passed out, but I'd catch her sneaking a few pills from my stash and then seconds later, I'd hear the toilet flush. I'm too fucked up to care, but I know I'm running low and will need to find more today.

I roll out of bed, the sheets stained from sweat, and stagger into the bathroom. I turn on the faucet and splash cold water on my cheeks. Catching a glimpse of my reflection in the mirror I'm disgusted at the face staring back at me. My normally tan complexion is washed out highlighting the dark circles stamped beneath my bloodshot eyes. The patchy scruff on my face has grown out and follows the drooping of my cheeks. My lips are dry with pieces of skin peeling off, probably a sign of dehydration.

Anger swells in me as I realize I have fallen victim to the one thing I despise—weakness. I was never supposed to cover up the hurt. I didn't deserve to feel numb. I promised her that I would always live through the pain.

Unable to bear the piece of shit I am looking at through the mirror, I lean over the sink struggling to find my breath. Visions of her lifeless body flash through my mind and I squeeze my eyes shut to try to shake them away. I can't bear the guilt of being responsible for her death. And I am fucking too much of a pussy to accept the pain that is intended for me. The same pain she felt when the other car crashed into hers and ejected her from her seat. Clenching the sides of the sink, I pull back my fist and unleash it on the mirror. I scream at my reflection as pieces of it falls into the sink, shattering into pieces. But I can't stop. I continue to launch punches as I watch the blood spurt out and feel the shards of glass peel the skin off my knuckles.

"Oh my God, Cole. Stop! Please stop!" Heidi's cries pass right through me unsuccessful at ending my attack.

She wraps her arms around my knees and they buckle driving me to the floor. I lay on my side defeated, gasping for air, as I press my face against the coldness of the tile floor and watch blood drip down from my hand staining the cracks of grout. I can feel Heidi's body trembling against me as she refuses to loosen her grip around my knees.

Once she steadies her own breathing she meekly asks, "Can I let go, yet?"

Beaten down by my own doing, I just stay motionless on the floor staring at the blood pooling around my hand. I wish I would just bleed out and be done with this life.

I'd never be that fucking lucky.

Instead I'm meant to live, to exist without her here, to pay the price for my sins. To accept that I'm part of the reason she's dead.

"Cole, talk to me. Please. I'm begging." Heidi's pleas are turning into desperate cries. "I'm here for you. I promise."

Whether it's the blood loss, the week of shit I've been pumping through my body, or the fact that I have completely lost it, I begin to laugh. I sound like a fucking hyena. Heidi, still attached to my legs, jumps up and releases her grip at the sound of my lunacy. Confusion mixed with a bit of terror, Heidi stares at me open-mouthed, probably trying to grasp some kind of understanding of my actions. I'm not sure what I'm laughing at, but I have to be fucking mental.

My moment of insanity is stopped when our dad stumbles into the bathroom. He glances from the damaged wall to the shattered mirror onto my bloody hand. Peering from me to Heidi he slurs out, "What the hell's going on?" He bends down closer to inspect the blood on the floor and his head shoots back to Heidi. "What? You finally trying to pay back the selfish little shit for killing your mom?" A sardonic laugh escapes from him. "Sorry, kiddo. Looks like you didn't hit the right spot."

He shakes his head and staggers back out into the hallway, while Heidi yells out, "Cole's not responsible for mom's death. You're an asshole, dad."

My dad stops dead in his tracks and turns back around to my sister who is now standing in the doorway of the bathroom. He glares at her and through clenched teeth bites back, "Excuse me? Who the fuck do you think you are talking to me like that? I'm the father and you're the daughter, you little bitch."

Heidi crosses her arms across her chest. "A father? Really? Then act like it."

Before she can get the last word out, our dad is leaping toward her and grabs her hair yanking it hard enough for her to yelp in pain. With the little strength I have, I crawl off the bathroom floor and launch my body into him tackling him to the floor. Pinning him beneath me, I raise my bloody fist in the air and pause as I gaze down at my dad who is defenseless under my weight, wondering how the hell it came to this.

"Do it. Just throw the punch, son." He mockingly chants.

Holding back my urge to hurt him, I whisper, "No. I won't let it come to this."

I roll my body off his and crawl to the top of the staircase while my dad continues to taunt me. "Hurt me, Cole. You know you want to. Hurt me like you hurt her."

I inch down each step trying to escape from his stinging words that keep playing like a broken record. His words that speak the truth. I limp to the front entrance, reach for the doorknob, and slam the door behind me. Hiding my bloodied hand in the pocket of my dark jeans, I turn the corner onto the sidewalk. Heidi catches up to me and grabs my elbow, pulling me into an embrace.

"I'm so sorry, Cole." Her voice quakes trying to hold in her sobs. "He doesn't mean it. Any of it. He's just so messed up right now." She hugs me tighter. "I need you...*we* need each other. Please just come back home with me and let's figure it all out."

I push away from her. "Heidi, don't you see it, yet? We don't have a home. No family. No nothing. It's over. Everything is gone."

I turn away and leave her sobbing on the sidewalk, this time not letting the sound of her cries to affect me.

Desperate to erase my dad's voice from my head, I make my way to Tara's house. Knowing Derek Chambers could be lurking nearby I walk to the corner of the block and call Tara's cell phone. She picks up on the first ring and tells me to meet her at the park a few blocks away.

Sitting on a bench at the park waiting for Tara, I watch as kids run around the bases on the field. Their infectious laughter carries through each other as they cross home plate. They are so carefree—not a worry in their perfect little worlds. Their moms are huddled together in the dugout involved in their own conversations occasionally peeking over their shoulders at their kids playing.

My mom was never one of those moms who stood around and gossiped. She'd be the one at this very park rounding up all the neighborhood kids for a kickball game, initiating a game of HORSE on the basketball courts, or surprising me and my sister with a picnic dinner on the tiny slab of grass behind the mostly dirt baseball field. She never once sat on these park benches while we played because she always wanted in on the action. And now I'm at the very same park trying to score my next fix—trying to forget everything about her.

Two arms snake around my shoulders breaking my reminiscent thoughts. Tara leans into my neck and gently kisses it before she whispers in my ear, "Missed you all week. I've been dying without you next to me in bed." She lays her head against the back of my shoulder. "Guess I got used to having you around."

Uninterested in a heartfelt reunion, I hop up from the bench breaking through her clasped hands. When I turn around to face her, I notice a startled look on her face.

"Not really looking to hang out today." I look down at the wet spot my bloody hand is leaving on the pocket of my pants. "I just need some more pills. To get me through the next few days."

Fury replaces the look of shock on Tara's face. "You've got to be fucking kidding, right?" Her raised voice causes a few looks in our direction and I lean in closer to try to quiet her outburst. "I'm your girlfriend, Cole. Not your *dealer*."

"Whoa…wait…girlfriend? When did that happen?"

Tears well up in her eyes and she reaches out to me, but I back away from her grasp. "How can you live in my house for weeks, sleep in my bed with me every night, and do the things we do to each other in that bed and then say it means nothing? Her tone turns desperate with each word spoken.

"I just thought we were having some fun, you know, forgetting the shit in our lives." I pause when I see tears streaming down Tara's cheeks. "I really need some more pills. Can you please just help this once and then I promise I'll never ask you again."

She reaches into the messenger bag draped over her shoulder and pulls out a small plastic baggie. Holding back her sobs, she throws it at me. "You're an asshole."

As she turns to leave, I grab her arm and she whips back around to face me. "I'm sorry, Tara."

Shaking me off, she spits back, "You're just like him. You make me feel worthless. The only difference is that he has the balls to throw the punches."

I step back troubled by the comparison she just made of me to her asshole father and watch, as she storms away never once glancing back in my direction.

****

I manage to stay hidden all day from my dad and

Heidi on our rooftop deck. Polishing off a six-pack I lay on the lounge chair staring aimlessly at the starry night sky. Tara had hooked me up with only a few pills, so I have to space them out and can only get a weak buzz. So, the beer is a perfect way to strengthen it. My phone vibrates in my pocket and I see Brady's number flash on the screen. Flipping it open I answer, "Yo, dude, what's up?"

"What the fuck did you say to my sister today" His tone is threatening.

Defensively I snap back, "What the fuck do you mean? I said jack shit to her." I'm straight up lying to Brady.

His voice raises into the phone, "Well, you prick, she's in the hospital because I found her laying in a pool of blood on the bathroom floor. Right after she snuck out to see you at the park."

The line goes dead and I go numb.

Chapter Nineteen

Present

Leaving the hospital and cutting off this unhealthy connection to Tara didn't give me the sense of relief I've been searching for since the day I got involved with her. Somehow, I know I can never ultimately be free of her, not with our pasts so intertwined, and definitely not with her still using me as her crutch. She knows too much about me, about my weaknesses, and she plays into them without one sense of remorse or guilt. Somehow, in her twisted mind, I'm still that weak sixteen-year-old who doesn't give a shit about anything, just drowning in pills, alcohol, and sex. And what scares the hell out of me, is I sometimes feel exactly like that kid, getting swallowed up by the shit that I've somehow allowed to define me.

Starting up the Jeep, my mind wanders to the disappointment I just saw on Camryn's face, and her attempt to hide behind her unyielding support of me, and then the frustration she tried to mask in her voice. Even during our most difficult times last year, the ones that drove us apart, I never once questioned Camryn's devotion to me. And I sure as hell won't ever take that part of her for granted, will never expect her to just accept this aspect of me. But the truth is, Camryn will, and she'll do it even if it hurts like hell.

As the visions are on a continual playback button, I slam my fist into the steering wheel, irritated with the past that I spent so many years recovering from making a comeback. I was supposed to be free of it, but the memories of my mom laying lifeless on a hospital bed because of me, then Tara still and pale with bandages tightly wound around her wrists because of me, and finally, Rose, her tiny body invaded by tubes, hooked up to machine because of me, would always flash back on. And then the claws of guilt would sink in deeper, taking hold of me.

Reaching the southernmost point of the island, I park along the sand-sprinkled road and jump out, hoping a for a quick escape from all that consumes me. I trail onto the desolate beach, with only the crashing waves singing out a slow melodious tune. Climbing over a sand drift, I land onto the jetty, a place that holds soothing memories, all of which Camryn is the center of them. I find the one rock and rub my thumb over Milena's etched initials. When I first came to Sea City, Camryn's mom was a positive force in my life, one that took me farther away from the darkness and showed me healing was possible within the waves. And then, after her death, she brought Camryn and Gavin to me to continue that job and show me that I was worthy of love again.

"Really could use you right now, Coach," I whisper out into the sound of the waves slapping up against the jetty. "The qualifiers are coming up, but I can't seem to get my head straight. Can't fully let go of the darkness."

I sink down and sit on the rocks, allowing myself to take in the peaceful escape this place has always been. I peer out to the edge of the jetty, the exact spot where Camryn and I released our past demons into the ocean and then moments later, proposed to her. Those past mistakes and painful memories were supposed to be gone, allowing us to move on with each other. But somehow, mine didn't want to leave. Mine wanted to come back to remind me I've hurt too many people to be given a second chance.

My phone buzzes in my pocket and I pull it out to see a text from Camryn.

Tara is stable, bleeding is under control. She is being admitted and will be undergoing withdrawal management. Cole, you saved her life today. That's who you are.

I smile, inspired by my wife's strength. She somehow cares about Tara, the person who conspired with Todd to take Gavin away, and who still continues to come between our family, the person she should hate. And somehow, she still sees me as a hero, even after my past is slowly revealing itself to her. I text back,

Baby, you're the lifesaver, not me. And right now, I'm sitting at our place thinking about the day I made you mine forever.

Camryn quickly responds,

I know. I'm looking at that same spot too.

I hop up from where I'm sitting and turn around to see Camryn, pieces of her long dark hair coming out of the wool cap on her head, and her arms wrapped across her long, winter coat. I saunter to her, feeling the heat that never seems to fade between us. Her eyes are set on mine and her lips are curled up in a gentle smile. When I reach her, I take her into my arms and hold her for a moment, no words need to be spoken between us. I lead her back to the jetty, helping her up, but never letting go of the hold I have on her.

Camryn looks up on the high rock getting a glimpse of her mom's initials. She blows a kiss up to it, and then turns to me. I brush some blowing pieces of her hair away from her face, and say, "I just told your mom I could use some help right now, and she sent me you."

I smile at the way I can still make Camryn blush. "That's because she knows I'd never let you fight alone."

I pull her into me, my lips against her ear, "You, Camryn Stevens, will always be what I need, and everything I don't deserve." I kiss her gently on her ear and work my mouth down to her neck, finding the bare skin beneath her coat. She tilts her head back, letting me in and I can hear a slight moan escape from her. I smile against her skin and relish in the goosebumps that I cause on her neck.

She presses her hands on my ears and pulls my face down to her. She gives me a kiss, catching a bit of my bottom lip between her teeth. She whispers to me, "Well, you, Cole Stevens, are completely and utterly wrong." A sly grin crosses her face. "You have yet to see that you deserve everything." She leans in for another kiss, lingering a little longer with my bottom lip. "But don't worry, I plan on showing you how much you deserve every day for the rest of our lives."

And now it's time for my body to tingle, to savor the effects Camryn has always had on me. I tighten my arms around her waist and lift her up, cupping her tight, little ass in my hands. She lets out a playful shriek and holds around my neck. I carry her off the rocks and toward the sandy trail leading off the beach. I trail kisses up her neck again, driving more squeals out of her. When I reach her ear, I sneak in a nibble of her ear lobe and then whisper, "How about I get your sexy ass home and you can start showing me exactly what I deserve right now?"

I can feel her cheek against mine, the heat radiating from it, making me aware of what I have the power to do to her. I continue with my barrage of seduction, "And if I could have my way, I'd take you here, right now in our special little spot next to the jetty." The memory of our summer night spent in our little cave right here gets me jolted up. It was that very night when I knew I had her, that I was somehow breaking through the barricade that she had built around her heart. There was no doubt that I could've dropped down to one knee and proposed to her that night.

Her breathing becomes heavy against my ear, and I race off the beach to my Jeep, carrying her in my arms. I place her in the passenger seat, and help her put the seat belt on, barely able to separate my mouth from any part of her body that I can get to. I stroke her cheek and revel in the pure desire I see in her. Flushed cheeks, swollen lips, and hooded eye-lids. Before I shut the door, I lean in and devour her mouth, our tongues forceful and needy, and the sweet taste of mint lingering long after I am racing down the Drive to get home.

When we're in the driveway, I throw the car into park and jump out, racing around to the passenger side. I scoop Camryn out of the seat before she even has a chance to get out herself, and kick the car door shut with my foot. I'm frantically stripping off her wool hat and winter coat, anything I can get my hands on, while I struggle with the key in the front door. I need this. I need her.

Camryn's words come out between short, gasping breaths, "Hurry. Up. And Open. The. Door."

With her body draped in my arms and her needy hands frantically trying to find a spot on my body to touch, there is nothing I want more, at that moment, than to fulfill every single one of her needs, to be the last man she ever craves. I answer my wife's request by throwing the door wide open and rushing down the hall to our bedroom. I place her gently on our bed and remove the clothes I couldn't already tear off of her in the hallway. Her perfectly plump lips are parted, a touch of pink streaking her cheeks, and those dark eyes, wide, and fixed on me. She reaches for my clothes, and I help her lift the shirt over my head and unbutton my jeans, letting them pool to my feet. I stand at the foot of the bed, just looking, admiring all that she is. Leaning over her, with my hand I trace down the length of her body, her back arching, begging for more. I place my fingertips between her legs, brushing lightly across her center. Her body jolts and she's grabbing fistfuls of sheets beneath her, greedy for more than what I'm offering.

"Tell me what you want, beautiful." I push my fingers further in, a cry escaping as her body rocks against the bed, and then bring them back out. I continue, "Tell me what you need from me."

With lust and desire written all over her face, and in every part of her writhing body, she stammers out, "Please. Oh God, please, Cole. Just…please."

177

I back away from her body, savoring my ability to tease her, but at the same time, wanting to take her all in again. *Goddammit, this woman is my world, my fucking existence.* She reaches out to me, her tips of her fingers gently gliding down my chest, tracing over my stomach, and stopping below my waist. Her smooth fingers graze over the shaft, taking hold of it, and my body falls victim to her touch.

I drop to my knees and crawl up the bottom of the bed, my lips finding every part of her. Hovering over her, I brush a few loose hairs from her face, exposing those alluring eyes that have enraptured me from day one. Leaning down, I meet her mouth, kissing her, grazing my teeth over that that plump bottom lip I love so much. I whisper in her ear, "Sweetheart, tell me what you want."

She pulls me down and steals another long kiss before she replies, "I want you, Cole. In *every* way I can possibly have you. Right now, and forever."

I smile at the depth of her words, the eternal strength they hold. "This is right now, baby girl." I slide down her body, my lips leading the slow assault, sucking and biting her hardened nipples, her body jostling with each touch my mouth makes on it. I follow the path of her hip bone, leaving tender kisses over the slight swell of the growing life in her. Her one hand grabs the bed sheets, the other my head, pulling at the short strands, as I begin to tease her with my tongue. With short, quick licks, her body thrusts toward me, imploring me to go deeper. I look up to Camryn, her cheeks flushed, lips parted, pleading eyes on me, and huskily repeat, "Right now."

I plunge my tongue in, keeping my eyes set on her.

Her moans cry out, her back arches off the bed. She's running both of her hands through my hair, tugging harder as my tongue moves faster and deeper in her. Her legs tense around my head and her body quakes as I bring her over the edge, tasting every bit of her orgasm.

I let her body recover, climbing back up on the bed over her. She is staring at me, with heavy breaths. I place a kiss on each of her cheeks and whisper, "And this is forever."

I plunge into her, both of us crying out in pleasure. Our bodies find a rhythm, the heat of our skin penetrating off of each other. Camryn's hands are restless, rubbing down my back, grabbing my ass and pushing me further into her. I obey her wants and grab a hold of the headboard, thrusting deeper and faster. Sweat beads begin to trickle down our skin, our bodies rocking as we climb to our highest peak. And with our gazes held on each other, we fall over the edge, giving in to every bit of the pleasure.

I collapse down next to Camryn, take a minute to catch my breath, and savor in the bliss of the moment. Pulling what covers remain on the bed over us, I curl in next to her body wrapping her in my arms. I kiss her cheek and notice her jawline arch up into a smile. Embracing this moment of healing, I whisper into her ear, "I love you, Mrs. Stevens. Right now, and forever."

Chapter Twenty

Past

It's insane how quickly life can go from an amazing ride to a fucking time bomb ready to explode at any second of any given day. With Brady hiding Tara away, I've been stuck to the confines of my house, staring at the piles of unopened late bill notices, listening to my dad stumbling in at all hours of the night with whatever skank he picked up at the bar, and the occasional stop-in from Heidi and that douchebag, Liam. Most of the time, they stay downstairs, and I hear the vacuum cleaner and washer running, but for some reason, they're hanging upstairs tonight in Heidi's room and the laughing, moaning, and other noises are making me fucking sick. So, I take my six-pack, climb out my window and escape to the roof until they leave.

The July air is still and heavy from the late summer humidity, but it's less suffocating then being trapped inside. It's hard to believe that this house was once not such a toxic shithole, that at one time there were the sounds of laughter, games, and family meals in it. The smell of chocolate chip cookies that greeted you when you walked through the door is a distant memory compared to the smell of stale smoke and whiskey. I twist the beer cap off and flick it angrily behind me. *How the fuck did I get here?*

Just then I feel something hit me in the back of the neck. I swat at it as if it's just a pesky mosquito, but instead Liam appears in front of me. I take the beer cap he just hit me with and toss it at him. "How about you leave me the fuck alone and go in there and keep ruining my sister." I snarl at him and then take a swig from my bottle.

He bites back, "There's nothing I'd rather do than not have to look at the pathetic piece of shit you've become, but I love your sister too much to give up on what she wants. And all she wants is her brother back."

I sneer at the word love coming from his mouth. "*Love?* Tell me what the hell you know about love? You destroy everything you touch and you're going to end up destroying her."

Liam takes a deep sigh and reaches over to me taking the beer bottle from my grasp, "How about you just stop punishing yourself and let her back in. Let her help you. She's your sister, man."

I quickly snatch the beer back and take a swig right in front of him. "What you see is what you get, prick. And you can tell Heidi you made me this way."

He howls out a sarcastic laugh and shakes his head at me. "Go ahead, Cole. Blame me, blame her, blame your dad, blame the fucking city of Philadelphia." He spans his arms across the city skyline which is in our sight. "But one day you'll realize it didn't have to be this way. That you have no one to blame but yourself." He starts to turn to walk away and murmurs, "When did you become such a pussy?"

The minute I hear him, I go ape-shit, and leap at him, tackling him. The beer bottle shatters, splattering all over us. He manages to hold my arms hostage, and he rolls me off him, pinning me down under him. I'm thrashing, trying to get an arm loose. There's nothing more I want than to drop him and wipe that self-righteous look off his face. But between the binge drinking, dabbling in pills, and lack of any physical activity, I can't throw down like I used to, especially when I'm trapped.

His face his beet red, a vein protruding from the side of his head and his eyes are wide, anger seemingly radiating from them.

"Lose the fucking pity party, Cole. It's time to step up and be the man for your sister, because your dad sure as hell isn't doing that. Hate me all you want, but don't hurt her. She doesn't deserve it you selfish little shit." He let's go of my arms with force and pushes them away. He grabs an unopened beer and then climbs over the side of the roof back into my bedroom window. As I lay on my back, I look up to the sky and tell myself he's right. Heidi doesn't deserve any of this. She's innocent. It's Liam and me who have my mom's blood dripping from our hands.

I must have dozed off because when I wake up the city lights are illuminating the rooftop. I sit up and rub my eyes, trying to adjust them to the darkness when I hear a familiar voice. "So, this is where you've been hiding out for the last week?"

Tara's sitting up next to me leaning against the side of the brick chimney, her legs in front of her, crossed at the ankles. I gaze up and down her body as if she's a figment of my imagination, but I stop and focus on her wrists, bandages wrapped around them, and reality slams right into me. Tara must notice, because she quickly tucks them into her lap and says, "The scars are just tender."

I nod, not really knowing what to say and hoping this awkward moment slips away. She must feel weird about it too because she quickly changes the subject and asks, "So, what's up for tonight? Any parties worth going to, or do you want to have our own little celebration up here?" She smiles and shakes her purse, a pill bottle very evidently rattling.

I stare at her with confusion and ask, "I thought you were drying out. Anyway, Brady seems to have you under lock and key."

She laughs and brushes my cheek with her hand. "Brady means well, but it's so easy to sway his attention another way. I mean just have Cassidy show up and I'm scot-free. Besides, I get the whole addiction thing. I mean I can go off these any time I want." She flicks her hand as if the idea of addiction is completely absurd. "You know, I did last a whole two weeks without them and didn't crave them once."

She slides in closer next to me and brushes the back of her hand down my chest to my stomach. "But what I did crave was this." Her hand is unzipping my jeans and sinks into my boxers. She grabs hold of me and begins to slide up and down my erection.

I tilt my head back and let out a small moan reveling in being able to finally feel something again. In the two weeks that Tara's been gone, I've gone through the motions just to get through each day, even laying off the pills to bring the feelings back. I think back to a few hours ago when Liam dropped the word love, and all I can do is roll my eyes. *What the fuck is love anyway?* It sure as hell doesn't exist for me, anymore but I'll settle for what this is with Tara, because for the first time since that night my dad called from the hospital, I can finally feel something. And, *fuck*, right now it feels pretty damn good.

Once Tara gets me amped up, I drag the shorts off of her body and slip my fingers beneath the soft lace of her thong. I tease her for a bit sliding my fingers in and out of her, listening to a few moans escape her. I whisper, "No need to crave anymore. Take what you want. I'm right here."

Tara reaches for my T-shirt and lifts it over my head throwing it behind us, while I wiggle out of my already unbuttoned jeans. I remove the rest of her clothes, finding a condom tucked into her bra. I lift it up in front of her and she laughs and shrugs her shoulders. "I grabbed it from your bedroom on my way up." I grin and roll her over, gathering all of our clothes into a pile beneath her to lay on. I allow myself to succumb yet again to the force that is Tara. I pin her arms above her head and feel the cloth of the bandages around her wrists, realizing I'm part of the reason for them. I know damn well that with her I'm in the danger zone, that whatever this is between us will probably one day destroy me. But does it really matter anyway? Hope is a distant memory and when you've already sold your soul, there's no one that can save you.

****

The last two weeks of July seem to be back to the same way the summer began with Tara—hiding away from the rest of world. Brady has even given up on keeping her away from me, or maybe he's just so wrapped up in his own all day drinking fests to really care what we're doing. Although, I know Tara's been slipping more and more pills each day, making her idea about addiction completely bogus, but who am I to judge. Even though I gave up on the pills, I drown my problems into plenty of other vices.

Sitting on her bed, counting my most recent winnings from another Skate Wars, Tara comes up behind me and leans over me hooking her arms at my chest. She moves her face in closer and starts kissing my neck. I flinch, trying to push her away by shrugging my shoulder at her. She doesn't get the message because she attempts it again, but this time I place the money in my bag and turn my attention to her. "Come on, Tara. I'm in the middle of something here."

She glares at me, her eyes enraged, but the cloudiness in them only tells me she's high. She spits out, "Only when it's convenient for you, right Cole? I don't see you pushing me away when I'm sucking you off."

She rushes over to her dresser and pulls open the top drawer. She pulls out a half empty pill bottle and holds it up to me. She rushes back to me and jabs the pill bottle continually into my ribs, unleashing her anger physically now. She slurs out, "And I don't see you pushing me away when you need these from me." She throws the pill bottle across the room. It hits the mirror and lands on top of the dresser it came from.

Confused by her accusations and the scene going down between us, I back away from her with my hands up in surrender. "I haven't touched those in weeks. That's all you, sweetheart."

Tara charges me and I lose my balance and fall onto the bed. She jumps on top of me and starts to throw weak punches at me, not landing any of them. I manage to catch her wrists in my grasp, stopping her assault on me. My fingers graze over the scars on her wrists and guilt washes over me. I let go and pull her down to me and start kissing her, wild and crazed. Her rage quickly fades, and her hands are all over me, restless and in search of a way under my clothes.

Suddenly, she lets out a scream and her body is lifted off of me. I see her dad toss her backward into the dresser, her head hitting the handle on one of the drawers. She's crying and curls up into a ball right as Derek drives his foot into her legs, which she is holding to her chest. She begs and scream, "Please, stop...please, dad...stop."

Derek spots the pill bottle on her dresser and grabs them. He bends down to her and shakes them in her face. "Aww, do you need these now? For the pain, you weak little bitch." He unscrews the cap and pours them out onto the floor, crushing them with his foot, while Tara is peeking out from her hands watching Derek ruin the last of her stash. "You're pathetic, Tara."

Tara sobs out, "Please stop...Daddy....Please."

Derek looks at her for a moment, a look of disgust on his face, and launches his fist to the side of her face. She cries out at the force in which it lands, and I see a welt already growing on her cheek.

In that instant, I leap off the bed and tackle Derek to the floor. Not expecting me to come at him, I'm able to pin him, straddle over him, with his arms trapped under my knees. I start to unleash on him, throwing punches at his face. Tara's screaming out for help, and suddenly, two arms wrap around my chest and pull me off him. There is a trickle of blood dripping down from his eye and a definite bruise forming on top of his cheekbone. Brady looks from me to Derek to Tara and then back again. "What the fuck just happened?" he asks.

Derek, with spite written all over his smug face gets up off the floor and wipes the blood off his face with the back of his hand. He glances at Tara who's being tucked behind Brady, and then he glowers at me, but there's no mistaken the smirk hidden in his expression. "Well, son, I walked into the room and this piece of trash had Tara pinned down and he was smacking her." He points to me and I hear a gasp escape from Tara. "So, of course, I jumped in to protect your sister and he attacked me." He raises his voice in anger. "And I find out he was after these." He reaches down and picks up a piece of pill that's not completely crushed up. "Brady, this hoodlum has Tara hooked to this poison again."

Tara is quietly sobbing behind Brady, and he's got his arm in front of her seemingly trying to keep everyone in the room away. Derek continues to rant lies, "Look what damage this street trash did to our family? Tara's already bruised enough without him interfering in our lives. And then he attacks me just because I'm trying to protect my daughter."

I'm in awe at the fucking lies spewing from his mouth, and I'm stunned to silence. Tara's sobbing louder and louder and Brady is trying to calm her.

Derek speaks directly to Brady, "Do me a favor and clean up this mess. Flush the remnants of the pills and do *whatever* you need to get him the hell out of my house."

Brady just nods, still looking around the room at the scene.

Derek brushes past me, leans into my ear and

whispers, "You just bought your one-way ticket out of this town."

Under my breath, I mumble out, "It was worth it."

His icy glare cuts right through me as he stomps out of the room and slams the door behind him, causing the frames on the wall to shake.

Tara lets out a louder sob and tries to get to me but Brady's body is blocking. He grabs her shoulders and looks at her in the face bending down a little to be at her level. "You know he has to go, Tara. Let him go."

His words seem to hold more meaning than what's on the surface because Tara stops struggling. She turns around and collapses to her bed her head in her hands, while Brady picks up my belongings for me. He tosses them over to me and shrugs his shoulders, saying, "Probably a good idea to head out."

I nod in understanding and head toward her bedroom door.

Brady calls out, "Hey, Cole." I turn back around. "Why don't you climb out the window, instead? Even a fall would be safer than that way."

I walk to the window and push it open. As I start to climb out, I stop and look back to Tara who's curled up with stuffed giraffe on her bed, her teary eyes set on me. I stare at her, not really able to comprehend what I'm feeling. But whatever it is, it doesn't matter. I am ruined in this city, and Derek Chambers will make sure of it.

As I begin to climb out, Brady leans out over me and says, "Hey, Cole, don't wait for the fires to burn out on their own, extinguish the hell out of them."

Confused, I nod and wave goodbye before I climb down to the small patch of grass below her window. I know I can't go home, just in case one of Derek Chamber's shady cop friends decides to show up on his behalf, besides there's nothing there for me anymore. I walk a few blocks to the skate park where Liam and I used to spend hours as kids trying to land the newest trick. He used to get so pissed because I somehow always figured it out after a few tries, and he would just struggle with the easy tricks.

The park is empty, especially since Skate Wars attract the skaters to other places, but I, with my skateboard, sit on the edge on the highest ramp and look across it. I think about the fires in my life, the ones I started, the ones that seem to just start burning on their own, and I wonder if it's even possible to smother them for good. I stand up and place my foot on the back of my board tilting up. I count to three in my head and hop on the board, soaring down the ramp, letting go of some of the pain for the moment. But for now, all I can do is let it ride.

Chapter Twenty-One

Present

"These wetsuits are pretty sick, Carter." Dusty is staring in the three-panel mirror at Carter's shop, turning his body all around as he checks out the team suits he designed for The Winter Qualifiers. "I mean, seriously Car, these are tight. Sweet design." Dusty lets out a *whoop* as he continues to admire himself.

As Carter finishes fitting the hood on my head, he looks over his shoulder to Dusty and says, "This distributor knows his shit when it comes to winter suits. He dominates the whole northwest territory where the waters are frigid." Carter rarely takes full credit for his work, even though his designs and builds have completely upgraded the East Coast surf scene, mirroring that of the West Coast and even Australia and New Zealand.

I peek in the mirror for myself. "Carter, your designs are insane. I mean the east coasters have never seen this before."

His cheeks redden, probably embarrassed by all the compliments, and just shrugs his shoulders. "Thanks, man. It's the next best thing to being in the water on competition days."

Carter was going all-pro a few years ago until an accident that ended his surfing career. He got into teaching and building boards after that, and somehow created a brand for himself with his shops. I have no doubt his business will become an empire, especially with the response he's gotten in his first year here.

"But, I definitely would rather be doing this than surfing forty-degree waters in March." He points to Dusty then to me. "If I didn't know you, I'd think your certifiably crazy."

We laugh, and Dusty challenges him. "I give you a year until you try one of your new fancy boards in the cold waters. If you can get past the first shock, you'll never want to come back to shore."

I nod my head in agreement with Dusty. "He's right. Ain't no other feeling like it. The winter swells are indescribable."

Carter just surrenders to us because since the season has changed, we've been on him to come out with us for winter training. We're starting to break him down, especially after he's watched Gavin do it all winter. But, I always joke he still has the California thin blood and he needs maybe one more winter become one of us.

A few customers come in and Carter heads downstairs to take care of them. I strap my booties on and shout over to Dusty, "Stop flexing and let's head out to test these suits. We're only two days away from Qualifiers."

Dusty throws one of his wetsuit gloves at me and laughs. "Not my fault, I have to flex to look somewhat like you. I mean how can I be buff Cole Stevens without a little help?"

I smile and shake my head, throwing the glove back at him. "if you're lucky, maybe one day I'll teach you."

Dusty secures the glove over his hand and takes one more look at his reflection. "All right, let's do this." He approaches me and gives me a high-five. "Glad to have you back, man."

"It's good to be back."

I know it's Dusty's way of referring to these last few weeks. With Tara tucked away in rehab and Liam busy with the financials of the clinic, my life has found balance again. Training has been intense with the upcoming competition, and I've immersed myself in the waves once again, the same way I did seven years ago when I arrived. The only difference is that this time, I have the girl who I saw in the cafeteria that day, the one who forever changed me in front of the lockers.

After spending the morning training, I spend the afternoon in my office finishing some contracts for a few new businesses starting up Memorial Day Weekend. Since Dusty won The Atlantic Classic last year, and Carter's business has been getting national recognition, Sea City has been in the news a lot, causing more and more people to want to come here, especially during the summer season. I also think it has helped Camryn find her love for this place once again, and has shown Gav what home really is.

I finish up with the contracts quickly because I'm anxious to get to Gavin's school to pick him up. Ever since the day I forgot to get him and, instead, was at the bar with Tara, I made sure to be at his school on time, if not earlier than dismissal. He never found out about that day, thanks to Heidi and Dusty, but I will never let myself forget it. I vow to never be that dad to him again, to never be that husband to Camryn. *Anything to protect them.*

I arrive in the pick-up line early, my Jeep being the first car there. I take the time to read through a couple of emails on my phone regarding some possible new properties to invest in. Out of the corner of my eye, I notice a figure coming out of the main office door, however, he turns the opposite direction of where my car is parked. His short stature resembles that of Liam's, and the sandy hair flipped out beneath his hat could be him as well. But, I try to think why he would possibly be here? He doesn't have kids, and, at this point, he doesn't know many people in town. Moments later, I spot Heidi leading a few of her students outside toward the parent line that is now filling up with cars. My breath hitches and the idea that Liam came here to see my sister comes to the forefront of my mind. I'm having memories of the past, ones that I would like to forget, of the days where Liam poisoned her mind against me, days where I was falling apart, and she chose Liam. As I see her approach, with Gavin's hand in hers, my negative thoughts melt away. My mind must be playing evil tricks because we both got past that part of our lives when we moved here. We somehow let it all go and found what truly matters to us in Dusty and Camryn.

Gavin stops in front of the Jeep and looks up to the sky, squinting his eyes in confusion. I jump out to help him get in the back seat and buckled up. "Gav, what's up? Are you okay?"

He continues to look around, "Yea, I just want to see what it looks like when the sky falls."

Heidi gasps and lets out a laugh. She grabs Gavin and tickles forcing unstoppable giggles from him. Heidi explains, "What I said, Mr. Gavin, was that my brother here is first in carline three days in a row. The sky must be falling because your dad is never on time to anything."

Gavin nods at the explanation, but I'm not sold that he understands it still because he's still looking up suspiciously to the sky.

I defend myself to these two. "Well, it so happens that when it comes to my boy, I will make it a point to be on time. Besides, I need his help at the grocery store." I look to Gavin and ask, "We're in charge of dessert for family dinner tonight, bud. So, I need your baking expertise."

He excitedly jumps up into the Jeep and starts shouting out different desserts he wants to make. I buckle him in and turn back toward Heidi as she is helping another student into the car behind me. Still bugged out with the nagging vision of Liam walking out of the school, I question my sister. "Hey, Heidi, did anyone come see you today?"

She gives a quick wave to the parent in the car behind me, and then looks at me seeming a bit taken back by my question. She furrows her eyebrows and repeats my question, "Did anyone come to see me today?"

Getting a little annoyed, I snap back, "Yea, Heidi. That was my question." I feel the anger rise, thinking that my previous notion might be true. "Let me be more specific. Did I just see Liam walking out of the school a few minutes ago?"

Heidi starts to stutter, "Umm…well…it's not what you think." She begins to wave all the cars lined up behind me out of the parking lot. I give Gavin a notepad and paper from my briefcase to make a list, while I try to get more information out of Heidi.

She finally returns her attention back to me and says, "I'm helping him with something for the clinic."

I bite back, "Helping him? What the hell is that supposed to mean?"

Gavin interrupts, calling me out, "Language, Daddy."

I smile into the rearview mirror and say, "Sorry, buddy. I'll throw ten cents into the swear jar when we get home." He gives me quick thumbs up. "Soon, you're gonna catch up to Aunt Lila."

I laugh, "Woah there, little man. Now, I think that's impossible." He giggles and nods with agreement managing to strip away any anger that was building in me.

I look back at my sister and she's staring off into space rubbing her thumbs together. It seems like she's nervous, so I let up a bit. "Heidi, what are you helping him with?"

She sighs and explains, "Cole, It's really nothing. They are designing the children's wing for the clinic and Liam thought it would be great idea to use children's art as part of the decorations in the hallways and rooms. So, he thought maybe my students could help out with making some of it. And he figured it would be a great surprise for Jack and Camryn to see Gavin's work hanging in the clinic."

I stare at her, my mouth gaped, and completely horrified by my initial annoyance. "I'm sorry, Heids. I wish he wasn't part of something so special for my family, but involving Gav and your other students is a really great idea." I look in the rearview mirror to see

Gavin and he's preoccupied with writing a grocery list. I lower my voice and say, "I'm just having a hard time with him being back and such an important part of my wife's career and dream." I shake my head in disappointment. "I just wish he would've stayed the hell in in my past life."

Gavin's little voice calls out from the back seat. "Language, Daddy. That's another ten cents for the jar."

"Woops, sorry again, bud."

I see him shrug his shoulders. "It's okay. Just more money for our trip to Disney World." His cute lisp when he says world brings a smile to my face.

"Just have Aunt Lila come over more often, and we'll get there before you know it." I joke with him regarding the swear jar he and Camryn set up as a vacation fund.

He gives me a thumbs up, and I return my attention to Heidi. "Just watch your back with him."

In a timid voice, she responds, "People can change, Cole. I mean, look at you now. Maybe he deserves his second chance."

I shut down her attempt to save's Liam's reputation. "He's the same con artist he was ten years ago, manipulating everyone and everything for his own benefit. Don't fall for his shit. We've come too far to go back there."

Heidi just nods, probably realizing how useless it is to convince me any differently about Liam. He may have shown up in my present life, but he's been long gone in my past. He became dead to me the day I turned fifteen.

I give one last check on Gavin's seatbelt and we

wave to Heidi as I drive out of the school parking lot. My mind is reeling at Heidi's idea of giving Liam another chance. In the past, she was always so soft when it came to him, but she never really saw the real Liam, the one I knew. The gambler, the manipulator, the liar, the selfish shit who only cared about himself. He proved it the night our mom died when he made her go out to save his ass from yet another problem he got himself in to.

Gavin's voice brings me back to the present. "Daddy, this is the last family dinner until after your big surf competition, right?" I nod at his question, and peek in the rearview mirror to see a mischievous expression taking over him.

After pulling into a parking spot at the grocery store, I turn around in my seat and ask, "What are you planning back there, little man?" I laugh knowing that he has something up his sleeve.

A wide grin stretches across his face. "Well, I was thinking some strawberry shortcake with lots of whipped cream."

I begin to break the news that it may be difficult to find strawberry shortcake in March and that we might have to rethink our dessert choice when it hits me what he's really thinking. I burst out in laughter, "So, are you thinking it's time for an occasional food fight?"

Gavin excitedly claps his hands and squeals in excitement. When Camryn moved back, she continued the tradition that her mom started for her as a young girl. Family dinners were every Thursday and Sunday evening and there were only three rules to follow: a crowded kitchen, loud conversation, and the occasional food fight. We've continued this tradition adding more and more family and friends and sometimes doing it more days than just the two. However, I'll never forget my very first one. Gav had his first surf lesson with me and he ended up inviting me to family dinner that night. I could see how nervous Camryn was about it, but I knew it was my way in and I wasn't about to let that pass me by. Well, I brought the dessert, strawberry shortcake, and it didn't take long for Lila to decide it was time to enact rule number three. In my opinion, it was perfect timing. The sound of Gavin's laughter that night amazed me, and I knew then I needed it in my life.

"Good plan. Let's see what we can do to get the baker to make us a double-sized cake." I hop out of the car and open up the back door, extending my hand out to help Gavin hop out.

He jokes, "About the baker...I got this, Daddy. Most people think I'm cute." He attempts to wink at me.

Jokingly, I ask, "What? Am I not cute enough?"

He waves his hand at me. "I guess so. Mommy sure thinks so." He points his finger in his mouth pretending to gag himself. "I mean I always hear her and Aunt Lila calling you and Uncle Carter spicy."

Confused I ask, "Spicy? What do you mean?

He shrugs his shoulders. "Yea, spicy, like the pepper."

I let out a howl of laughter. "Oh, you mean hot." I love this kid more and more every day.

He blushes and after we stop in front of the bakery counter he looks up at me. "Same thing. They're called cinnamons. That's what Aunt Heidi taught me."

"You're right, bud. Spicy and hot are synonyms.

And I like that I'm spicy according to your mom." He furthers his gagging motion by adding the upchucking sound to it.

Happy with my response, he smiles his toothless grin at me and then returns to the task at hand — to schmooze the baker into making a strawberry shortcake. Twenty minutes later, we are leaving the store with an Angel Food cake transformed into Gavin's strawberry vision. His eyes are lit up with excitement as he walks out of the store with the box in his hands. I'm impressed with the little man's skills, and I'm thinking I might need to start worrying now about those teenage years. We head home in excitement knowing that not only are we celebrating tonight with a family dinner, but an epic food fight awaits.

Chapter Twenty-Two

Present

The sun is shining, but it doesn't do much to mask the brisk wind that is blowing across the beach. Today is Winter Qualifiers, and Dusty and I came up to the beach early to stretch and warm up our muscles. However, with Carter's wetsuit already making me sweat, I don't think a warmup is needed. I know how much he hates the cold, but goddamn, these suits aren't letting anything in.

While Dusty helps me with a few stretches he taught me while I was with him in physical therapy last summer, he confesses, "I'm stoked you're here, man."

"I know. The Quals are a sweet competition. Will say it over and over again, but there is nothing better than being out in the winter waves."

Dusty nods. "And no doubt that the disappearance of a certain little leech helped with your training the past month. I mean I hate to even bring her up today, but I hope you see the difference it makes for you."

I know Dusty is right about Tara. Both Milena and him would constantly be in my ear about her, but back then I was so screwed up and I didn't really listen. Then, once she became pregnant, I had committed myself to her, and even the shit storm she brought with her. Besides, I'm man enough to admit I'm reason for many of Tara's issues.

"Damn right it's been different. With her being out of touch in rehab, I have definitely felt a sense of relief."

Dusty adds, "See what I've been telling you all these years? I knew the minute I met her she'd suck the life out of you. Damn well came close to it, too. If not for Milena's secret, little trail to Camryn you'd still be with Tara feeling responsible for every one of her issues."

While everything Dusty says is true, he wasn't around to see the damage I did to Tara before we were in Sea City. He didn't see all that I *was* responsible for. "I always knew it, man. The first day I met her I knew she was trouble. But there's no denying I was trouble too. That I am responsible for some of the shit she feels."

Dusty is forcefully shaking his head at me. "This is the last thing I will say about that bitch because I refuse to let her ruin another big day for you. Cole, you were fifteen when you two met, you were broken and desperate, and poor teenage decisions were made by both of you. But there's a point when you need to grow up from that. When the high school bullshit is put to rest. It's called adulthood and she never seemed to get there. And for that, you owe her nothing."

While I see where Dusty is coming from, I can't let go of the guilt I hold. I made a choice to be with Tara back then, knowing full well we were toxic together. I'm man enough to admit that I was part of the problem, part of Tara's madness. By the time Dusty and Milena helped me get control of my life again, I was too far in with Tara, tethered to her through Rose.

I secure the straps on my gloves, tucking them tightly under the sleeves of my wetsuit. I peer out ahead, to the dark mass of sea that is left untouched for the moment, and confess, "I never really had the chance to say thank you for this."

Dusty steps up next to me, our eyes fixed on the ocean, our playground, our very own solace. He throws his fist out to me and says, "Bro, all I did was forge the path. You found your own way."

I return the fist pump and pull my wetsuit hood up over my head. "You ready to do this or what?"

Dusty jokingly asks, "Do you mean, am I ready to kick your ass in qualifiers?" He laughs. "I'm always ready for that."

"I think you're forgetting one thing, man." I pick up my board from the sand. "You know those tricks you used to win the Classic last year? He nods. "Well, they're mine."

His laughter howls, echoing across the vast stretch of beach and as we start toward the ocean, our boards in tow. The quick shot of cold hits me the second I dive in, but nothing can overshadow the warmth the waves bring me. I paddle out, through the breakers, with only one more practice run between me and my comeback.

After a solid practice, Dusty and I make our way down to Wavers Beach, the spot for all of the big competitions. The crowds are already forming as they huddle into the heated tents that are set up on the sand. I immediately spot Gavin, sporting a "Team Cole and Dusty" winter hat. He insisted our team logo be positioned against the blue and red Spiderman pattern. So, we went with it, even as far as Carter designing our wetsuits with that same pattern. Besides it makes my son happy; it no doubt made us stand out among the competition.

When Gavin spots us walking up, he takes off in our direction, with Camryn and Heidi a few steps behind him. Camryn's dark hair under her winter hat gets caught in the wind, blowing back to expose the pinkness in her cheeks. Her smile widens as our gazes meet, and I can't help but to sneak a peek down her body. Even bundled in a winter coat, I can make out her perfect curves, the ones that accentuate every part of her body, the ones I love to grab hold of. Gavin wraps his arms around my waist and squeals out, "Daddy, Daddy, the waves are huge! I counted between the swells and it's the biggest number ever!"

I scoop him up in my arms and kiss his cheek because he's just so damn cute. I love that he's watching the ocean so closely and knows his surf mechanics. No doubt he'll look to the sea for his own peace one day. I squeeze him and say, "I know, kiddo. Uncle Dusty and I just got in from our practice run and the waves are the best." I place him back down on the ground and whisper in his ear, "I think we got this, buddy. What do you think?"

Gavin cups his chin with his hand and peers out toward the ocean, as if inspecting the scene. He looks to the left, then to the right, and then back up to me. "Well, from what I can see, I think..." He looks from side to side again and clearing his throat and trying to act professional. "As I was saying, I think you totally got this." A huge smile stretches across his face.

I pull him into a hug, grateful for this moment with my son, the one I fought so hard for to be mine. As I hold him in an embrace, I realize how much my comeback to surfing, after my injury, is for him. I want him to see that no matter how hard you fall, you need to keep getting back up.

After I let Gavin loose to go play with a few kids he knows from school, I stand back up to the beautiful sight of Camryn. She's watching me, with a glint of tears in her eyes. I draw her into me and place my lips over hers. I take as much in of her as I can stand on this cold, very crowded beach. She places her hand on my chest and leans back, away from our kiss and says. "I love that you love him."

I place my hand on her stomach over her winter coat. "Well, I love that he lets me love him." I lower my voice so only Camryn can hear. "And the three of you are everything I need and want."

I pull her in for another tender kiss, tasting the cherry of her chap stick, yet another *Camryn-thing* that makes me love her and want her even more. Breaking apart from our very obvious public affection, I tease, "How about we skip this and have our own little competition at home?" I lean in and whisper into her ear, "You know we can try to break the record of how many times I can make you scream my name."

Her cheeks flush a deeper red, and her smile takes on a devious form. I love tempting her and opening up that sexual side of her that has been hidden so long behind the mistrust of men and the realities of raising a child on her own. Every intimate moment together is new, raw, and fucking perfect.

She cups my cheeks in her hands, her wool gloves bringing warmth to my stinging skin. "While that is an extremely enticing offer, I didn't nurse you back from your injury last year to let you miss this chance."

"Nursed me? Oh, I thought that was you allowing me to perform every sexual desire I've ever had on you."

Camryn squeals, quickly covering her open mouth with her gloved hand. "What am I going to do with you, Mr. Stevens?"

"Well, I can think of a million things, Mrs. Stevens." I steal one more kiss from my wife before Dusty is pulling me away.

"Break it up, love birds, it's time for some serious winning to happen for Team Dusty and Cole."

I joke, "Ahh, you mean Team *Cole* and Dusty, right? I mean I do carry us, old man."

Dusty gives me a playful punch in the arm. "Only one year older and one year more experienced." He calls back to Heidi, "Right, Heidi?"

She shakes her head and laughs, "You got that right."

I cup my hands over my ears, "Dude, that's my sister."

The four of us howl in laughter and it's nice to feel the easiness again, to feel like I might have dodged those innermost demons yet again. After hugs, kisses and wishes of good luck from Heidi, Camryn, and Gavin, Dusty and I make our way to the warm-up tent, while they head to the promo tent, where Carter's shop will be selling merchandise form the store.

Today, Dusty is really only surfing for a better run time. After winning the Atlantic Classic back in August, he automatically earned a spot back to this year. He begins to stretch me out and run through our visual exercises out loud. I keep my focus on the waves, watching them rise, roll, and then finally crash. As I feel the calm set over me, my name is announced over the speaker. With Dusty urging me forward, I adjust my wetsuit hood and gloves, grab my board, and head down the path that leads to the start line. Dusty walks with me, talking through possible scenarios, and throwing out tips as he sees the other surfers in my heat. Before the horn sounds, I turn toward the merchandise tent and immediately spot Camryn and Gavin, who's on top of Carter's shoulders, with their eyes set on me. I blow a kiss and give Gavin a thumbs-up, a sign between us that has always meant one thing—victory. It started the day he conquered his fear of the huge boardwalk Ferris wheel, and ever since then a thumbs-up has been our thing. He flashes his toothless grin and raises his own thumb to the air. With those two giving me everything I need, I turn around and start jogging to line. I get set and once the horn sounds, I dive in on my board and start paddling out, well ahead of the other surfers.

Because this is a winter competition, surfers are only given fifteen minutes in their heats, which is different from the Atlantic Classic thirty-minute heat times. I let a few waves pass by, the other surfers trying to make something out of them, but not really succeeding. Knowing time is ticking, I paddle sideways toward the fishing pier, and hope that something will form from there. Most of the other surfers are hugging the jetty, waiting to cash in on something there. Off in the distance, I spot a small swell beginning to form under the legs of the pier, I peek behind me to see if anyone has spotted it. With their attention focused the other way, I begin to move toward the swell, trying to place the wave once it forms. I stop paddling and begin to set, the swell rising higher than I had anticipated. I faintly hear the two-minute warning bell right before I stand up. The wave rolls and I'm cutting and carving, blocking my opponents with the speed I build up. I ride the wave all the way to the jetty, the other surfers slapping the water in frustration. As the wave breaks, I slow down and take a turn before the rocks of the jetty, finishing every bit of the wave. I pump my fist in the air, knowing it was the best run of the heat. Shortly after, the horn blares and I body board the rest of the way to shore.

Gavin is the first one I see, darting down the beach, a huge smile stretched across his face. As soon as he reaches me, he leaps in my arms as I catch him midair. He's delirious with excitement, his words tumbling out of his mouth at record speed. Camryn rushes up to us soon after, tears streaming down her face, and she throws her arms around the two of us. Seemingly overcome with emotion, she chokes out, "*Paddle to piers...*it's the very first lesson my mom would teach her students."

I tilt her chin up and brush my thumb against her wind-streaked face. "It's something I'll never forget from a woman I'll never forget." I wipe a stray tear from her and gently kiss her on the cheek where it landed.

She whispers, "I'm so proud of you. You're a fighter."

I stand for a few minutes with my family, embracing each other, the trials of the last year flashing through my mind. I couldn't have gotten through the darkness to this very moment without these two. And I never want them to have to endure that darkness again.

Anything to protect them.

We start our way back up the beach toward the merchandise tent to watch Dusty's run. With the final heat at the starting line, I catch his attention and flash him a hang ten sign with my hand. He acknowledges my sign, and lips to me, *"Paddle to piers."* I nod and flash him a smile.

Once back at the tent, I place Gavin down. Dusty follows the same advice and manages to already catch a killer wave within his first few minutes out there. Carter tosses me our team swim parka and pats me on the shoulder. "Epic…fucking epic."

Lila cuts into our *bro-moment* and congratulates me. "You killed it out there. Who would've thought Milena would still be making our decisions for us?" We all laugh, knowing that Milena has, in some way, had control over each one of us.

I spot Heidi, who is standing at the corner of the tent, facing ocean toward Dusty's run, but looking a little distant. I walk over to her, and peer out to see that Dusty is far ahead of his heat in both time and waves caught.

"He has a gift, you know" I look over, but her eyes remain glued on Dusty.

"So, do you, Cole." She smiles, yet I catch the glimpse of unrest in her as she's hugging her arms close to her waist, rubbing her gloved hands against them.

"Are you okay, Heidi? You seem off lately. Even Dusty mentioned it a few times."

She turns to me, but quickly masks any turmoil she may be feeling with a smile. "I'm fine, Cole. Just crazy happy for you. Your life is amazing." She looks back toward the ocean, but I know when Heidi is lying. She never was good at it and I can always call her out on it.

"I don't buy it, sis. What are you keeping from me? From Dusty?" I don't mean to be forceful, but I can't help it. I hate to see the ones I love struggling with something.

The announcer calls the two-minute warning on Dusty's heat, and Heidi returns her attention to the water. She shrugs her shoulders and says, "I just kind of feel stuck, that's all. Dusty is going to be traveling the world for surfing, and you, you're moving on with your family, your career, your surfing. And don't get me wrong, I am so, so happy it's all happening. It's all I ever wanted for you. I just feel like I'm left behind in all of this." She instantly shakes her head and pulls herself back together. "What am I doing? Throwing myself a pity party? I'm good, Cole. I promise. Just going to be missing Dusty when he heads out on tour after the summer."

While I am not sure I believe her, I tell her I understand and let her know that Camryn and I will always be here for her, especially when Dusty goes on the Champions Tour. The horn blows, and my attention draws back to the beach where the run times are being displayed, placing Dusty in first place ahead in his heat. He is holding his fist up in the air as he makes his way to shore. I see Gavin on his way down to congratulate him, Camryn catching my eye as she follows behind him. Just as I step out of the tent to join them, I peek back to grab Heidi's hand to drag her down to the celebration, but her attention isn't on Dusty now. Instead, she's staring off in the distance toward the rock jetty, and there looking back at her is a part of our past who won't seem to leave us alone. Anger with a twang of worry stir within me—Liam's definitely not here for the victory party.

Chapter Twenty-Three

Past

I hang out in the park until sunset, letting my skateboard take me away from the reality of the situation. I attacked Derek Chambers. *What the fuck was I thinking?* He's got enough connections in this city to make me disappear without a trace left of me, but as I glide up and down the ramps, I come to grips with what I did. There's no telling what damage he would've done to Tara if I didn't step in, and given the fragile state she's in, it's better that I became his target. Besides, what can he possibly take from me? Everything that mattered is already gone.

I take the long way home from the park, walking up the crowded sidewalks of South Street. People are milling about everywhere, throwing back drinks and eating dinner at the many restaurants and bars. Lines form outside of the clubs, girls in shiny tops with tight skirts hanging on to guys wearing tight-ass shirts over their ripped muscles. My mom used to love coming here to people watch and drink one of those frozen drinks from *Bourbon*, the bar on the corner. She would drag my dad, Heidi, and me here on any random night in the summer, and we would just sit outside for hours making up crazy stories about anyone we saw. I remember the way she'd tilt her head back in laughter when me or Heidi added a detail to the story.

Now, as I make my way past that same bar she loved so much, I feel nothing but hatred for these people who are laughing, drinking their frozen drinks, and probably making up a story about me as I walk through with my skateboard. They don't deserve it, not when she doesn't get to. With the anger that seemed to have left at the skate park setting in again, I hurry across the street and turn down the first alleyway to avoid any more people. I set my skateboard down and hop on it riding the bumps and grooves in the unpaved back roads. I feel like everywhere I go in this city, memories just pop up on this reel in my head, and all it does is spur the rage inside me. I picture those pills Derek crushed up with his foot in Tara's bedroom, and begin to crave the numbness they can bring. I skate faster and harder, trying to shake the desire, the need that's building. After Tara's time in the hospital, I made a vow to myself to stop hiding behind the pain, to endure everything I deserve to feel. No fucking way will I allow myself to crack, and definitely not at the hands of Derek Chambers.

As I approach the back of my house, I notice Heidi sitting on the recliner on the back patio, hugging her knees into her chest. Her noticeably red, blotchy face against her bright blonde hair is evidence that she's been crying. Even though things between us have been rough lately, it still kills me to see her upset. And if that asshole, Liam, had anything to do with it, I will tear him apart, especially given the mood I'm in tonight. When I reach the patio, her head snaps up, and she stares at me bringing her hand over her open mouth. Within a second, her tears start flowing. Startled by her breakdown, I sit down on the edge of the recliner next to her and pull her into an embrace.

In between sobs, she chokes out, "I've been looking for you all day."

Confused on why she's crying I try to calm her. "Just hanging at the skate park. No big deal."

Her eyes widen in what looks like anger, and she hops up from the recliner and hovers over me. She wags her finger in my face, the tears still streaming down hers, and shouts, "Everyone I know in this godforsaken city is talking. Talking about how Derek Chambers found drugs on you, ones you were pushing Tara back into after her coming out of the hospital clean. Talking about how you beat him up for them. Talk, talk, talk. That's all I'm hearing." She collapses back on the recliner next to me, her tears now in steady stream, her sobs shaking her entire body. "What's going on? This isn't you, Cole."

I place my arm across her shoulder and pull her into me, trying to at least stop the tears from streaming. I think about how shitty of a brother I've been toward her this last year, how much pressure I've put on her for every decision she's made since our mom died. As I wallow in my own anger and self-pity, I've failed to remember that my sister lost her mom, the one woman who would be there with her through her teenage breakups, who would help her plan her wedding one day. The selfish prick that I am has only thought about what I've lost and the pain I've been feeling since she's been gone.

"Don't listen to them. You know it's all lies, just made up shit by people that don't have anything better to do with their lives."

She wipes her eye with the back of her hand. "What about the drugs? Is that true? I mean you have been drinking a lot since mom died."

I sigh, knowing I can't lie to my sister, but not really wanting her to know about what I've really become. "I stopped the pills weeks ago, after Tara went into the hospital. They were just prescription drugs, something to take the edge off." I shrug at my confession.

Heidi cringes at my confession but calmly continues, "And what about Tara's dad? Did you attack him?"

She looks at me like a wide-eyed child while she waits for my answer. "It wasn't like that. I didn't *attack* him."

Her mouth gapes open and a low shriek escapes from her.

"Listen, the douchebag was going after Tara. I stepped in to try to stop him from hurting her. Then, Brady showed up and broke it all up. I jetted and landed at the skate park to unwind for the rest of the day."

She nods slowly, looking like she is trying to process it all. "Cole, what were you thinking? Derek Chambers practically owns this city. He can destroy you"

I pause and just stare off in the direction of our house. Some cushions from the outdoor furniture are missing and the umbrella over the table is ripped and faded. Flower pots that line the patio and the window boxes are all empty, once full of color. Ivy climbs up the brick wall of the house, overgrown and blanketing the rain spout that trims the edge of the wall. Our home, no longer the envy of the neighborhood, no longer full of life, is now just a constant reminder that she's gone.

Feeling that pain of losing her wells up again in my chest, I quietly confess, "There's nothing left to destroy." I slowly turn my head away from the house back to Heidi. "There's nothing more that Derek Chambers can take from me that matters."

Heidi nods, tears still pooling in her eyes. She leans closer into me and wraps her arms around my waist, clasping her hands together. She rests her head against my shoulder and says, "But there's *so much* he could take from me."

"Cole. Heidi. You out there?" Our dad's roaring voice interrupts our brother-sister moment. And for once, he isn't slurring.

Between his nightly drinking binges and my own distance from everyone, I'm surprised, almost startled, that he's looking for us. Heidi must feel the same way because she jumps at the sound of his voice. We look at each other, confused, and neither of us answer him back.

Heidi whispers, "Did I really just hear that?"

"What the hell could he possibly want from us?" I shrug my shoulders at my own question. "A year too late, in my opinion."

Heidi flashes me a comforting smile right before our dad approaches us. He's not dressed in the ripped jeans and dirty, outstretched band T-shirt we've been accustomed to seeing this last year. Instead of his usual barhopping, whore-finding garb, he's wearing pressed jeans, a button-down shirt, and his loafer shoes, the ones my mom picked out for him to wear to some fancy party they were invited to a few years ago. His face his cleanly shaven, and his hair gelled and neatly combed back. I feel like I'm looking at a different person from the football tossing, skateboard teaching guy I used to know. Now, all I see is the one who had no qualms abandoning his children, the one who honored his wife's fallen legacy with drunken nights, random whores, and unpaid bills. The longer I look at him, the more I feel the storm inside of me build. I tense my jaw, and with clenched fists, I stand up and move toe-to-toe with him, poised and ready for battle.

Heidi must notice my seething anger because she pops up from the chair and squeezes in between me and our dad. Before I can spew any venom at him, she asks, "What's going on, Dad? I mean, is there something you need?"

Although Heidi is in the middle of us, trying to quell the fire that's rising, all I notice is my dad's glare set on me. His expression is cold, eyes full of contempt or disappointment, I can't really tell which one. Probably both. What I do know is there's no amends here, no chance for our family again.

Heidi repeats, "Dad? Dad? Did you need something?"

He turns his attention toward her and his expression softens. I even catch a shadow of a smile appear, and I can't help but feel the dagger of guilt drill deeper into me. His look of fucking disgust at me just confirms that he blames me, that he thinks I'm the reason my mom isn't here anymore.

"What's going on, Dad?" She looks up and down him at his clean-cut appearance and adds, "You look nice. Do you have plans tonight? "

"Well, actually *we* have plans tonight." He flashes a genuine grin at Heidi and continues to explain.

"We're heading to Sea City for a few days. Grandma and Grandpop have been asking to see you both for a while now."

Before Heidi can respond, I blurt out, "You've been non-existent for over a year and now you want to take a family vacation? What the hell!" Heidi reaches over to me and pinches the crook of my elbow, something she'd always do growing up when she wanted me to stop doing whatever it was that bothered her.

My dad scowls at me and snaps back, "Well, I guess there hasn't been much to celebrate in the last year, has there, Cole?" He turns to Heidi and continues, "But it's not fair to keep you away from Grandma and Grandpop and being it's another hot as hell summer in the city, I think Sea City will be the perfect getaway." He turns back to me and angrily mumbles, "Or, perhaps, a perfect hideaway for some of us."

And there it is, the real reason for this *family* getaway—all at the recommendation of Derek Chambers, I'm sure. My dad used to have balls, waving his middle finger at anyone who would mess with him. But, here he is, bowing down to that almighty douchebag, running like a scared pussy.

Noticing that Heidi clenches her fists by her side and tenses her shoulders, I hold back on saying anything in response to him, to spare her any more awkwardness that this confrontation with our dad is causing. I notice a smug look directed from my dad to me. The asshole probably thinks he shut me down, but really, I was looking out for Heidi—something I've failed to do for the last year. I stare back at him, giving a quick head nod just to prove I'm not intimidated.

He frowns at my reaction and turns around to head back in the house. Over his shoulder he calls out, "Pack your bags and be ready to leave in an hour."

The door slams and we both stare in that direction. Part of me is relieved to get the hell out of here for a little, let the smoke I caused with Tara's dad to clear. But, on the other hand, I'm pissed off that my dad is running scared from Derek Chambers. Besides, what the hell is in Sea City for us? We haven't been there for a while and, without my mom, it really isn't the same. That was her summer hideaway, *her* sacred place.

I turn toward Heidi and she's still staring at the door, tears welling in her eyes. I'm not sure what's affecting her most from all of this, but it's obviously my fault. I'm the one who got involved with Tara knowing full well how shady her dad is. I'm the one who went at Derek never considering how he would strike back. The only positive thing about hightailing it out of town is that she'll be apart from that shitbag Liam for a little while, and I'm sure that's why she's about to shed tears right now.

Attempting to show her some comfort, I say, "Don't worry. He'll pretend to be a good dad for a week, and then we'll be right back here, to the same old shit, again."

She sighs, looks over to me, and chokes out, "But I don't want the same old shit anymore."

I nod in understanding and just stare back at her, because no matter how much we try to escape it, the *same old shit* will continue to just pull us in.

Chapter Twenty-Four

Present

My head is swirling, anger seething at the sight of Liam, and then I look at the way Heidi gazes at him and it's like my pulse radiates out of me. I can't find a way to string together words at the moment, wondering what the hell is going on with him, and between them. Nine years. Nine fucking years since we've been in Sea City without a trace of Liam or anyone else who we left behind in Philadelphia. I thought she moved past whatever fucked up connection they had with each other, but given the way she's looking at him, I am dead wrong.

I let my rage take over and leave the tent, charging down the beach toward him. Heidi is yelling to me to stop, her shouts a faint plea, but I can't. I have to end whatever this is before Liam destroys more in my life. When he sees me coming, he hops up from the jetty he's leaning against and we come face to face. Every part of me wants to wreck him, wants him to feel pain from my fists. Heidi catches up to me, and she steps in between us. While she tries to catch her breath, I notice Liam's hand brush over the small of her back, and I fucking lose it. I clench my fist and pull it back, ready to unleash it on him. At that moment, a hand catches my arm and I hear the words, "Cole, own your breath."

Those simple words, the ones I once used for Camryn during her months of turmoil with Todd, instantly extinguish the fury and I drop my arms to my side. Camryn, who is behind me, wraps her arms around me, and holds me in her possession. Dusty comes up next to me, shoving his hands in the front pocket of his parka, and looks back and forth between Liam, Heidi, and me. He finally stops at Heidi, who's staring at the sand beneath her feet, and says in a tone that is unusual to his normal laid-back way, "You want to tell me just what the hell is going on here?"

Heidi shifts her weight from one foot to another and looks up to all of us, and then back to Liam. Her expression is pained, her eyebrows furrowed and a tear escaping down her cheek. Dusty, seemingly frustrated for the lack of an answer from Heidi, takes a step toward Liam and gets in his face.

"Why are you even here? I mean didn't you get the fucking point when no one called you all these years? Move the hell on."

"Is that really what you think?" Liam spits back. "Maybe you should check your facts before saying shit."

Heidi gasps and breaks out in a cry, and just as Dusty lunges at him, I catch him in my grasp and whisper, "Not worth it, Dude. You have too much riding to let him drive you into the ground. Work this out with Heidi behind closed doors."

Dusty nods, however his glare still set on Liam as I drag him away. Camryn's tending to Heidi, who's sobbing and repeatedly saying "I'm sorry."

A small crowd begins to gather around us, probably to see what all the commotion is with Dusty, who's definitely a fan favorite here. In the distance, I see Lila and Carter, who has Gavin on his shoulders. When he spots me, he points and excitedly taps Carter's head. The three of them make their way in our direction.

Once Camryn has Heidi calm she walks her over to us, and Dusty snakes his arm around her waist. The motion seems awkward with what was just exposed, and I can tell a lot of shit has to be hashed out between them tonight. Then after he's done with her, she's got some explaining to me too. But I'm letting it drop for now, especially when I see a smiley kindergartener running to me, with that excitement he always seems to possess. He jumps up in my arms and Lila follows behind him, giving Camryn the look I know all too well—the one that guarantees them a long phone call later. In an attempt to end the spectacle that's beginning to happen, Lila takes charge of the crowd and shouts, "All right, all right! You got your look at the first and second place Qualifier winners, and yes, they are quite delectable. But, the merch tent is open to get what they are wearing and so much more."

A random guy in the crowd shouts out, "You for sale in that tent? If so, I'll be there." A bunch of guys start howling in laughter.

Lila, the sassy shit-starter that she is, shuts him down immediately. "Oh honey, you couldn't afford me. And being that you came here with your little sausage party over there, I am guessing you really can't *afford* any female."

Carter yells out, "Whew, that's my girl!"

She succeeds at changing the mood as we find humor in the guy's friends taunting and teasing. Gavin stares at me looking confused, and I can only be grateful that he doesn't understand most of Lila's kid unfriendly banter.

Carter and Lila, who blows us all a kiss, start back to the tent as the crowd dissipates, some heading in that direction, and others heading off the beach to probably get into a warm place.

I shout over to Dusty, "Let's get out of here." He's whispering something to Heidi, who's staring listlessly at the ground beneath her.

"Definitely. The vibe is feeling a little murky right now." Dusty says back as he scowls at Liam who, for some reason, is still standing here staring at Heidi.

I nestle my nose into the side of Camryn's face and whisper into her ear, "Let's go home, baby. And we can celebrate this win later." I kiss her gently on her cheek, while Gavin makes puke noises.

"Sure but give me a minute. I have to take care of something first." Camryn pulls away from me and walks over to Liam, causing him to direct his attention away from Heidi and Dusty. She says something to him that I can't seem to hear over the cold wind that is blowing across the beach. His shoulders slump and he shakes his head toward the ground, his reaction defenseless, his disappointment evident. That's when I see a different Liam. Not the cocky and tough, but rather lonely and broken.

She rushes back into my arms and I pull her in. She leans over and kisses Gavin on top of his snow hat and looks up to me, smiles, and says, "All set now."

"What was that about?"

"Nothing, really. I just told Liam that my dad and I will find another sponsor for the clinic."

I guide Camryn out of my arms and turn her to face me, which breaks Gavin free to run over to Dusty and Heidi. "I don't want that for you, Camryn. I refuse to ever be the person that holds you back from your dreams. We'll make it work with Liam."

She cups my face with her gloved hands. "Well, *I* don't want this for you. And the only dream I have is *you*—you, Gav, and our baby." She pulls my face down and kisses me. "He doesn't matter, you got me? There is always another donor out there."

"I love you so much, Camryn Stevens. Not one minute goes by where I don't question how you are mine." I place my hand on the back of her head and pull her into me, claiming her mouth with mine. I pull away and ask, "Are you ready to get out of here?"

Her lips curve up and she nods. We get Gavin's attention and begin to walk away, Dusty and Heidi following behind us.

"Oh, so that's it? That's how *this* ends?" Liam arms are extended out next to him. "I continue being the bad guy and you all live your perfect little lives." We stop in our tracks and turn around to Liam who's in mid-rant. "Well, if you think I'm going to keep going like this, you're all wrong."

Dusty steps up, closing the space between them. "Just go. Go back where you came from and move the hell on. We sure as hell are going to."

Liam looks at Heidi and lips, *I'm sorry*, before he yells back, "No, not this time. Not again. Because it's time you hear. It's time Cole knows the truth." Heidi gasps and covers her mouth with her hand as she shrinks back away from everyone.

I cringe at Heidi's reaction. "That's enough, Liam.

223

No matter what you say, I wouldn't believe you anyway." I place my hand on his shoulder in attempt to calm the tension that's rising. "Just walk away, go back to your life in the city. And leave our lives alone. I think we all made it pretty clear that we don't want you here."

I turn away from attempting to take my family home finally, when he calls out, "What about me though? My family is gone. All because I've been living a lie." He backs away so that my arm drops from his shoulder. "You see I never called her that night, Cole. I never called your mom."

I stop in my tracks, Camryn urging me to ignore him, trying to pull me along off the beach. Gavin is begging to go home and complaining about his frozen toes and fingertips. But once he mentions her, once he brings up that night, my body tenses and I instantly go on guard.

I slowly turn back around and see Liam, his arms out next to him in defense. Out of the corner of my eye, Dusty is trying to calm Heidi down, who is in full sobs, and at the same time he is trying to see what is going down between me and Liam.

Through gritted teeth, I bite back, "Twelve years. Liam. Twelve years since she died, and you still can't let her rest." I wave my hand at him, brushing off his reveal. "She's gone and you can't bring her back. And no matter what bullshit you've construed in your head, she's gone, and you are one of the reasons why."

With a little more confidence, Liam steps closer. "Come on, Cole. You really believe I'm the toxic one?" He's glaring into my eyes, his hot breath spreading over my face. "Do you really want to go here?"

Before I have time to answer back, he takes a step back and addresses Dusty, Heidi, and Camryn, who's trying to shield Gavin, but not leaving my side. "You all want to know the real Cole? Because I sure as hell would love to tell you about him." He lets out an ominous laugh, like he's been waiting for this moment to come.

Camryn jumps in to my defense. "Liam, I think you're angry and need to walk away now before you regret anything."

"Regret? I have lived my life regretting, thanks to him." He points directly at me. "It's my turn now, to tell the story."

Camryn calls out to me, "Let's go, Cole. We don't have to stay for this. Let's just walk away."

But I'm frozen, never able to walk away, and my wife knows this about me. It's one of my downfalls, the one thing that would always get me into trouble.

Liam ignores Camryn and continues to expose whatever he wants to let out about me. "You think I'm so capable of hurting people, that I'm responsible for her death. What the hell, Cole? She was the closest I ever had to a mom growing up. And you think I called her that night, that I dragged her out of her sleep and needed her to save me from the betting sharks and gamblers I always seemed to get involved with? You actually think I would do that to her? Well, the truth is I didn't. I never called her, never asked anyone to help me that night. Only you. Only you to bail me out at Skate Wars." He starts to choke up, his anger driving him to tears. "I wanted to protect her, protect her from the assholes who followed me to the party, who were touching her, who were hurting her that night. That's all

225

I wanted to do. I went after them for her, and she was able to get away. But then it was three on one, and I was in trouble. She called for help. She wasn't thinking Cole. She had no clue what would happen."

I stare at him in shock, confused as to what he's telling me, or maybe just in utter disbelief of the lies he's construing. Who else would've called my mom that night? Who else would've wanted Liam to be saved?

With tears streaming down his cheeks, he confesses, "I saved Heidi that night and she saved me. But after that night, after the guilt finally sank in, I also wanted to protect her from you. To make sure you didn't turn on her, to make sure you didn't abandon her like you did me. I loved her enough to do that, and I took the shit you dealt me because she was worth it. She still is."

I look at Heidi and her reaction tells it all. Liam's telling the truth. He saved her from the party that night, and for all these years he took the fall for it to protect her from me. From the angry, out of control person I was, or maybe still am. And I'd like to think that she is my sister and I would have never blamed her, but who the hell knows. I did it to Liam, who was my brother.

Liam gazes back to me and that anger returns and he unleashes, "But what about everyone else *you* ruined, Cole? Your dad, who couldn't stand to even look at you after everything and just one day dropped you off here and never came back. Oh yea, and Tara. Poor Tara is still feeling the effects of your poison. It sounds like she's in the same place she was when we were teenagers. Remember that day? The day you drove her to kill…"

I cut him off, "Shut the hell up." My body clenches and I feel heat swarming my cheeks. Camryn's calming words are drowned out by the rage and I can't do anything to control myself. I leap at him and grab him by the coat collar. Heidi is screaming and Dusty is attempting to pull me off, but I am too strong, too driven by my temper. I register the smirk on his face, and all I can think of is how to get it off him. Without another thought, I hold him with my left hand and pull my right arm back and send a right jab into his left cheek.

I let go of him and he falters back. Dusty wraps his arms around me to pull me back and Camryn is begging me to stop. Her voice registers, sinking through the fury that just consumed me, and my head snaps up realizing where I am. Camryn's hands are over her mouth and I can see her fighting back tears. And that's when I see him, my little superhero, crying and shaking at Camryn's side. My sweet little boy, my Gavin—*how could I let myself get to this point?*

I reach out to him and he shudders back, sinking into Camryn even more. At that moment, my heart shatters, seeing that my son, the one I vowed to protect, is afraid of the menace I just became. My gaze travels to Camryn and I see the pain in her eyes, which I am sure I put there. "Take him home, away from me."

She reaches her hand and grasps my wrist, pulling me with her. "Come home with us."

I pull my hand away and begin to back away from them. "Take him home without me. Right now, he's afraid...of me." I can't bear to stay here and look at what I did to Gav and Camryn, to see that the old Cole has never really left. I rush off the beach, away from my family, the ones I disappointed again with my thoughtless actions. I try to grasp the realization that I'm no longer the superhero Gavin once thought I was. Today, I became the villain.

Chapter Twenty-Five

Present

That first night Liam showed up on our front door step I lost my shit, like I did today, and ended up with shots of Jack at *Twisters,* the same place I'm headed right now. I rush through the door and the warmth from the small local bar greets me. I need to figure some shit out before I go home, before I face the two people I love most. I know I'm being a coward, but in all honesty, there's nothing scarier than being a parent, especially one that shattered his kid's world.

I unzip my large parka overcoat, exposing the top of my wetsuit and take a seat at the bar stool closest to the window that overlooks the bay. The bartender approaches and before he takes my drink order, he asks, "Did you make us proud out there today?"

I stare at him for a moment thinking about how to answer his question, especially with the way I am feeling right now. "Sure, if punching a guy in front of your son is something to be proud of." I let out an uncomfortable laugh as I replay the memory in my head.

"I was just talking about the surf competition." He points at my wetsuit top that is showing. "But on that topic, as long as that punch carried meaning with it, then you should be proud." He casts a comforting smile.

I nod at him and say, "A Jack on the rocks, please."

"I'll have the same thing my son-in-law is having, Alan." I swivel around to see Jack, Camryn's dad hopping up on the stool next to me. He's wearing scrub pants, but has a Sea City Island hoodie on, which is telling me that he's coming off his shift at the hospital.

"Sure thing, Dr. Singer." The bartender, apparently named Alan, chirps out. "And remember first round is always on me, for you and your family. That's just in case you need to save my life one day. You'll remember that I'm the guy who bought you a drink." They both laugh.

Two rocks glasses are quickly placed in front of us and Jack takes a sip and then turns toward me. "So, I hear congratulations are in order?"

If only he knew I yet again fucked up and ran away from his daughter and grandson, leaving them alone while I grovel in my own pity. Then, I think his tune would change. I just shrug my shoulders and say, "I had a lucky run."

He smiles against the rim of the glass as he takes another sip. "Luck? I don't think the two of us experience luck too often." He places his glass on the bar top and asks, "Did I ever tell you about my early years as a surgeon?" I shake my head at his question and he continues, "Well, I was in my first year of my fellowship with this amazing hospital in Philadelphia, probably close to the neighborhood where you grew up. I'm sure you know that being placed in the city, especially Philadelphia, was a young surgeon's dream come true. I mean the hospital was busy, and surgeons were in constant need at all times. Man, any young doctor would think they hit the jackpot with that placement, and I was no different with how lucky I thought I was." He stops and looks ahead to the window that faces the bay, as if he's deciding whether or not to finish the story. "The hospital was short-staffed one night, and there was this woman who had just given birth and was experiencing complications, she was basically bleeding out. Well, I got called to the OR, they said it was a pretty standard procedure. I mean a fellowship in a huge Philly hospital and being put into the OR that quickly? How lucky was that? But, like many other times, luck wasn't on my side that night. I was told that it was a hemorrhage, a very common after birth hemorrhage. So, I stopped the bleeding and stitched up the tear caused by the placenta." Jack's eyes well with moisture as he continues to reveal this story to me. "But, you see Cole, I made a mistake and missed the rupture, the rupture that was behind the small tear I stitched. You see the stitches I did became a barrier that hid it, and she ended up bleeding to death. She became my first—my first fatality." He takes another sip just as a stray tear escapes behind the glass he's drinking from.

"Jack, I'm sorry that happened, but think of all the kickass surgeries you've completed where you were successful? I mean, they far outweigh that one time." I try to comfort him as best I can.

"Ahhh, yes. You're right. But no matter what, there's always that one mistake, that one mishap that comes to define you. It somehow sneaks into your life and becomes your identity. You think that nothing you do greater will ever erase that mistake." He looks directly at me and places his hand on my shoulder. "Son, what I'm trying to say is that you can never erase the mistakes, but you can sure as hell stop them from defining you."

I sigh and take my own sip, welcoming the singe down my throat. "Yea, well, let me know if you've figured out a way to do that."

He squeezes my shoulder, "Simple. Acceptance. Accepting that you can do better for the next. And from what I see, I think you are doing a hell of job better for your next, who happen to be my daughter and grandson."

Jack reaches for his wallet from his back pocket and drops a fifty-dollar bill on the bar. He gives me a pat on the back and says, "I'm pretty sure there is a beautiful young woman and an amazing, almost six-year old little boy waiting for their champion to come home right now."

I stand up and give him a hug. "Thank you, Jack."

"No problem. It's all part of doing better for my next. Now go on and get out of here." He gives a quick tilt of the head and walks toward the exit.

"Hey, Jack. That story you just told? How'd you do better for the next?" I ask.

A wide smile stretches across his face. "Well, what I left out was that woman ended up having a healthy baby boy that day. And then, twenty-seven years later, I helped her son find his way home."

I look at him with confusion.

"Oh yea, I forgot to mention...that woman's son...his name is Liam." He nods his head, the smile still spread over him, and gives me a wave before he heads out the door.

****

The house is mostly dark when I pull up the

driveway, except for a dim light on in Gavin's bedroom. I sit in the parked car in the driveway for a few minutes before I head inside to again try to make things better with my family. I know Camryn sent Jack to find me and bring me home, but I'm having a hard time stepping foot through the door. I'm ashamed of how I acted in front of them, of the person I became in my son's eyes.

However, the need to make it right far outweighs the terror I'm feeling to face my family. I can't run from this, can't hide from my mistakes any longer. I've spent years blaming—blaming Liam for my mom's death, blaming myself for Tara's choices, blaming my thoughtless actions on my past heartache. But tonight, I'm taking back control, I'm doing better for my next.

I quietly enter the house and walk to Gavin's bedroom door, which is cracked open. Camryn reads him a book, and I stop next to the door to listen for a few minutes. Gavin giggles at the poem repeated through the story as Camryn recites it with a high-pitched voice. Nothing beats the sound of them, and I know I must find the strength to face this and make it right.

I quietly peek my head in and Gavin spots me first. "Daddy, your home!" The excitement in his voice calms me a bit. Camryn turns around and I instantly notice the worry in her expression, but she casts a soft smile trying to cover it up.

Gavin reaches his arms out to me, "I thought you wouldn't come home like that one night, and I wouldn't get a good night hug and kiss again."

And just like that, my heart shatters at his words. The night Liam showed up here, I ran away and hid from my mistake, the same way I did when I was fifteen and found Tara, the same way I did tonight. The only difference is now I have someone depending on me, and I have to do better for him.

I sit down on the edge of the bed next to Camryn and pull Gavin onto my lap. He squeezes his arms around my neck and I hug him back, placing a kiss on top of his messy hair. "Gavin, what I did, how I acted both times, was wrong. Fighting is never the way to handle a problem. I'm sorry you were there to see it. And I'm even more sorry I wasn't there for you after it happened." I sigh at my confession and pull him in against my chest. Camryn places her hand over mine and squeezes it, giving me the reassurance to move forward. "You see, buddy, I made a lot of mistakes in my life. And then I met you and your mom, and you made everything better, you made *me* better. Lately though, it seems I stumbled again. And…well…I have to find a way to make it better."

Gavin hops out of my embrace and goes over to his backpack, pulling out a piece of paper. He looks at it for a moment and holds it out in front of me. I look at him and ask, "What do you have there, little man?"

Gavin smiles and begins to describe. "Well, Mr. Liam came to school a few days ago and asked us to make a picture of our favorite memory for the clinic he's setting up with Mommy and PopPop." He looks at Camryn and flashes her a toothless grin. "He said that these pictures will help the sick people feel better. But, I was having a really hard time with thinking about my favorite memory because Mommy and me have so many since we met you, Daddy. I couldn't pick just one." He shrugs his shoulders and I can't help but smile at that confession. "So, Mr. Liam came over to my desk to help, and he told me he has the same problem, too. So, he said to think about the best time I ever had with someone else and to draw that. That was a whole lot easier because I loved the time you took me on the Ferris Wheel last summer."

I agree with him exclaiming, "You're so right. That was the best night, ever." I point at the paper in his hand. "Is that the picture you drew?"

Gavin shakes his head and says, "Not my drawing, because that one had to go to the clinic. But Mr. Liam drew one to help me think of an idea and I think you might like it."

Gavin walks over next to me and hands me the drawing. Camryn peers over my shoulder to catch a glimpse as well. It's a pencil sketch of a skateboard ramp and a person on that ramp. On top of the ramp, is another person sitting and facing the skateboarder. There are no features drawn on faces, but at the top of the page it says, *"Watching my brother do what he does best."*

I stare at the picture, for a moment, allowing my thoughts to go back to that place, where I had it all. Looking back up to my wife and son, I realize I can have it all again. I just need to let go of the pain, the guilt, the blame. Camryn hooks her arm around me and kisses my cheek. She whispers, "Looks like a pretty great memory."

I turn my head and kiss her on the lips. I ruffle my hand through Gavin's hair and say, "It sure is. We had a lot of great times together." I squeeze Gavin even closer into me. "Thanks, buddy for reminding me."

He escapes from my hold and jumps on top of me,

pushing both Camryn and me down on his bed. He's swarms us with kisses and hugs. We're all howling in laughter, and it feels damn good to be with them. Gavin, who's piled on top of me says, "Daddy, you know, sometimes even superheroes need to be saved."

Chapter Twenty-Six

Past

"He has to bring us home now, right? I mean with school starting in a few days, he has to plan on picking us up." Heidi is sitting on the edge of the bed in the room that I've been sleeping in for the past month. She is trying to rationalize our dad's disappearance over three weeks ago when he dropped us off in Sea City Island, a small beach town where our grandparents live, and then one day didn't show up at the breakfast table. Our grandparents haven't said much about it, but at the same time, they don't seem surprised about it either—like maybe it was planned or something.

I'm attaching new wheels on an old skateboard I found in the shed. It was mine from when we used to vacation here in the summers. And I'm listening to Heidi whine about our current living status. I'm not sure why she's dying to go home, I mean the last year has been shit. At least here, the bills are paid, and we have more than just rotting fruit and open beer cans in the fridge. I'm sure it has to do with Liam, who I hear her talk to for hours in the middle of the night. I can't wait until our grandparents see the phone bill.

"I think you better get used to beach life, Heidi. Looks like we're not leaving here anytime soon." I feel my own frustration start to take over. "I mean, do you really think he's coming back? He's a fucking wreck and hasn't given two shits about us since Mom…" I stop abruptly, still unable to come to grips with her not being here.

"I know, Cole. But he wasn't always a bad dad. He used to be great, and if you were once great, it still has to be there, right? He just needs some time to get over mom." Heidi's reaching for some explanation but I shut it down.

"Great? Time? Are you delusional? I mean most *great* dads would help their kids, you know support them through tough times. But he'd rather drink his profits and stick his dick in any woman that walks into his bar. Great dad, my ass." I tighten the last wheel and stand up, holding my new and improved skateboard at my side. "Face it, Heidi, he doesn't want us anymore, he gave up on us, and now we're Grandma and Grandpop's problem." I start to head toward the hallway and turn back to her. "Maybe you should take up surfing or something? I mean it's what all the locals do."

She throws the anchor-shaped decorative pillow on the bed at me and I dodge it, letting it soar into the hallway. Her face drops, a sad expression taking over. "How are you okay with all of this? I mean our life is in Philadelphia, not here?"

"I'm not okay with it, but what the hell do you want me to do about it? Go find dad and beat the shit out of him until he finds his *greatness* again?" I let out a sarcastic laugh. "Besides, our life in Philly ended the day mom left us."

Heidi yells out, "She died, Cole. Please, just say it!"

I gnarl back, "Yea, I know, and I know who we can *thank* for that." Completely over the conversation, I flick my hand up to give a quick wave and head out.

I hear Heidi shout something back about it not being Liam's fault or something, but I head out the front door and shut her out. Shutting everyone out— yea, that's the one thing I'm good at.

****

We pull up in the drop-off line of Sea City High School, me in the front seat and Heidi behind me. She skipped Grandma's homemade breakfast of blueberry pancakes and hash browns and is sitting in the back seat with a bitchy scowl on her face. I notice our grandma keeps eyeing her in the rearview mirror. I just roll my eyes at Heidi's drama. *Get over it, we're here for a while.* Before we hop out of the car for the first day of school, Grandma stretches her arms and places a hand on my shoulder and one on Heidi's knee.

"I know it's been a tough few weeks with your dad leaving, but you have to understand he had to go. He needs help and you two need stability and love. We will get through this as a family, okay?"

I snap, "Never knew family could just throw away their kids, like a piece of trash. I'm sure he's finding the help he needs right next to his latest bimbo of the week and a bottle of whiskey."

Grandma winces, probably not used to hearing the real deal of her son-in-law, but squeezes my shoulder. "You're angry, Cole, and it's okay and normal. We will work through it, I promise." She flashes me a comforting grin.

She looks back to Heidi and says, "And you, sweetie. You will be the most gorgeous senior at this school. Trust me, it will be a memorable year. I have total faith you will love it here."

Heidi nudges our grandma's hand off her and folds her arms across her with a *humph.* "I don't belong here." She looks at me and repeats, "We don't belong here. We have a home and it's definitely not here."

Our grandma nods in understanding and calmly says, "For now, this is your home. So, let's try to make the best of it." She reaches out again to Heidi and her hand lands on her thigh. "Grandpa and I love you two with all our hearts and want nothing more for you than to somehow find happiness now. We will all get through this together."

I force myself to nod, not really believing the happiness part, but not wanting to fight with my grandma. Besides, she's not responsible for the asshole our dad has become. If anything, she's stuck with cleaning up the mess he made.

"All right, Heidi, let's go." In a sarcastic tone, I add, "Don't want to be late for our first day, do we?"

She huffs as she opens the car door and slams it shut. When I'm out, I peek back in the car at our grandma and shrug my shoulders at Heidi's little fit and give her a wave goodbye. Heidi's already walking into the school when I turn back around. I start jogging, trying to catch up to her, but stumble into someone on the sidewalk. I blurt out an apology but am startled when the person turns around and squeals, wrapping her arms around me.

"Oh my God, I thought I'd never see you again."

My body is stiff, my hands hanging down at my sides. She steps back, away from me, and still in shock, I ask, "Tara, what are you doing here?"

She smiles and says, "I'm going to school. I moved here with my brother and mom a week ago."

Sighing in relief to hear that her dad's not here, my eyes are wide as I look up and down her tight, little body that's she's barely covering with a jean skirt and tank top. I smirk at her and say, "Looks like I'm in for it now."

I place my arm round her waist and pull her in close to me, as we walk together through the doors. Maybe it won't be so bad here now. I laugh at myself. Who am I kidding? This screams nothing but trouble.

****

"Cole, come and help us decorate the Christmas tree," Heidi yells down the stairs to me. I look in the mirror at the dark bruise on my cheek and rub my hand over it. The punk got a lucky shot, but it didn't stop me from laying him out on the ground.

"Can't. I'm heading out. Have to finish a project for Science class," I shout back. I can hear Heidi complaining about Tara to my grandparents. She blames her for the fights I've been getting into, and now my first suspension. But what was I supposed to do? I wasn't going to let the guy stick is hand up my girlfriend's shirt and not face the consequences.

I hear Grandpop calm Heidi down and tell her that I'm going to be okay. I guess they're all crazy, thinking I still have a chance. Heidi might have made a quick turnaround, finding a new love for this small beach town, but to me it's the same shit just different place. And with Tara here now, it's like I never left Philly.

I leave the house with my family trying to figure out a way to save poor, broken Cole and I run into Heidi's friend, Dusty, in the driveway. He's the epitome of this town—long hair, captain of the surf team, and totally laid back. I can't complain though, he got Heidi out of her funk and the late-night calls to Liam have ended. He doesn't seem like a bad guy either.

"Woah, dude. I'm afraid to see what the other guy looks like." He's pointing to the bruise on my face.

I laugh and reply, "Not sure. I left him flat faced on the ground before I could notice."

He only nods at my response. Dusty is definitely not the type who pursues a fight, but I have no doubt he'd wreck someone if he was pushed too far. "So, when are you hitting the board with me?"

"Really, man? You're still trying to get me to surf? Since your daily visits to the skate park haven't worn me down yet, maybe you need to look for another recruit."

A sly smile spreads over his face. "How about we make a deal? If I can get your sister out there on a board, then you have to come, too?"

I laugh and put my hand out to shake his, "That's a deal. Ain't no way my sister will ever go out in the ocean. She thinks Jaws is a real shark."

Just after he shakes my hand to seal the bet between us, Tara walks up behind him and calls out, "Ready to go, Cole?" I notice Dusty's grin turns to a scowl when he sees her, and an icy glare remains when he says goodbye to me and heads into the house.

Tara, who probably notices it too, says, "Aren't surfers supposed to be all laid back and free? Looks like that guy forgot to hit the peace pipe today."

I shrug my shoulders, and before she really thinks too hard about it, she wraps her arms around my neck and guides me down to her lips. I pull away quickly and say, "Let's get out of here before my grandparents figure out I'm not doing a project."

As I'm leaving with Tara, I look back at the house and notice Heidi and Dusty are on the front porch watching us. Heidi's bitch stare at Tara is apparent, but Dusty is leaning into her ear whispering to her. He's probably trying to convince my sister to go out surfing with him. Too bad he doesn't have a shot.

A few days later, on our first day of Christmas break, Heidi comes barging into my room, pulling the covers off of me. I grab a pillow and put it over my face and in a muffled voice, I yell, "What the hell, Heidi. We don't have to get up today."

In an annoying, overly cheerful voice, she sing-songs, "We're going surfing today."

I throw the pillow from off my face and quickly sit up in bed, staring at Heidi, wondering if I heard it correctly. "Say it again. Because what I thought you said was *we* are going surfing."

A smile that creases her eyes stretches across her face and she repeats, slower this time, "Get out of bed. We're surfing with Dusty today." She laughs, obviously amused at the stunned look I'm giving her.

"You're kidding, right. You? On a surfboard? In the ocean? With sharks?"

She waves her hand at me, brushing away the comments. "Oh, stop, Cole. I was afraid of sharks when I was like ten. Besides, a few months ago you did tell me to go try surfing."

I toss up my hands in frustration, "I said you should try. There was nothing about me doing it."

Heidi puts her hands on her hips and leans her

weight to one side. "Well, a bet is a bet. And, you lost. So, get up, and get ready. The wetsuits are in my room. Dusty is letting us borrow them."

I fling my feet over the side of me bed and am cursing under my breath. I'm not sure if I am angrier about losing the bet or having to hop into a cold ocean in the middle of December. Heidi must want this guy pretty hard, if she's willing go past her knees in the ocean, and on top of that in the winter. I traipse over to her room and grab the wetsuit hanging from her doorway. I can hear Heidi downstairs talking to our grandma.

She says, "Dusty really thinks that it's going to help him deal with everything." My grandma replies, "I always have said the ocean can do wonders to someone's spirit." There's a pause and then she continues, "We'll get him back, sweetie. I can promise that." There's another pause and then she says, "Get yourselves going. I can't wait for Cole to find some peace and love through surfing."

I zip up the top of the wetsuit, amused by the conversation, and say to myself, "Don't count on it. This is one and done."

Chapter Twenty-Seven

Present

Camryn and I stay with Gavin until he falls asleep. I watch his chest rise up and down, and listen to the hum of his tiny, child snores. I take in his innocence, his complete goodness, and I know that I have to give my best self to him. No more excuses. *Anything to protect them.*

Camryn stands up from of the side of his bed and takes my hand into hers. She eyes the length of my body, her eyes turning seductive, and whispers, "Let's get you out of this wetsuit, and into the shower."

She guides me out of Gavin's room and down the hallway into master bathroom. After opening the shower door and starting the water, she turns back around to me and starts to slowly unzip my wetsuit. As my chest pops up, she places her lips delicately on it and kisses it, with every hair on my body standing up. *God, I love this woman.* She looks up, and says, "It's the biggest heart I have ever known."

She then reaches up on her tiptoes, her round belly brushing against my stomach, and kisses my lips. "The sweetest lips I will ever taste."

That's when I lift her up, her legs wrapping around my waist, and place her on top of the counter. I kiss up her neck, her head lifting up to allow me in, and a giggle arises from her. "Well, that's the greatest sound I will ever hear."

Camryn brings her hands back to my chest and pulls the top of my wetsuit completely off, and I help her by stepping out of the rest of it, baring down to my naked body. As she drags her fingernails down my back, I instantly go hard, my need for her growing by the second. Taking her sexy ass in my grasp, I lift her off the counter and back her into the shower, letting the warm water run down her back. With the spray of water on my face, I allow my mouth to explore her body. "God, Camryn. I need this. I need you."

She cups my face in her hands, and when our eyes meet, she says, "Then take it. Take all of me."

I take her arms pinning them against the tile wall above her head, having her grasp hold of showerhead cord that hangs down. Trailing a line of kisses down her body, I take each of her round tits in my mouth one-by-one, I fall to my knees, the water rushing over my head. Lifting one of her legs, I place it on the shower sitting ledge and spread her wide open. Her back arches before I drag my tongue up her legs. I love that she fully submits to me, trusting me with every inch of her perfect body. Very slowly I circle my tongue over her heat, feeling her legs go weak at first touch. I thrust my tongue in her, lapping and caressing every bit of her. The sounds of her moans mixed with the streaming water makes me go faster, as if I've been starved of her. One of her hands comes down under my chin, lifting me off my knees.

"Cole, I want you inside of me. I need to feel you." Camryn begs.

"Whatever you desire, sweetheart, I will make a

reality."

I turn her around place her hands against the wall, her sexy ass tilting up toward me. I push inside of her, the tightness swelling around me. With my hands grasping the sides of her ass, I thrust into her, our rhythm slow and steady. As her body tenses, my movements become more hurried, spilling over with pure lust, but layered with the deepest love. Love for her. Love for us. With the warm water pouring down our bodies and hanging over the edge of pleasure, we both surrender together, our reality with each other.

Cuddled in bed together, I hold Camryn who's asleep in my arms. My body is awake because our shower session, but my mind is reeling with everything that's gone down the last few months. I watch as Camryn sleeps soundly, remembering when only a year ago the nightmares of her past would never allow this. I love that she let me in to help her slay those demons. It was the truth when I told her that her pain was caused by others. But for me, I'm the only one to blame for my past. I'm the reason for my own pain.

I brush a piece of hair out of Camryn's face, then drag my hand down to the swell of her belly and circle my hand gently over it. I never thought I could have this, not after my mom died, not after Rose died. I've fucked up with so many people in my life, but I can't this time. I need to do better for them. *Anything to protect them.*

"Our little bean is already perfect, right?" Camryn's says groggily.

I smile, widening the circle I'm tracing with my hand over her stomach. "No doubt in my mind our bean will be all you." I kiss Camryn gently on top of her head. "You are so full of goodness and beauty."

Camryn shimmies up, elevating her back so she's in more of a sitting position and face-to-face with me. "Do you remember that day we met? That day in the cafeteria?"

"Will never forget it. It marked the first day of my journey to you."

She flashes me a grin, her cheeks pink streaked from my compliment. "Well, let me tell you what I remember. There was boy, and in his eyes, I saw that he was hurting, that something or someone left him empty. But he was able to cover that hurt with anger and detachment. That boy couldn't fool me, though, because in him I saw my own struggle. That somehow we connected through our pain." She brings her hand to my face and strokes my cheek. "And then, years later, I saw that boy again, now a man, with the same ache. But this time, I was smarter, I knew a little more. That ache…it wasn't because of the emptiness he felt, or the void that his past left in his life. No. It was because he couldn't find a way to forgive himself. That somehow, he made himself believe he was responsible for those things that were out of his control. That he was destined to suffer for that. And, he doesn't see how beautiful he really is. But I see it. Every day, I see my beautiful, broken man." She leans into my mouth and our lips meet, along with a few trickling tears.

With her warm breath on my face, she chokes out, "Cole, your mom's death, your dad's abandonment, your relationship with Liam, your need to fix Tara—that's all part of me now, too. And I want in on all of it. You see, the day I met that boy in the cafeteria, he became a part of me. That day, you and I became an us."

Her slow, trickling tears are now streaming down her face, and she needs to stop and take a breath from the emotions she's showing. I pull her into my chest, resting her head against my heart. A heart that will always beat for her.

"Camryn, I never wanted you to know about that side of me...the anger, the emptiness, the destruction I caused with my friends and family. But, what I forget is that day in the cafeteria, you saw me already, actually you saw right through me. And you still wanted me, broken and shattered. I wanted to protect you, Gavin, and our baby from that, from me. Now my past is catching up to my present and I feel like I'm spiraling, falling out of control again."

She looks up, clasps my face in her hands and finishes my confession. "But this time, I'll be there with the safety net to catch you."

She claims my mouth with hers, declaring her unconditional support. It's the moment where the fuck-ups of my past start to become a distant memory, when the years of guilt and anger I've been harboring for so long begin to drift away. Oh, sweet Camryn, my wife, my gift, the one who has saved me.

****

I roll over to an empty bed, the sheets wrinkled and the pillows still holding that intoxicating strawberry aroma of her hair. I squeeze the pillow, sucking in every bit of Camryn's sweetness. The bedroom door opens, and the sound of Gavin's whispers fill the room.

"Mommy, I think he's still asleep."

Camryn answers, "Well, that only means one thing..." Her voice fades off and within a few seconds I feel a certain little boy piled on top of me, trying to reach under my arms to tickle me. But I'm too fast, and I circle my arms around his body rolling him down to the bed. I unleash major tickle bugs on him, and Camryn joins me. We drag the biggest giggles out of him and as he's thrashing from side to side trying to escape our attack, he yells out, "Surrender!"

I help him into sitting position and ask, "You thought you could get me, didn't you?" I raise my arms up in victory. "There's no beating the tickle master."

I see him give a quick nod to Camryn and all of a sudden, she has me on my back, pinning my arms down. Gavin hops on top of me and does the same thing I just did to him. I'm laughing so hard that I can only garble out the word surrender.

Gavin jumps off and holds his hand in a V above his head and taunts, "Oh yea? I think the tickle master just got beat." We all laugh together, Camryn giving our son a high five.

"Hey, you set me up." I look to Gavin and jokingly say, "Mommy's a traitor."

He nods his head with pride. "Well Daddy, *I* was the first boy in her life." I pull them both in to a hug and revel in this moment with them.

When they finally coax me out of bed, I walk up to the kitchen and am greeted by an amazing breakfast spread of eggs, homemade chocolate chip waffles, fruit, and toast. Hanging across the breakfast room window is a sign, obviously homemade by Gavin, that says, *"Way to Go! Atlantic Classic Here We Come."* All around the words are pictures of me surfing with Gavin. He must have worked on it yesterday when I was gone. It warms my heart to know that he was thinking of me yesterday, even after what he saw on the beach with Liam.

I turn to Gavin. "Did you do all this?"

He'd nodding his head quickly, with a proud smile spread across his face. "Well, I got a little help from Mommy." He points his thumb toward Camryn. "Just a little."

"Well, it's perfect. Thank you for this."

Camryn hooks her arm around mine and rests her against my shoulder. "Well, our champion deserves it."

Gavin airplanes toward the dining table and squeals, "Atlantic Classic here we come."

I follow him, doing my own impression of an airplane and shout back, "Let's get our grub on, little man!" I catch up to Gavin and scoop him up, swinging him into his chair.

As we begin to devour delicious food, I look around the table at my little tribe, the home we built, and the love we've brought into it. And for the first time since my mom died, I don't feel like I'm trudging uphill anymore. Somehow life is finding balance. My family has declared their unending support, and it sure as hell came at the very time I needed it.

Chapter Twenty-Eight

Present

After we eat breakfast and play some video games, we get Gavin dressed and ready to go out with Jack. On his days off from the hospital, Jack has made it a point to spend time with his grandson, especially after missing so many years with him. As Gavin says, they go on "mega-awesome adventures, *secret*, mega-awesome adventures." It's become a tradition that when they come home, we have to try to guess what they did. And every time, Gav just shakes his head with a big grin on his face, and Jack gives him a wink.

Camryn and I wave goodbye to Jack and Gavin from the front porch as they leave for their mega-awesome adventure. She clasps my hand, guiding me to our porch swing to sit with her. The March air is still brisk, but you can feel a hint of Spring warmth as the sun shines and the season approaches. We swing for a few moments in silence, my hand circling over our baby's bump on Camryn. Her pink lips are pursed in a soft smile, and her eyes are watching my fingers circling her stomach. Just a year ago, Camryn never thought she could find this peace, and then she was able to shed the evil and secrets in her life. That's the day I knew she was completely mine.

Camryn breaks into my thoughts. "Remember that

day on the jetty last year?"

I slyly grin as some dirty thoughts come to mind. "You mean the time we were *under* the jetty?" Her cheeks flush and she nudges me in the ribs. "Because I definitely remember everything about that day." I lean into her the crook of her neck and give it a quick nibble, feeling the pores on her skin elevate.

She bats me away, her giggle infectious, and says, "Not that time. The time when you proposed?"

I wrap my arms around and pull her into me, her head resting against my chest. "Of course. One of the greatest days of my life."

I feel her cheekbone move against me, knowing that she smiled at what I just said. "Well, right before that, my mom had guided us, through her last letter, to let go of the past." She looks up to me. "Do you remember that?'

I squeeze her tighter in my embrace. "Of course. It was the moment I was waiting for. The day you'd be free, yet all mine."

"The day *we* were free." She corrects me. "We let go of our shared past and found peace, with each other. But that day I failed. I failed at helping you release your guilt. The deep-seeded guilt that came before me, before us." She lifts her head off of my chest and looks at me. "Well, Mr. Stevens today we begin to take that away, piece by piece."

I steal another kiss from her. "Well, start chipping away sweetheart. Because God knows you are the only one who can." I lean in in and whisper, "And you know what it does to me when you call me that?"

A sly grin slides over her face like she knows exactly what she's doing. "How about you show me,

Mr. Stevens."

I sweep her up into my arms and nudge the door open with my foot. She's laughing at my quick response to her, and I never want to stop hearing that giggle from her. I lay her onto our bed and plan to take every bit of her, as much as I can, because there is no way I'm ever letting go.

****

Camryn is practically dragging me through the double glass doors of the rehab center. When she told me our plans for the afternoon, I thought she had gone crazy. I mean for me to visit Tara at rehab is one thing, but to mention that she wanted to join me, well, that's just insane. But her persistence is inspiring and now we are both getting clearance at the front desk.

Camryn leans into the front desk receptionist, talking quietly so I can't hear. Being a nurse in a small-town hospital, she pretty much knows everyone involved in the health field. The woman nods at her, gives Camryn a pass, and unlocks the door that leads to a dining area and other communal rooms. Hand in hand, we pass by one room where a few women are sitting in meditation poses on a mat humming and chanting. I laugh to myself, knowing prissy Tara would never be caught dead doing something like that. She always had a status to uphold and that would surely fall below it in her mind. As we walk by more rooms with more people involved in activities, I wonder if Tara is even allowing herself to experience any of them. She's stuck in the past, always hanging on to hope of us, of Rose. When in reality, we never had love, we had loneliness.

Camryn and I stop in front of the elevator and she

pushes the up button. Her voice breaks in, "A penny for your thoughts?" She's watching me with a comforting smile on her face.

"Oh sweetheart, you deserve much more than a penny." I give her hand a squeeze.

She kisses my cheek, her lips so soft and gentle and whispers, "I promise to help you find your peace."

The elevator doors open, and I say, "I already found it—you."

We travel up to the fourth floor, no words between us, but that overwhelming sense of support. I know why she wants me to come here, I'm just not sure what it's really going to do. Any interaction I've had with Tara has been dramatic and toxic. Yet, I can't shake the feeling that she's here because of me, that I'm the reason for her fall again.

We round the hallway to room 422 and Camryn knocks lightly on the door, still holding tightly to me with her other hand. Nerves quickly build in me as I'm not exactly sure what type of person is behind that door. When it opens, we're not greeted by a bitchy blonde, but instead by her dark-haired twin, Brady. He looks the same, just a bit bulkier, and no one can miss the shiny gold ring on his finger. I step back, shocked to see him, wondering why he's back. After he graduated high school, he left for college out west and made it quite clear he was never coming back. After everything their dad put them through, who could really blame him?

Camryn releases her grip on my hand and hugs Brady, "Thanks so much for coming back." I stare at them, confused on how they know each other enough to hug. "How's she doing?"

Brady responds, "She's coming around." He smiles at Camryn with a sense of gratitude for her concern about who I assume is Tara. He then turns to me and explains. "Hey, Cole. I guess your confused by this." He' pointing back and forth between himself and Camryn.

I slowly nod and respond a little more tough guy than I wanted, "Yea, you could say that."

Brady laughs. "I see you're still on attack mode." He waves it off, "It's cool, man. I get it. But *your* wife, Camryn, reached out to me and my wife. About Tara. And you."

I snap my gaze to Camryn who's grazing her nails over my lower back and sending a comforting grin my way.

I look back to Brady and he continues, "Camryn brought to light everything that's been going on with Tara since I left. And to be honest, I was stunned. I always knew she was conniving. I mean I watched how she controlled you in to doing anything she wanted. But, honestly, when Camryn filled me in on what she and Todd did to you guys, and then lately, using your past together to try to guilt you away from your family." Brady sighs. "Man, I'm sorry for this, for all of it. And when I heard everything, I knew she was using. And then Camryn verified that when she told me she was here in rehab. That you, again, picked up her pieces and got her here."

I stare at Brady, my mouth gaping at his comment. I mean his voice is still ingrained in my memory the day he blamed me for her attempted suicide. And now he's claiming I helped her. *What the hell is going on?*

"Tara's no longer your responsibility. She will no

longer be a burden on your family. And, Cole, I hope she will no longer be a burden on your memories."

Finally, finding my voice, I ask, "Where is she now?"

"She's out in Colorado right now with my wife. We're going to get her back on track. She cut us out of her life years ago, but that's not going to happen anymore. My mom is close by and she will help, too." I stare at Brady in shock, as Tara told me that her family shut her out. That her mom left her without a trace. "This should have never been on you, man, and I'm sorry about that. I promise she won't be back. I'm extinguishing the hell out of this fire." He winks at me after saying the same thing to me as I climbed out the window of his house that one day.

He packs up the rest of Tara's belongings and as he walks by he hands me a key and an envelope. "I hear you're a realtor here. You mind handling the sale of the house for me?"

"No doubt, Brady. I got that." I hold up the envelope and look at him questioningly.

He shrugs his shoulders, "Your lucky to have Camryn." He looks from her back to me. "You're lucky to have each other."

He walks toward the door, a bag in his hand with the last of Tara's belongings. He gives Camryn a kiss on the cheek and she thanks him, tears in her eyes, and he then approaches me. "You know, Cole, we've had our ups and downs over the years. But, it was always at the expense of my asshole father. Tara suffered the most because of him. And as fucked up as Tara may seem, if it wasn't for you all these years, my family probably wouldn't even have the chance to help her now." He sticks his fist out to mine. "So, thank you for giving us a second chance. This time to make it better." He smiles as I return the fist pump.

We watch him walk down the hall and disappear into the elevator, and somehow, I feel a bit lighter, like the weight that Tara has had strapped to me for so many years is lifted a bit. I shake the envelope in front of Camryn, curious as to what is written inside, and she leads me over to the bed in the room. Guiding me to sit down next to her, I fumble a bit before opening the letter. She wraps her arms around mine, her chest leaning against my shoulder, and I begin reading the letter aloud.

Dear Brady,

You don't know me, but you know my husband, Cole Stevens. And while the sound of his name may leave a bitter taste in your mouth, I ask that you read my entire letter, and maybe that taste will change about my husband by the end.

Camryn goes in to detail about Tara and her antics, starting from her cheating with Todd, her using Rose to always get to me, and the plan to destroy me and Camryn through Gavin. She talks about finding her pills in my jacket pocket and knowing that I continually blame myself for her unhealthy need to use and her suicidal thoughts. I can feel every bit of Camryn's emotion and heartbreak as I relive these moments with her in the letter. The anger for Tara and Todd, the pain of losing Rose, the helplessness of Camryn and Gavin against Todd are all raw, open wounds that still threaten to bleed me out.

As you can see, Tara is slowly sinking, struggling to stay afloat, crying out for someone to save her. But,

Cole can no longer be that someone. I ask you, her twin brother, to step up and be the man who helps Tara find ways to cope. Cole must not carry that burden anymore. You see, Brady, some of us need to be forgiven, some need to be saved, Well, my husband needs both.

Sincerely,

Camryn Stevens

****

I slam down the phone and massage my temples, trying to figure out where to begin. I came to the office today thinking it would be quiet and I could write up some of the contracts that are due. Since Dusty's recent success in surfing and Carter's well-known brand, this little seaside town has seen some action with businesses wanting to come in and have a piece of real estate here. I can't complain, though. It keeps me in business and pays the bills.

The phone rings again, and I push the folder away that's in front of me. At this point, a quiet office isn't going to happen, and I've accepted the fact that work will be coming home with me today.

I answer on the third ring. "Cole Stevens."

"Hey, babe. How's work today?" Camryn's sweet voice registers over the phone.

"Well, now that I hear your voice, it's definitely taken a turn for the better."

I can practically hear her smile over the phone. "I have some good news. I may have a buyer for Tara's house."

I shuffle through the paperwork on my desk and find the listing for Tara's beach front property. "It's only been two weeks since I put it up for sale and you have a possible buyer? Maybe, you should be in real estate."

She giggles and says, "No way. Besides, you look too sexy sitting behind that big, old desk with a pen tucked behind your ear."

I reach up and feel for a pen behind my ear and smile. At the moment, my office door opens and Camryn comes through, with a flirty grin and her phone still up to her ear. She continues, "And I can never resist a man at work."

She pushes off her cell phone and sneaks around my desk, sinking into my lap. Hooking her arms around my neck, she pulls my face down and her lips meet mine. She pulls away, her nose still touching mine, and whispers, "I missed you, Mr. Stevens."

I can't help but smile at the little vixen she's turned into. I mean I should've seen it last summer when she set up that little flirting game between us. "Oh yea, Mrs. Stevens? Just how much do you miss me?"

"Well, we have a half hour until we have to meet the potential buyer." She stands up, saunters over to shut the office door and locks it. "I think that's the perfect amount of time to show you exactly how much I missed you today."

Camryn slowly unzips her jacket, tossing it to the floor. She saunters toward me, slowly unbuttoning the tight, little plaid shirt she's wearing. Ahh, my sexy country girl. Camryn lifts her leg over me, straddling my lap. She grabs my hands and guides them to her open shirt, dragging my fingers over the plumpness of her tits that is spilling over the side of her lacy bra. This little bit of contact makes me needy, completely rock hard. My hands get frantic, wanting all of her at this second. I slide my hands to her shoulders and before I can rip off her shirt to catches my wrists and says, "Uh-uh. We're taking this one nice and slow."

Camryn climbs off my body and slides down, unzipping and pulling off my jeans. My erection pops right up, only shielded by thin boxer briefs. She slips those off my body and I jolt when I feel her plump lips wrap around me, the warmth of her breath spreading through me. I recline back in my desk chair, my hands grabbing through her hair as the arousal in me builds. Nothing will ever feel more perfect than Camryn.

Before I allow myself to go over the edge, I pull Camryn up to her feet, push her unbuttoned shirt off and slide her jeans off. I stop and take her all in, the curve of her panties around the growing swell of her belly, her long hair sweeping over the sheer lace that covers her breasts, her eyes penetrating through me, making me feel like I am the only man for her. I can't believe this woman is mine.

I stand up, towering over her, and tilt her chin up to me, I lean in and kiss her neck, watching the goosebumps spread over her skin. When I reach her ear, I whisper, "Camryn, I want to make love to you, and I'm going to do it nice and slow."

I push the things off of my desk and gently place her on it. We spend the next half hour making love on top of my desk. Camryn's my medicine, the cure to everything that ails me. We take it slow, allowing every moment to be ours. Too bad that potential buyer will just have to wait.

****

We make it to Tara's house a half hour late, and I'm doubting this potential buyer would even stick around to wait. However, Camryn insists that it's fine and he'll be there waiting for us. When we arrive, no one is out front and I look at Camryn and shrug. "I guess we took a little too long at the office. Too much piled up on top of my desk." I pull her into me by her waist and give it a squeeze.

She smiles, her cheeks turning pink. "Now, why would he be waiting out front, when the real view is in the back."

Camryn leads me around the wrap around deck to the back that faces the ocean. I see Liam leaning on the railing, staring out to the water. A few fishing boats are setting out, probably getting a head start on early spring catches. I stop in my tracks and look at Camryn. She smiles calmly at me and squeezes my hand.

"Own your breath, then find your peace." She repeats the same words I would use with her often last summer. The same words Milena used with me.

I sigh, knowing what I need to face, realizing that I've kept this one part of my past hidden for too long. I haven't seen Liam since the day of Winter Qualifiers, but his confession has been on my mind constantly. The anger he bears because of it just another piece of my guilt.

I walk over to Liam, looking back at Camryn on my way, and lean on the railing next to him. "Remember when you wrote that letter to the ocean telling it how much you hated it?" I start the conversation between us.

Liam let's out a laugh and adds, "Yea, I had to write that on the first day of school in third grade. It was the first day back to school after summer vacation, and you guys had spent practically the whole summer down here. I told the ocean that I was mad at it for keeping you away all summer." He focuses his attention on me. "How'd you know about that letter?"

"My mom thought it was so funny and had it hanging on our refrigerator. She also knew that you only hated the ocean because you missed us that summer."

"Well, she was right. And I remember that I was so excited when she invited me down with you guys the next summer." He looks back out to the ocean and smiles. "That was the best summer of my life."

I smile back, thinking about all the times we spent together, those many moments we shared. "And then every other summer after that until…"

Liam, no longer smiling, quickly interjects, "Until she died, Cole." His eyes are focused on mine. "Until the worst night of my life, until the day I lost my family, until the day my best friend no longer wanted me in his life." His anger now replaced with pain.

"Liam, it's not your fault. It never was. I know that now." I concede to my own pain and guilt.

"I know that, Cole. But being blamed by you for so many years, I actually started to believe it. Then, I would see Heidi or talk to her over the phone, and I would remember the truth. The truth that I did it all for her. That I protected her from those assholes that night, that I protected her from you. You have to know that I was willing to die for her if it helped take away *her* suffering." He looks down at his hands as if this is a difficult proclamation. "I'm still willing to do that for her."

"My sister was lucky to have you, because I sure as hell wasn't there for her." I turn my body toward Liam and continue, "Listen, I know that I'm twelve years late with this, and I don't expect you to forgive me, but I'm sorry. I'm sorry for shutting you out, I'm sorry for putting her accident on you." I shake my head. "I was toxic back then, and I made you my excuse, my scapegoat. I was wrong."

"Nah, man. I sure as hell wasn't innocent. I was pissed at you and I stoked the flames every chance I got. I watched you fall apart and didn't do a damn thing to stop it." He looks over to Camryn who's standing away from us, watching intently. "It took an angel to get me to see that. *Your* angel."

I look back at my wife, my angel, and she smiles and blows a kiss to me. I wink back at her, never more grateful for her than right at this moment.

"Damn right. She came in to my life right when I needed her the most. Right when I needed to be saved."

Liam nods and then looks around Tara's property. "So not a bad price for this off-the-hook view."

I agree and add, "Looks like it's close to your family too, man."

He looks at me, relief flooding his face, and a little of that darkness gone behind his eyes. "Think we can make it work?"

"Hell, yeah. Let's do it." I put my hand up to him and he high fives me back. I guess that's Camryn's cue because she's jumping up on my back, squeezing me around my neck.

She leans over and kisses me cheek and then says, "Welcome home, Liam."

A big grin spreads over his face and he replies, "Thanks to you."

I tell Liam I will write up the contracts and let

Tara's family know the deal. They will most likely allow him to move in right away, since it's empty. As he's leaving, I call out, "Liam, you know Camryn and Jack need you at the clinic."

He nods his head. "Wouldn't have any other way." He turns his attention to Camryn and says, "I'll see you at work tomorrow."

She gives him a thumbs-up and we watch him walk out, hearing the rev of his engine drown away in the distance. I carry Camryn to the lounge chairs set on the higher part of the deck and place her down in one. She moves over and pats the open space next to her, wanting me to join her. She cuddles up next to me and we take a moment to enjoy the current calm of the ocean. She reaches into her coat pocket and hands me an envelope. I look at it and then to her.

"I've been holding for a while. But I think it's time you have it." I take the envelope from Camryn's hand and open it, pulling out the paper inside. I unfold and I begin to read it, with Camryn's chin resting on my shoulder.

Dear Cole,

It's been years since I first saw that broken boy in the school cafeteria. But the truth is, I never once believed that broken meant forever. You came to me at a time in my life when I felt unfixable, but in that one short encounter, I had hope. Hope for you and hope for me. The years between that moment and the day on the beach when I fell into you, both literally and figuratively, somehow made us believe that our past choices lead to consequences that will forever define us. But together, we have proven that wrong. We now live this life of ours knowing that we decide the outcome. We control our fate. It's become clear to me that I wasn't meant to save you. We were meant to save each other. Welcome to our happily-ever-after.

I love you, Cole Stevens.
Camryn

Chapter Twenty-Nine

Past

I grab the shitbag by the collar of his shirt and just start pounding him with my fist. Blood squirts up and I know I jacked up his nose, most likely broke it. I hear Tara whimpering over me, trying to pull me off, but she's too weak to do that. A low moan comes from whichever Murphy brother this is, whose face I'm messing up. So, I wind my fist back, ready to deliver one more blow, but instead of swinging, my arm is stopped.

The principal, Mr. Mack, is holding my arm tightly, making it impossible to move in any direction. He's pulling me off and lifting me off the hallway floor. It's a wonder he wasn't here sooner, but in the year I've been here, I managed to figure out which hallways aren't watched often.

He pushes me back toward the lockers and commands me to stay there. He helps Tara and sends her down the hall with the guidance counselor who accompanied him. After calling for the nurse on his walkie-talkie, she shows up a few minutes later and helps my victim off the floor guiding him down to the nurse's office. I snicker at his mangled face, probably unable to see through his swollen eyes.

"Report to my office now, Mr. Stevens." I watch

Mr. Mack's finger point in the direction of the principal office.

He's following close behind me as I walk, the tips of his shoes hitting the back of my heels. I can tell by his heavy breaths he's not happy to find me in yet another fight on school grounds. But, I couldn't help it. If a guy is going to hit a girl, he should be prepared for a major beat down. Just another deadbeat dealer, who hides his stash in mommy and daddy's BMW. These rich fucks are all the same here. Put them in the city for a day, and they wouldn't survive.

The principal's office is the same scene, just a different day. I get lectured on choosing the wrong path, violence isn't the answer, and then get slapped with another in- school suspension and participation in anger management classes with the guidance counselor.

"Mr. Stevens? Excuse me?" I jolt, bringing my attention back to the drone sound of his voice. "Are you even listening to a word I'm saying"

I give a pretty unconvincing nod, which causes him to huff in frustration.

"I asked you, what your grandparents would think of another suspension?"

I shrug and respond, "Probably that they're happy I didn't get expelled."

His cheeks turn flaming red and the vein in his forehead is popping out. Looking completely pissed off, he just points his finger toward the door. I take the hint and slowly walk away, but before I can make a full escape, he calls out to me, "And Mr. Stevens? One more incident and you will be expelled. You think *Granny* and *Grampy* will be so proud of you then?"

I stomp out and slam the door, hoping his stupid,

Principal of the Year banner falls off the wall. Must have paid off the judges, because his fat ass is the farthest thing from what that award says.

I pass by the guidance office, and Tara is sitting on the couch with her knees pulled up to her chest. I can tell she's non-responsive to whatever is being said to her. She's probably pissed because she ruined her *relationship* with yet another pill runner. Can't believe she's still hooked on those things. I thought for sure that day with her dad would've kept her off of them. Oh well, it's her body, not mine. Who am I to judge anyone? I mean I find enjoyment in mangling people's bodies. The minute I'm noticed by the crotchety old counselor, a big wooden door is slammed in my face.

I burst through the cafeteria doors and stomp my way to the soda machine. Digging in my pocket for change, I notice the table behind me instantly stops talking. I slowly turn around and their gazes all drop down to their food. I know they were talking about me. Everyone always does. I've learned not to care. When I turn back to the soda machine, that's when I spot her, sitting at the table by the doors. The girl in the pink sweater. *Jesus Christ.* Something about her—I have to stop and stare. Everything about her glows, except for the obvious frown on her face. The guy next to her has his arm around her, but she's leaning away as he talks. And he's talking about me. I hear him calling me "white-trash," "a fucking head case." Nothing I haven't heard from these douchebags before. Suddenly, the girl throws his arm off of her and she yells, "He's not crazy. Maybe he's misunderstood. Maybe someone that was supposed to love him broke him." And then she storms out of the cafeteria, leaving the table of assholes just staring at the doors.

I wait to see if the guy with the arm around her would go after her, but he doesn't. Instead, he just sits there and shoots the shit like his girlfriend just didn't run out upset. *What a total jackass!* I grab my soda and head for the doors determined to find her. I have no clue what I will say to her, but something is drawing me to see if she's okay, to find out why she would defend someone she doesn't even know, to thank her for not being one of them.

I turn the corner to the hallway where I was just pounding on one of the Murphy brothers, and I see her walking, or maybe hiding. I rush up toward her to stop her.

"Hey." She jumps a bit when I shout out and turns to me, backing into the lockers. "I'm sorry, I didn't mean to scare you."

"You don't scare me." She forces a smile, but only half of it shows up. I notice she's absolutely gorgeous, with her long, dark hair, soft cheek bones, and *Jesus,* that sweater. It makes her silky skin glow. I think pink may be my new favorite color.

I look behind me to see if asshole boyfriend took the hint, but lucky for me, he didn't. When I look back to the girl, she's staring at me, her eyes filled with questions, but somehow hollow at the same time. She relaxes, leaning her weight against the row of lockers behind her.

Nervously, I shuffle back and forth and say, "Listen, I—I. I just wanted to say thank you." She looks at me with a bit of surprise. "Thank you for not being them."

She looks down to the floor and mumbles, "Well,

I'm not them. And I never will be them."

Sensing her anger, I gently tilt her chin back up to me, "Remember, it's okay to feel the anger, just don't live with it for too long." Her mouth opens, and it takes every ounce of willpower not to lean in and kiss her. Instead, I turn and walk away, but somehow, I know I won't ever forget the girl in the pink sweater.

****

"Coach, I can't do another," I groan as I'm doing what feels like my thousandth surfboard push-up. "This is child abuse. Don't you have children?"

I hear my surf coach, Milena, just laugh. "I do have a daughter. But she's not at school beating on everything that walks, so I don't have to abuse her. It's only fifteen more, Cole."

I grunt in pain because push-ups suck on flat ground, but trying to do them on an unbalanced surfboard in the ocean is just plain torture. When I finish my last one, Milena grabs my board's leash and drags me to shore. She motions for me to come sit with her on the sand.

Before Dusty left for college, he and my grandma set me up with his surf coach. After that first day surfing, I'm not going to lie, I was hooked. So, Dusty had no problem taking me under his wing to show me the ins and outs of the sport. And I picked up on it pretty quickly. However, when he decided to head to upstate New York for college, he wanted to make sure I continued my training.

"So, what's the deal, Cole? Another fight? What happened this time? Did the kid look at you funny?" I laugh at Milena's question, but quickly stop when I see her glaring at me. My arms can't take anymore push-ups.

"Coach, he's a low-life. He's just some wannabe dealer who drives his Daddy's expensive car. Tara got mixed up with him and I was left to settle it." I pick up a broken shell next to where I'm sitting and fiddle with it in my hand.

Milena sighs. "Tara. There's her name again. The girlfriend that seems to be in the middle of every problem you face." She puts her hand on my shoulder. "What is it about this girl that makes you feel it's all worth it? The fights, the suspensions, the anger. What is so great about Tara?"

I take the shell and begin to trace in the sand as I think about what Milena is asking me. I know how Tara feels about me, but I also know I don't nearly have the same feelings for her. After a few minutes of thought, I answer, "She's had a shit life. I feel like I owe her some form of happiness."

Milena nods to me, as if she understands what I just revealed. I know she and my grandparents have discussed my past, but I doubt Tara was really mentioned. My grandma tries to ignore the fact that Tara is a part of my life. She barely talks to her when she's over, and she always brings up names of different girls to me, telling me I should ask them on dates and all. I let it go because Tara is definitely not your girl-next-door type, and I don't expect that she would impress my grandparents.

"Cole, you know you can't fix her problems. They're not meant for you. You're not meant to save each other." Milena gives my shoulder a squeeze and stands up. "All right, grab your board and let's catch some waves."

I hop up and carry my board down to the water's edge. As I adjust the leash on to my wrist, I look out to rolling waves, watching them rise then fall. There's nothing better than riding the high of the wave, and then somehow surviving the low of it, and coming out on my two feet. I guess life works the same way, and right now, I'm stuck in the low part of the wave, hoping to come out standing. Milena's words ring in my ears, and as I stand at the water's edge, I'm left to wonder, who is meant to save me?

Epilogue

Present—Five months later

"Wake up, wake up!" Gavin barrels into our bedroom and jumps on top of us. He stands up in the middle of our bed and sing-songs, "It's Atlantic Classic day!"

Camryn just moans, completely exhausted from being nine months pregnant. I pull him down, cuddling him into me. I peer at the clock next to the bed and say, "You mean it's Atlantic Classic too early in the morning." He looks at me funny and I explain, "It's 6:00 in the morning, bud. We have two more hours until go-time."

Gavin face drops with disappointment. "This is the longest night ever. And I thought Christmas Eve was bad. This is worser."

I brush his head with my knuckle and give him a kiss above his ear. "Just close your eyes and I promise you next time you open them, we'll be ready to go." He's already dozing off as I'm saying this to him.

Once I get him back to sleep, I decide it's is now impossible for me. I slip out of bed quietly and make my way up to the kitchen. After filling a glass of water, I head out the back door to the part of the beach that connects to our backyard. I sit in the sand and pull my knees up to my chest. The twilight of the morning has a calming glow, and while hints of the sunrise are starting to show, the silence of night still prevails. The day of the Atlantic Classic has been a source of pain in the past for me, first with losing my baby girl on the day, then last year recovering from Todd's stab wound after our fight.

I'm determined this year will be different because Camryn and I will make it different. *We* are in charge of our outcome. As I listen to the early morning seagulls singing their tunes, watching the waves gently roll into shore, I can feel her behind me and my world is just a bit more complete. I turn around and there's Camryn with her round belly, a part of it popping out from under her tank top. Her hair is gathered on top of her head, with pieces falling in her face. She is absolutely breathtaking, and she is mine.

"I heard you get up after Gavin's early wakeup call." She is smiling, probably thinking about our overly excited son. "I was worried about you."

I put my hands out to her and help her down to the sand. Wrapping my arms around her, I rub over her belly, searching for the movements I love to feel from our baby. "No worries today, baby girl. I'm right where I need to be."

She snuggles her head into my chest and says, "*We* are where we need to be, Cole. Always *we*."

I squeeze her against me to let her know I agree. Going forward it will always be us, never alone. *Anything to protect us.*

Squawking seagulls and rolling waves are interrupted by a *"Mommy? Daddy? Where are you guys?"* coming from the deck behind us. I wave my hand in the air and shout back, "Down here, buddy. On the beach."

Within a few seconds, Gavin's running to us, his Batman pajamas all twisted and hair sticking up in all directions. When he reaches us, he squeezes right in between, looks up to us and says, "Are you two hiding from me?"

I laugh and just start tickling him, messing up his hair even more. "We're not hiding from you, little man. Just out here enjoying the quiet before the big day."

He looks back and forth between Camryn and me. "You were out here kissing, weren't you?" He makes a gagging gesture with his finger.

I lean over Gavin's head and kiss Camryn in front of him. "Maybe we were. What are you going to do about it?"

He leaps on top of me and uses his bat powers on me, and I play along pretending to be frozen. Camryn joins in and throws her melting Superwoman powers my way and we take our little Batman down with tickle torture. When he's covered with sand and laughing so hard he's crying, we call a truce.

I hop up, brushing some sand from Gavin and then reach down to help Camryn off the sand. As she gets on her feet, she holds her pregnant belly and groans. "Cam, is everything okay? Are you in pain?" I ask with concern as I place my hand overs hers.

"I'm two weeks until Bean's due date. Everything is in pain." She smiles to console my worries. "All normal aches and pains."

I lean over and kiss the spot that hurts her. I whisper to our baby, "Bean, we're all ready and waiting. Come any day you want."

Camryn lifts my face up and says, "But not until

after the Classic."

Gavin interjects, "Mommy's right. First, we surf. Second, we win. And then Bean can come."

I give Gavin a high-five and shout, "All right, then. Let's go do some winning!"

****

The beach is a mob scene today. Since Dusty is gaining national recognition, this is probably the largest crowd the Classic has ever seen. In the past, the Pacific was better known for surf competitions, but between Carter's brand presence and Dusty's kick ass surfing success, we're getting noticed.

Dusty and I are on the beach, headphones on to drown out the distractions, and trying to stay loose through stretching and conditioning work. Carter is with us, checking our wet suit tops, and helping us wax the boards. I keep peeking behind me to see our fan section. They're not hard to miss, especially since Gavin insisted their team shirts this time be neon pink. They're the brightest fans on the beach. I notice Liam has Gavin on his shoulders, and I'm grateful he's back in my life. I know Dusty's having a hard time with it, and Heidi is still acting weird now that he's around, but he's family and we have a lot of time to make up for.

My heat's up and I blow a kiss to Camryn, who gives me a sexy, little wave. It's exactly what I need to get me revved up and ready to go. The competition is stiff, everyone stepping up their game to be a match for Dusty. In earlier runs, my qualifier time is well ahead, but the later heats tend to bring the stronger competitors.

The whistle sounds and I'm out paddling. I see some going toward the piers, my strategy last time, but they won't get anything there. The waves are rolling smoothly, so the piers will only make them choppy. I'm sticking to the center, keeping the jetty at a good distance. A few quick waves come in and some of the competition catch them, but nothing that would give them major points. I'm eyeing the distance and I suddenly remember one of Milena's tips. She always said that when your competition paddles out, you sit back. I would have to endure the small breakers and stay atop my board, but I have a better chance to spot the big ones. I back up, closer to the shoreline, while the others are drifting out by the pier. Times ticking, but I see something in the distance that looks exactly what I need. The ones out by the pier won't even spot it until it's past them. I start to paddle toward it, and right when I reach the perfect spot, I hop up. I cut and carve the wave, riding it all the way through. As I get closer to land, I can hear the shout and cheers. Pretty sure I can here Gavin's squeals. With ten minutes to spare, I end up catching three more, a bit smaller than the first, but enough to knock out everyone in my heat. As I leave the water, I see the standings put me well ahead in first place.

On his way down to the water, Dusty passes by throwing his fist in my direction. I return the love right before I'm tackled by Liam and Gavin. They are shouting, but not about my run. I hear the words *baby, hospital, it's time,* all coming out between their heavy breaths. And then it registers, Camryn's in labor. I look up to their spot in the crowd and see Heidi holding Camryn's hand. She's smiling, but I can see the pain she's feeling, most likely from the contractions.

I drop my board, knowing Carter will grab it for

me, scoop Gavin in my arms and rush up the beach. When I reach Camryn, she gives me the nod and I ask Heidi to stay with her until I grab the car. In what feels like seconds, I have Camryn strapped in the car and we're speeding down the Drive heading to Shore Memorial. Gavin is yapping in the back seat about all the surfers and doing the play by play for the waves I caught. But I'm in a panic, trying to hide it from Camryn, who's so calm you'd never know she's about to have a baby. But that's my Camryn—a fighter.

As we pull up to the hospital, I spot Jack, sporting his scrubs, probably coming off a twelve-hour shift. But he's there with a nurse, who I instantly recognize as Melva on Camryn's floor, a wheelchair, and a huge smile on his face. I know he's not missing the birth of this grandchild.

I help Camryn out of the car, and Melva whisks her away, but I hear her oohing and ahhing the whole way to the door. Jack tosses me a duffel bag, then hops in my car, letting me know he has Gavin. When I walk into the hospital, Camryn's already checked in and heading to her delivery room, total five-star treatment, a perk of working there. I rush through the door, and there's my Camryn watching the monitor. As the lines go up, she cringes in pain, and I rush to the side of her bed. She reaches for my hand and squeezes it hard as she struggles through the contraction. When it subsides, she simply looks up at me and smiles, assuring me it's okay.

After a few hours, the doctor comes in and lets us know it's time for Camryn to push. She's been a trooper through everything and I haven't left her side once. Jack's been texting, letting us know Gavin is in good hands. And, of course Lila and Heidi are blowing up our phones every few minutes. As the doctor preps, I lean down and kiss Camryn's sweaty forehead. "Just a little bit longer, okay."

With tears streaming down her cheeks, she declares, "I love you so much, and I can't wait to have this baby with you."

I kiss her again. "Remember, it's us. Always us. Are you ready to do this?"

She nods, and I wipe the tears from her face. In that moment, everything flashes before my eyes—the cafeteria, the pink sweater, Rose, Tara, Todd, the day on the beach, the running away, the coming back, the jetty, the day I made her my wife. Our path. Our journey. Our outcome. Before I realize it, I hear the beautiful sound of crying, and the doctor announcing our baby girl to the world. There she is, our tiny bundle with a head full of dark hair, and the perfect little button nose. Camryn reaches for my hand as the doctor places the baby on her chest. I look down to Camryn and our daughter and whisper, "Welcome to the world, Mila Rose." And just like that, I fall in love.

****

"Mommy, is Aunt Lila ever going to put my sister down?" Gavin is hanging out on the bed with Camryn, while the rest of our crazy family is huddled around. We've been told by three nurses that we're over the visitor limit, but no one is budging, and at this point they've quit holding us to the visitor rules.

"Gav, you know she'll be handing her back the minute she starts crying." Camryn tells him.

"I can hear you, and I'm totally offended." Lila jokes, "Besides, who do you think held you, Gav, when you would cry three hours a night?'

"Umm, probably mommy or me-mom," Gavin replies.

"Well, you're right. But I'm a changed woman." She looks at the baby in her arms and in a sing-song voice says, "And Aunt Lila is here for you all the time."

Mila begins to fuss, and Lila passes her to Carter. "Here, Uncle Carter wants to see you."

Everyone in the room laughs, and Camryn reaches her arms out to Carter. "Carter, I can take her. Especially since you look like a statue holding her."

Stiff and wide-eyed, staring at Mila he asks, "You want me to actually walk this tiny thing over to you? You're kidding, right?"

I step over to Carter and take my daughter from him. "I got her, Carter." He gives me a thumbs-up, and slowly backs away to sit with Lila.

I make my way over to Camryn and pass Mila over to her. Gavin's leans over her, playing with her tiny little hands. He's made a smooth transition into his new role as big brother. I look around the room to Jack and Liam, who haven't stopped snapping photos, then to Lila and Carter holding each other by the window, at the end of the bed is Heidi, who hasn't stopped crying since she met her niece, and Dusty, who just keeps passing her tissues. I never thought I could have this, not after all I had lost.

Dusty calls out to me, "Hey, Cole? Don't you want to know who won the Classic today?" I peer around the room, my gaze locking on Mila, Gavin, and Camryn. "Nah, man, I already won."

A word about the author...

Kimberly Daniels is a middle school English teacher who took the advice of her students to pursue her writing hobby as a career. When she's not at her laptop dreaming up new happily-ever-afters, she can be found glued to the TV or Kindle, consumed with a new show or book addiction.

She lives with her husband and two daughters in the suburbs of Philadelphia, spending weekends at basketball games, softball fields, and dance recitals.

https://www.kimberlydanielsauthor.com/